# THE BIG, BAD WOLFE FAMILY

Cameron Wolfe, Sr. **m.** Matilda "Maddy" Simmons

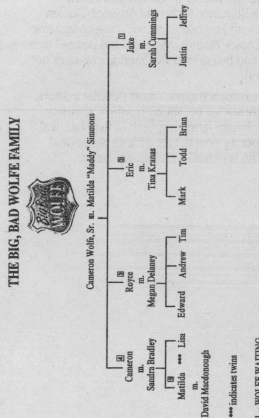

**4** Cameron
**m.**
Sandra Bradley

    **5** Matilda *** Lisa
    **m.**
    David Macdonough

**3** Royce
**m.**
Megan Delaney

    Edward   Andrew   Tim

**2** Eric
**m.**
Tina Kranas

    Mark   Todd   Brian

**1** Jake
**m.**
Sarah Cummings

    Justin   Jeffrey

*** indicates twins

1 – WOLFE WAITING
2 – WOLFE WATCHING
3 – WOLFE WANTING
4 – WOLFE WEDDING
5 – WOLFE WINTER

**JOAN HOHL**

was born, raised and still lives in southwestern Pennsylvania. The winner of numerous awards, including the Romance Writers of America Golden Medallion Award and two *Romantic Times Magazine* Reviewer's Choice Awards, Ms. Hohl has penned over forty novels and boasts over five million copies of her books in print!

As one of the romance genre's most popular authors, she is well-known for her strong conflicts, dramatic style and her heady sensuality, both in her historical and contemporary novels. Her widespread appeal proves that she is indeed a master storyteller.

# JOAN HOHL

## BIG, BAD WOLFE: READY TO WED?

Published by Silhouette Books
**America's Publisher of Contemporary Romance**

SILHOUETTE BOOKS

ISBN 0-373-48396-1

by Request

BIG, BAD WOLFE: READY TO WED?

Copyright © 1999 by Harlequin Books S.A.

The publisher acknowledges the copyright holders of the individual works as follows:

WOLFE WAITING
Copyright © 1993 by Joan Hohl

WOLFE WATCHING
Copyright © 1994 by Joan Hohl

Visit us at www.romance.net

Printed in U.S.A.

# CONTENTS

Dear Reader,

Due to your wonderful and gratifying response to *Wolfe Winter,* the fifth, but not necessarily the last, book in my WOLFE series, Silhouette Books has decided to offer again the first four books in the BIG, BAD WOLFE series. There will be two volumes, with two complete stories in each.

If you have read *Wolfe Winter,* and I sincerely hope you have, you will know the stories are about a family of dedicated men and one woman, all in the business of law enforcement. This first volume, *Ready To Wed?,* contains the first and second books in the series, titled *Wolfe Waiting* and *Wolfe Watching.*

In *Wolfe Waiting,* you'll meet the youngest of the four Wolfe brothers, Jake. This former wanderer comes back to his hometown to serve as a small-town police officer. Then he meets Sarah, a lovely young associate professor.

In *Wolfe Watching,* you'll meet the second youngest Wolfe brother, Eric, a Philadelphia cop working undercover for the narcotics department, and Tina, the woman he suspects is involved in some unsavory business, yet still can't resist.

I hope you like them.

All my best,

# WOLFE WAITING

# One

She might have looked beautiful, if not for the big, round tortoiseshell glasses that gave her a wide-eyed owlish appearance.

Jake Wolfe sat at the counter of the off-campus hamburger joint, nursing a cup of coffee while surreptitiously appraising the young woman seated in the corner booth.

She had a good face, great bone structure, a mass of gorgeous dark brown hair tumbling in vibrant waves to somewhere below her shoulders. Her slim, elegant nose was pointed at the book lying open on the table in front of her.

"Refill?" Dave, the counterman, asked, coming to a halt opposite Jake, coffee pot poised over his cup.

"Umm..." Jake murmured, reluctantly shifting his attention to the man. "Who's the owl perched in the corner?"

"Name's Cummings," Dave said, not looking away from the dark stream pouring from the pot. "Sarah. She's nice."

A man of a few words was Dave, Jake mused, nodding his thanks for the refill. Getting information out of Dave was not unlike mining for hens' molars.

"New to the college?" Jake pried at Dave's closed lips. "A graduate student?"

"Nah." Dave shook his head. "Well, yeah, she is new to the college, but she's not a student. She's the new associate professor of the historical studies department."

"History teacher, huh?" Jake grimaced. "I was always bored in history class." A devilish grin played with his mouth. "Now, if I had had a teacher that looked like that..." He let his voice fade and shot a meaningful glance at the woman.

"I hear you." Dave chuckled. "Seemed like every one of my teachers was old, wore rusty-looking black dresses and serviceable black shoes with thick heels and laces. And every blessed one of them carried a ruler—used it, too."

A veritable mouthful for the taciturn Dave. Jake flashed him a sparkling white-toothed grin. A blur of movement caught his eye, and he cast a sidelong look at the corner booth. The owl had closed her book and was sliding off the bench seat.

"Er...Dave," he murmured. "Why don't you introduce me to the lady professor?"

"Dunno." Dave leveled a pointed look at Jake's uniform. "Ain't you on duty?"

"So what?" Jake retorted in a whisper. The owl was now standing, gathering her things together, taking off the glasses and confirming his speculation—she *was* beautiful. "Get with the program," he muttered. "I'll meet her sooner or later. I patrol the campus, remember? It might as well be sooner."

She was walking toward him. Jake held his breath and glared a warning at Dave. Dave got the message—and the implied threat.

"Oh, Miss Cummings." Dave stopped her at the stool next to Jake's. "Have you met the local law?"

She started and frowned. "The local law?"

Jake had to quash an urge to raise his hand and smooth the frown line from her brow with his fingertips. He released his breath in an exasperated sigh; why was he plagued by folks like Dave, forever honing their meager comedic talents on him?

Dave obviously heard the sigh, because he immediately pulled his act together. "Uh, yeah, this here's Jake Wolfe. He's one of the Sprucewood police. Patrols the campus." He laid a benign smile on Jake. "Jake, this is Miss Cummings."

Jake shrugged off Dave's smile and turned to Sarah with one of his own, his most charming. "Miss Cummings," he murmured, extending his right hand.

Sarah Cunnings didn't appear at all charmed; she looked wary, almost frightened. But she did give him her hand. "Officer Wolfe," she said, so softly he could barely hear her. She didn't return his smile, and she drew her hand back after the briefest contact with his palm.

Hmm... Now Jake frowned. Sarah Cummings was looking at him as if he were the devil incarnate. And she appeared on the point of making a dash for the door. What was this woman's problem? he wondered.

"Dave tells me you're the new associate professor of the history department," he said, sliding off the stool to stand directly in her path.

"Ah, yes, I...ah, am."

What in hell? Now Jake was really confused. Unless he was misreading her tone, Sarah was as nervous as a rookie cop on his first big case.

"You know, it's funny we haven't run across each other before," Jake observed in a neutral tone, careful not to betray his aroused suspicion. "Did you arrive just recently?"

"Yes." She nodded, and sent a quick glance at the door. "I, er...arrived two weeks ago."

"Yeah, that's right," Dave confirmed. "I remember you came in for lunch the day after you got here."

"That explains it, then. I was working the middle and late shifts the last two weeks," Jake drawled, favoring Dave with a get-lost look.

"Yeah, that's right," Dave repeated, all in a rush. "And I gotta get back to work." Grabbing a cloth, he began wiping his way down the counter.

Jake waited; nothing happened. Sarah Cummings just stood there, fidgeting and looking as if she'd prefer to be anywhere else but there.

"Are you from this area?" Jake asked, digging for a common denominator.

"No." Sarah Cummings shook her head. "I'm from Maryland..." She hesitated, as if she didn't want to give him any more information than was absolutely necessary. "Baltimore," she added, when he didn't respond—or move.

"Nice city," Jake said, trying another smile; it fell flat. "I've been to the Harbor Place."

"Oh, have you?" She didn't smile; she eyed the door. "Um, I, er... That's nice."

Great. Jake wasn't at all sure he could handle such scintillating conversation. What he felt certain of was her intense desire to get away from him. Why? Since he couldn't convince himself that she was overwhelmed by his masculine attractions, he was at a loss to explain her strange reaction to meeting him. Maybe she was shy? Retiring? In trouble? Jake dismissed the last consideration as springing from his occupational mind-set. Miss Owl Eyes looked too young and innocent to have the kind of trouble that would make her wary of a police officer.

Had his deodorant failed him? Mentally shaking off the flip reflection, Jake tried another gambit. "Can I buy you a cup of coffee?" he asked, flicking a hand at the stool next to her. "That is, if you're not in a hurry?"

"No…thank you…" She didn't even hesitate in refusing, and he wasn't surprised. "I, ah…have a class. Another time, perhaps." Sarah Cummings swept a telling look over the full six-foot-four-inch length of his obstructive body. "May I pass, please?"

What could he say? Or do? Swallowing a curse, Jake said and did the only permissible thing. "Of course," he murmured, dredging up a smile as he stepped aside. Inspiration struck as she started to move by him. "When?"

"When?" She paused to glance at him in consternation. "When what?"

"You said another time," he answered, shooting

a quick look at his wrist watch. "I stop in here for my morning coffee break every day about this time," he explained, moving his shoulders in a shrug. "How 'bout tomorrow?"

"Oh…well, I…" Her eyes shifted from him to the door then back to him. "I…"

"The invitation's only for coffee," Jake inserted, in a reasonable tone aimed at reassurance.

Sarah Cummings wet her lips. The nervous action sent an astounding shaft of heat sizzling through Jake's body, forcing him to breathe slowly while waiting for her response.

"All right," she finally said, with unconcealed reluctance. "Ten o'clock?"

"Fine." Jake smiled. "I'll be here."

Then she was gone. But she didn't scurry away, as Jake had expected her to. No. Sarah Cummings walked in a supple, long-legged stride, neatly rounded hips swaying just a fraction from side to side.

A goddess. She walks like a goddess. Jake rubbed his suddenly damp palms against his taut thighs and blinked himself out of bemusement, back into reality.

Whoa! You'd better be careful here, Wolfe, he advised himself. This woman is potent.

"Oh…those eyes!" Jake said, grinning at Dave as he slid back onto the stool.

"Yeah, they're brown," Dave retorted, obviously unimpressed by the subject of eye color.

"Brown? Brown?" Jake demanded. "Are you blind, man? Sarah Cummings eyes are not merely brown." He pondered a moment before continuing. "Her eyes have the look of spring pansies...that soft, velvety brown."

Dave grimaced. "Oh, brother."

"You have no soul, Dave," Jake said accusingly, keeping a straight face. "No appreciation for nuances."

"Maybe so," Dave allowed. "But I recognize a nice person when I meet one, and Miss Cummings is the genuine article."

"Hmm..." Jake concurred with a definite nod of his head. *But what is she afraid of? And why does she appear fearful of me? Because of the uniform—and what it represents?*

His interest piqued on several levels, Jake sipped his now-tepid coffee and kept his own counsel.

*Drat the man.*

Gnawing on her lower lip, Sarah strode along the campus walkway, heading for the humanities building. Distracted, she responded absently to the greetings called out to her by several students making their way to the class she would be conducting within the next fifteen minutes.

*Why had she agreed to have coffee with him?*

Sarah asked herself, smiling her thanks to the pretty young woman holding the door open for her into the lecture hall.

Because he was so darned intimidating, she admitted, moving to the front of the large room. An image rose to fill her mind, an overwhelming image that caused a tremor in her hands as she deposited her handbag and books on the table.

Even the image was intimidating. A frown creased her brow as she slid her glasses into place and set her stopwatch and her text on the lectern. She had not discerned an inch of excess flesh on his body, and with his tall frame and whipcord-lean form, Jake Wolfe was one formidable specimen of masculinity.

Handsome, too…in a rugged, chiseled way.

"Good morning, class. Shall we begin?"

Hair the shade of golden toast.

"Though the Western world was barely aware of it, the Chinese Empire was already great when the Romans began their quest to conquer the Mediterranean."

Eyes the dark blue color of a twilight sky.

"That is an excellent point, Mr. Kluesewitz. China did not fall far short of the power and wealth that the Roman Empire achieved, even at its zenith."

Skin tone a deep, tanned bronze.

"Yes, of course, I do agree that China left for

posterity a wonderful legacy of literary and visual artworks.''

So tall, so imposing, every solid inch of him an assault on feminine senses.

A police officer.

"…also known as the Period of the Warring States, nearly two hundred years of turmoil following the collapse of the Zhou dynasty.''

Purely by rote, Sarah somehow managed to conduct the class on the ancient Chinese Empire. The shuffling of feet directed her gaze to the watch; the period was over. Wondering if anything she had said made any sense, she thanked the students for their participation and dismissed the class.

A police officer.

Sarah sighed as she collected her things.

And she had foolishly agreed to meet him tomorrow morning for coffee.

Was she looking for more trouble…or for help?

Sarah worried the question throughout her remaining classes for the day and during the brisk fifteen-minute walk from the campus to the apartment she had rented on the second floor of a recently converted private home in the small town of Sprucewood. Since she enjoyed the walk, Sarah seldom took her car out of the tenants' garage in back of the house.

Not even the brilliance of the southeastern Pennsylvania autumn, the nip in the air or the tangy scent of burning leaves had the power to divert her attention from the mishmash of her own thoughts.

Sarah had a definite problem.

Could Officer Jake Wolfe be the solution?

No. No. Sarah denied the ray of hope. She couldn't confide in Jake Wolfe, or any other person connected with the law. Talking, speculating, was too dangerous. There were lives involved here, the lives of others—and possibly even her own.

*Silence is golden, Miss Cummings.*

The warning echo of the student's voice whispered through Sarah's mind, bringing a shiver to her flesh that was unrelated to the zip in the early-October air.

No—talking, especially to Jake Wolfe, was definitely not one of her options. In truth, she felt she had no options, no recourse at all in the matter.

Beginning to feel mentally and emotionally battered, Sarah entered her apartment, dropped her things onto a chair, kicked off her shoes and padded through the living room and into the tiny, utilitarian kitchen.

She had felt too tense to eat anything at lunch time, but even worry eventually gave way to encroaching hunger. With a sensation growing inside her of her stomach having taken on the dimensions of a huge hole in the earth, Sarah began gathering together the ingredients for a macaroni-cheese-and-broccoli casserole.

After placing the baking dish in the oven, Sarah set the timer, slid a bottle of white wine into the fridge to chill and headed for the bathroom for a long, scented and—she hoped—relaxing soak in the tub.

The oven timer was ringing when Sarah emerged, pink and glowing, from the bathtub. And so was the doorbell.

Now who in the world could that be? Grumbling to herself about visitors showing up unexpectedly at dinnertime, Sarah grabbed the garment hanging from the hook on the inside of the bathroom door.

Pulling the lilac-striped satin robe over her nude, still-damp body, she drew the braided belt into a tight slipknot as she crossed the living room.

The bell trilled again as she neared the front door.

"Yes, who is it?" she called, reaching confidently for the doorknob.

"Jake Wolfe." His voice was muffled but unmistakable through the wooden panel.

Her hand paused to hang in midair an inch from the knob. Her heart seemed to stop beating for an instant, then accelerated to an alarming rate. Her throat went dry; her palms grew moist. Her mind went blank.

"Miss Cummings?"

Sarah swallowed, opened her mouth, then swallowed again before she could force one word from her parched lips.

"Yes?"

"Are you going to open the door?"

Was she? Sarah frowned and glanced down at the thin, shimmery material covering her nudity. No way.

"I'm not dressed," she said, raising her voice to penetrate the door.

"So go get dressed," he shot back. "I'll wait."

Checkmate. Undecided whether to do as he suggested or tell him to buzz off, Sarah raked a hand through the steam-dampened, tangled mass of her hair and curled her bare toes into the soft nap of the carpet.

The timer bell was jangling away merrily in the kitchen; she didn't hear it.

"Ah...Sarah, are you still there?"

She started. Had he heard her breathing? Ridiculous. Sarah shook off the idea.

"Yes, I'm here."

"Is that a smoke alarm I hear?"

His query jolted her into awareness. The casserole! Sarah shot a glance at the kitchen, then back at the door. Since it was obvious that he was not going to budge, there was no help for it—she would eventually have to open the door.

Besides, she was hungry.

"Do I smell something burning?"

Burning? Her beautiful casserole! Jake's question galvanized her into action. Twisting the lock, she turned the knob and swung the door open, and then, without actually looking at him, seeing him, spun to dash for the kitchen.

"Come in," she said over her shoulder as she rushed into the tiny room. "I'll be with you in a few minutes."

A tingling sensation crept up Sarah's spine as she bent over the open oven door to remove the baking dish. She hadn't heard a sound, yet she knew Jake Wolfe had followed her into the kitchen and was standing behind her...too close behind her.

"Can I help?"

Even knowing he was there, Sarah started at the easy and too attractive sound of his voice. "No! Ah..." She grimaced at the fluttery tremor in her voice. "Thank you, but no." Her back still to him, she placed the casserole on top of the stove, closed the oven door, then switched off the timer.

The sudden silence rattled her more than the jangling sound of the timer had.

Jake had moved into the room, even closer to her. Sarah heard his slow inhaling and exhaling.

"Not burned," he murmured. "Smells delicious." He hesitated a moment before continuing. "Cheese? Broccoli? Right?"

"Yes," Sarah replied, on a sharp sigh. She

turned, and nearly jumped back against the stove; he was standing too damned close. "If you will excuse me?" Her voice now held a decided edge. "I would like to get dressed."

Sarah wasn't quite sure what reaction she'd expected from him. Perhaps a slow examination of her scantily clad person, followed by an insinuating, cocky grin. If so, she was off the mark. Jake Wolfe kept his eyes fixed on hers, and not by the wildest stretch of the imagination could his smile be described as anything but pleasant and friendly.

"Sure." He backed up, through the doorway, into the living room. "I'll wait here."

"You do that," Sarah muttered, sweeping by him on a direct path to her bedroom.

"Anything I can do to help?"

His question brought her to a jarring halt in the open doorway to her room. Uh-huh. Here it comes, the offer to zip a zipper, snap a snap, hook a bra clasp. "Like…what?" she asked through gritted teeth.

"Set the table." He responded, neatly throwing her off balance. "I mean, you can't be so cruel as to expose a man to such tantalizing aromas and then not invite him to stay for dinner."

Sarah slowly turned to give him an arch look. "Can't I?" she inquired coolly. "Why can't I?"

Jake Wolfe managed a woeful expression. "It

would be cruel and unusual punishment for a hungry man.''

It was at that moment that Sarah saw him... really saw him. And what she saw did quite a number on her senses and her nervous system.

Jake was out of uniform, which should have produced a diminishing effect. It didn't. On the contrary, the change of attire had the effect of a sensual power charge.

Whoever would have thought of denim as an electrical conductor? Sarah marveled, staring at him while trying to appear casual and unaffected.

And the denim clung so faithfully to every curve and contour of his slim waist, narrow hips and long, muscular legs. Her gaze rose, collided with a broad expanse of chest and wide shoulders, delineated by a snug-fitting knit pullover shirt. Below the hem of the short sleeves, his lightly haired forearms tapered to raw-boned wrists and long-fingered hands that rested loosely on his hips, just beneath a plain leather belt.

The overall picture Jake Wolfe presented to her was one of solid, blatant masculinity. His stance appeared casual, but Sarah wasn't deceived. He was coiled and waiting, silently challenging her to refuse his request for a meal.

Sarah wanted to meet his challenge, wanted to deny and defy him, but she didn't. And she wasn't even certain why she didn't—wasn't certain, or didn't care to question it. Instead, she caved in to his request.

"The plates are in the cabinet above the sink," she said abruptly, turning away. "The flatware in the drawer below. The napkins are on the table. I'll only be a minute."

"Take your time." His voice was low, soft, beguiling. "I'm not going anywhere."

That's what worries me, Sarah told herself, shutting the door between them. If she had only met him sooner, as recently as one week ago...but no, it wouldn't have made a difference, wouldn't have changed the situation.

What to do?

Sarah stood inside the door, unable to move for a long moment, fighting against the insidious and exciting sensation of anticipation that was dancing along her nervous system. She felt strangely exhilarated and exhausted at one and the same time. Eagerness vied with reluctance. Trepidation warred with daring. Eagerness and daring won the tussle. Honesty led the way.

She was attracted to Jake Wolfe, Sarah conceded, strongly attracted to him. The admission set her in motion. Allowing that she was very likely making a mistake, a mistake she would probably regret, she nevertheless hurriedly dressed, dragged a taming brush through her tangled hair and applied a quick pat of foundation to her flushed cheeks, a flick of mascara to her lashes, and a dash of lipstick to her mouth. Then, her heart racing, she made herself walk slowly from the bedroom into the living room.

The sight that met her surprised gaze brought Sarah to a dead stop three steps into the room. She had only been gone fifteen minutes or so, and yet in that short span of time, Jake Wolfe had apparently been a very busy man.

Jake was standing, waiting for her, on one side of the small table Sarah had placed in front of a window in the corner of the living room next to the kitchen. The table was set for two, with her best lacy place mats, dishes and stemmed wine-glasses. The steaming casserole held pride of place in the center of the table. The opened bottle of wine she had put in the fridge to chill sat to one side of the casserole, breathing, and a tossed salad in a wooden bowl was set on the other side.

Salad? Sarah shifted a glance from the bowl to Jake. How in the world had he accomplished all this in less than a half hour?

A low hunger growl from her stomach drew Sarah from her bemused reverie. In all honesty, it really didn't matter how he had managed to get everything together so quickly. What did matter was that he had. Still, she couldn't resist an impish urge to tease him, just a little.

"Everything looks lovely." She sauntered

across the room to the table. "But…no bread?" she asked, in a gently taunting tone.

"But…of course," Jake replied, tossing the taunt back at her. "I found some wheat rolls in the bread keeper. The oven was still hot, so I stuck them in to warm."

The smile he tossed along with the taunt wiped all thoughts of bread, casserole and salad from her mind. Sarah did think of the wine, but only because her throat suddenly felt parched and achy. The man possessed a positively electrifying smile, electrifying and energizing. Sarah felt singed, and she felt an overwhelming need to move…anywhere.

"Ah…I'll get the rolls," she volunteered, veering away from the table and escaping into the kitchen.

"I'll pour the wine," Jake offered, in a voice that contained a suspicious hint of suppressed laughter.

As she removed the rolls from the oven and placed them in a small breadbasket, Sarah was dismayed by the tremor in her fingers and the trembling sensation in her midsection. The thought struck her that her unusual physical reaction to a man she had so recently met did not augur well for a relaxing and congenially shared dinner.

Sarah's fears were subsequently proved groundless. Although she began the meal in a state of heightened nervous tension, within minutes of seat-ing herself opposite Jake Wolfe she found herself at ease, laughing at his dryly related anecdotes about the more amusing aspects of his work.

"The woman was beside herself, wanted me to take the dog into custody," he was saying midway through the meal.

"Custody!" Sarah exclaimed, laughing. "A dog?"

"Wild, huh?" Jake grinned. "And all because the mutt growled and scared her precious cat."

Jake was so friendly, so natural, Sarah found herself reciprocating without a second thought.

"I had a cat when I was in high school," she said, taking a sip of wine. "The darned feline was so independent...used to stand and stare at me as if to say 'Leave me alone, I'm simply too lazy to be bothered.'"

"Yeah, that's the way they look." Jake laughed, and served himself another helping of the casserole.

"Do you have to deal with many animals?" Sarah asked, absently breaking a roll. "I mean, must you cope on a daily basis, like mailmen?"

"No." Jake shook his head, then he grinned. "The only thing I cope with on a daily basis is Mr. Bennet's power cocktail."

"You lost me," Sarah confessed, buttering a piece of the roll before popping it into her mouth.

"Mr. Bennet lives outside of town, along my

patrol route. He's eighty-some years old, and in fantastic shape. He's alone since his wife died last year, and he's kinda adopted me. He knows my routine and waits for me in front of his house every morning with a drink that he calls a power cocktail." He made a face; Sarah giggled. "The stuff tastes god-awful, but damned if I'm not beginning to feel better for it."

"Really? In what way?"

Jake shrugged. "My energy level's up, and I have more stamina, that kind of thing."

"Incredible," Sarah murmured.

"So is this." He indicated the macaroni dish with his fork. "You're a good cook. It's delicious."

Sarah felt inordinately pleased, and flustered, by his compliment. "Thank you, but it's only a casserole," she said. "I tend to stick to simple fare."

"Well, in a world that seems to grow increasingly more complex," Jake observed, "I think there's a lot to be said for simplicity."

*Simplicity.* That one word dispersed the euphoric haze clouding Sarah's thought processes. Apart from her cooking, there was nothing simple about her life anymore. It had suddenly become very complicated, complicated and frightening. And absolutely the last person she should be relaxing with was a member of the local police force.

What if she had relaxed her guard to the point

of inadvertently letting something slip? Sarah silently upbraided herself, concealing a shudder by turning away to glance at the kitchen wall clock.

"Oh, will you look at the time!" she exclaimed, in a not-altogether-exaggerated tone of shock. "I hate to ask you to eat and run, but..."

"You have a date?" Jake inserted, in a not-altogether-pleased tone of voice.

"That's really none of your business," she retorted. "But, no, I do not have a date. I have classroom work to prepare for tomorrow."

"Oh." Jake didn't appear chastened in the least. "Okay, but I'll help you clean up before I go."

"That's not necessary," Sarah insisted, moving away from the table in anticipation of his following her. "It'll only take a minute to clear the dishes and stack the dishwasher."

He hesitated, frowning at her.

Sarah held her breath.

He exhaled audibly, but gave in.

Sarah resumed breathing, and led the way to the door.

"I really am getting the bum's rush," he said, giving her a wry smile as he came to a stop next to her.

Sarah opened her mouth to apologize, then immediately closed it again and opened the door instead. Telling herself that she had nothing to apologize for, since he had invited himself to dinner, she offered him a sweet smile, along with a word of advice to send him on his way.

"Don't go away mad."

"Just go away," he finished the old saying for her in a droll tone. "Right?"

"I'm afraid so," she admitted, laughing out loud at his dejected expression.

"But you are still going to meet me for coffee tomorrow morning, aren't you?"

Sarah had forgotten about that. Knowing she shouldn't get within a mile of him again, she made a firm decision to say no.

"Yes." So much for firm decisions.

"Good." Raising his hand, Jake gave her a slight wave. "I'll see you, then. Thanks for dinner."

Sarah watched him lope down the stairs before shutting the door and slumping against it. Suddenly feeling drained, she sighed and closed her eyes.

Within the space of a few hours, her problems had doubled. Because Jake was as nice as he was handsome, she had enjoyed their interlude more than she could recall having enjoyed anything in a long time. She felt a strong attraction to him, an attraction that could be dangerous to her well-being.

*Silence is golden.*

Wincing at the echo in her memory, Sarah pushed away from the door and slowly crossed the room to the cluttered table. Staring down at the plate he had used, she experienced a sharp pang of regret for what might have been, had they met at any other time.

It wasn't fair, Sarah complained in silent despair.

Why did Jake Wolfe have to be so nice?

# Two

Jake swallowed the last of the power cocktail, somehow managing not to gag or even grimace, and handed the tall glass through the open car window to the elderly man in the sweat suit who was standing by the side of the road.

"Thanks, Mr. Bennet." Jake made a show of glancing at the big circular watch on his wrist. "I gotta get moving. See you tomorrow morning."

"You betcha," the old gentleman called over the revving engine of the black-and-white. "And don't you go slacking off on your workouts."

"No, sir," Jake promised, checking the mirror before easing the car onto the macadam road.

Jake felt great. It was a spectacular autumn morning, the sunlight bright and warm, the air crisp and fresh. But Jake knew his feelings of well-being were not due entirely to the beneficial effects of the morning cocktail, or even the revitalizing results of the exercise program Mr. Bennet had suggested he try.

Jake was struck by the sudden, and mildly surprising, realization that his feelings of uncertainty and ambivalence about settling into a position as a small-town cop were easing somewhat—not altogether, as yet, but somewhat. It was a start on the road back to tradition for him. But even that startling realization wasn't the ultimate cause of his high spirits.

No, Jake was fully aware that the main ingredient supporting his inner sense of soundness and satisfaction stemmed directly from a human source.

Sarah Cummings.

Merely thinking her name brought a soft smile to tug at the corners of Jake's mouth.

Lord, what a woman.

With his outer eyes alertly skimming the area of his patrol route, Jake's inner eyes gazed at a memory image of Sarah, and the way she had appeared to him when she opened the apartment door the evening before.

Surrounded by a mass of steam-misted, gleaming dark hair, Sarah's lovely face had worn a becoming pink tinge from her recent bath. Her soft brown eyes had been shimmery, her lips moist, invitingly delicious-looking.

Jake unconsciously skimmed his tongue over his own suddenly dry lips. Damn, he had been forced to wage a fierce inner battle to resist the impulse to taste her damp hair and her flushed cheeks and her sweet mouth. Then, when he had lowered his gaze to her body, the impulse had expanded into a need to draw Sarah into his arms. He had experienced a physical ache at the sight of her slender form embraced by that satin robe, which revealed every delectable curve, yet concealed every tantalizing feminine secret.

Becoming uncomfortably warm, Jake lowered the car window all the way, allowing the crisp air access to his overheated flesh. Man, he had it bad, he thought, laughing softly at himself, at his erotically active imagination.

But the funny part was, Jake reflected as he drew the car to a stop at the side of the road near the grade school, Sarah had appeared every bit as appealing and sexy to him after she was fully dressed.

Keeping a sharp eye on the youngsters converging on the school, Jake mulled over the hours he had spent in Sarah's apartment, in an attempt to rationalize and understand the intense attraction he felt for her.

"Good morning, Officer Wolfe!"

The chorused greeting from a group of second grade girls distracted Jake from his introspection.

"Morning, ladies," he responded, as always, eliciting giggles from the girls. "Got your thinking caps on?"

"Oh, yes, sir!" They fairly sang the daily reply.

From there, Jake made the short run to the middle school, where the scene was reenacted—sort of.

"Hi, Jake." The less formal greeting came from a couple of eighth grade boys...who believed they were cool.

"Hi, kids." Jake gave the boys a wave. "Ready to wow the teacher with your superior knowledge?"

"Yeah, right," one boy retorted.

"I wouldn't want to give her a heart attack," the other boy joked.

Jake stuck his head out the window. "Yeah, but it wouldn't hurt to give her a surprise, now and then," he suggested in a muted shout.

Laughing, the boys scuffed along the walk to the entrance doors. Laughing himself, Jake drew his head back inside and once more set the car in motion; it was time to check out the kids arriving at the high school.

The routine never varied whenever Jake was on the day shift, and yet he was continually amazed at how tall and mature the high school kids seemed to be—that is the boys were tall, the girls were mature.

After the last one of the kids—an extra-tall, all-arms-and-legs, gangly basketball player—loped into the low, modern building, Jake felt a surge of adrenaline as he headed the car in the direction of the college campus.

Sarah.

Although Jake knew his chances of seeing Sarah were somewhere between slim and none, he could not contain the expectant tingle that skipped erratically through his body, or the thoughts that danced inside his mind.

What *was* the attraction? Jake mused, automatically cruising the perimeter of the college grounds, keeping a keen, hopeful eye out for a particular woman.

Sarah was good to look at, but, Jake reminded himself, he had known many good-to-look-at women. He had even shared mutually satisfying intimacy with a few of them.

So then, Jake had to surmise that the attraction was therefore more than merely physical.

She was intelligent. It hadn't taken him long to realize and appreciate her sharp mind.

She possessed a quick, rather dry sense of humor; dry, wry wit never failed to capture Jake.

She could cook. While Jake certainly valued culinary expertise, he didn't consider the skill a prerequisite in a woman. When it came to culinary skills, he had heard some testimonials to his own talents.

But, for Jake, she had one outstanding attribute; Sarah Cummings was just plain nice...nice to be around, nice to talk to and, he knew instinctively, nice to make love with.

All things considered, he concluded, Sarah had a lot of plus factors going for her.

The tingle bubbling away inside Jake awakened him to the here, the now and the time. He shot a glance at his watch, and the tingle bubbled over into an eager smile. Smoothly turning the car, he drove away from the campus, heading for the little hamburger joint.

It was five minutes until coffee-break time.

Five minutes until Sarah time.

Jake could hardly wait.

Anxious and excited, he glided the car to a stop inches from the curb in front of the hamburger joint—which bore the ludicrous name The Golden Spatula—just as Sarah crossed the street, in the middle of the block.

"I could cite you, you know," he said as he stepped out of the car, frowning in mock sternness.

"What?" Sarah wasn't wearing the big round glasses. Her soft brown eyes grew wide, and flickered with—fear? "For—for what?" she asked in a quivery voice. She made a misstep and stumbled on the curb.

Jake's quick reflexes saved her from pitching forward and landing on her face on the sidewalk. The minute she was upright and steady again, Sarah pulled her arm free of his grasp and shied away from him.

For crying in a bucket, Jake thought, staring at her in stunned disbelief. What is her problem? Last night, Sarah had relaxed with him, conversed, laughed. Now, suddenly, she appeared as nervous and apprehensive as she had yesterday morning—if not even more so.

"I...I asked you a question," she said, in a dry, crackling voice that was still rife with tension.

Confused by her turnabout, Jake had forgotten her demand for an explanation. What in hell had he said to set her off? He racked his brain, and then the answer hit him. Oh, yeah. He had teased her about a citation. Big deal.

"I was only—" he began, but she cut him off in a tone that contained equal measures of feisty belligerence and edgy trepidation.

"You said you could cite me. For what?"

"Jaywalking," he answered, shaking his head, as if trying to clear his thoughts.

"Jaywalking!" Sarah exclaimed. Now it was her turn to stare at him in disbelief.

"I was teasing you, Sarah." Jake didn't know if he should laugh out loud or curse under his breath. "You crossed in the middle of the block."

"Oh." The fight, and the fear, visibly left Sarah, leaving him relieved but no less confused.

"I need some coffee," he declared, crossing the sidewalk to open the door of the café and hold it for her. "What about you?"

"Yes." Appearing to drag her feet without actually doing so, Sarah joined him at the doorway.

What was she doing here, with him?

Sarah slid into the booth Jake indicated, using the ploy of depositing her books and handbag in the corner of the bench seat as a means of avoiding his probing stare.

Jake probably thought she was some kind of a fool, Sarah reflected. No, he probably thought she was *all* kinds of a fool. Just another flaky woman who couldn't make up her tiny little mind, blowing warm, then cool, friendly, then antipathetic, calm then jumpy.

And Sarah couldn't honestly say she could blame him, if in fact that was Jake's perception of her. Her behavior—yesterday, last night and now—hardly suggested a high level of intelligence.

But there was a difference between last night and this morning; Jake was once again in uniform.

"Oh, hi, Jake, Miss Cummings," Dave called, strolling out of the kitchen. "I didn't hear you folks come in."

"You need a bell over the door," Jake suggested.

"Nah." Dave shook his head. "I tried that when I first opened the place. The damn thing drove me nuts." His shrug conveyed unconcern. "What can I get you? Two coffees?"

"Yes, please," Sarah murmured.

"The same for me," Jake said. Then he added, "And one—no, make it two—of your famous Coney Island hot dogs." He glanced at Sarah. "You want a dog?"

"At ten o'clock in the morning?" Sarah grimaced. "I'll pass, thank you."

Jake's expression dismissed the consideration of time. "Hey, I've been up since five-thirty, and all I've had is a cup of coffee and Mr. Bennet's power cocktail. I'm hungry."

"For a Coney Island hot dog?" She shuddered. "With raw onions and sauce and...everything?"

"Yeah." Jake smacked his lips. "All that good stuff."

"Incredible."

Jake frowned. "What's so incredible about it?"

"Well," Sarah replied, unaware that the tension

was slowly easing from her, "I mean, to follow a health drink with a loaded hot dog seems counter-productive."

Jake tossed her a grin born of the devil. "What can I tell you? I'm a junk-food junkie. And my particular favorite happens to be Coney Island hot dogs."

"And cheeseburgers," Dave reminded Jake, coming to a stop at the booth, steaming mugs of coffee in his hands. "Don't forget the cheeseburgers."

"Yeah," Jake said, on an exaggerated sigh. "I love a good cheeseburger. Maybe I'll change my order."

"Too late," Dave informed him, turning away. "I already got your dogs on the grill."

Jake slanted a gleaming glance at Sarah. "Independent bas—son of a gun, isn't he?"

Sarah wanted to remain aloof from Jake, wanted to remain cool, distanced, but she simply couldn't. Despite her genuine apprehension at the thought of any involvement with him, a police officer, she simply couldn't resist. Dismay stabbed at her mind, even as a smile tugged at her lips.

Why did Jake Wolfe have to be so darned nice?

"Come out, come out, wherever you are," Jake sang, chanting the childhood hide-and-seek refrain.

"What?" Sarah blinked herself out of her reverie. "What do you mean?"

"You were hiding inside there," Jake explained, tapping his temple with his forefinger.

"Oh, I was...er, just thinking."

"About me?" he asked, brightly, hopefully.

"Certainly not," she lied, and in a reproving tone of voice, at that. Lifting her cup, she took a tentative sip of the aromatic and still hot coffee.

"Oh." Disappointment weighted his tone. "About your problems with your students, then?"

Sarah choked on the coffee. Did he know? The frantic thought flashed through her mind. She had to find out. Catching her breath, she blurted out, "What do you mean?"

"Mean?" Jake gave her a strange look. "Nothing in particular." His dark eyes probed her anxious expression. "I was led to believe," he went on, "that all teachers had problems getting their subject across to at least some of their students. Was I led astray—down the academic path, so to speak?" he asked teasingly.

The wave of relief that washed over Sarah was so forceful it robbed her of breath and speech. Fortunately, at that moment, Dave came up to the booth, bearing a plate containing two hot dogs that smelled positively scrumptious.

"Two Coney Islands," he intoned, sliding the plate onto the table in front of Jake. "Try not to wolf 'em down, as usual, Wolfe." Chuckling to himself at his own play on words, he turned and ambled back behind the counter.

"You're a card, Dave," Jake called after him. "Hopefully by the time you're fifty-two you'll be a full deck."

"Ha!" Dave retorted. "I turned fifty-two six months ago." And although he didn't voice it, his tone said, *So what?* Shrugging, he turned to go back to the kitchen.

"Some character," Jake said, sinking his strong white teeth into the first of the dogs. He chewed the bite, swallowed, then gave an appreciative sigh. "Man, that's good. Sure you don't want the other one?" He arched his dark brows.

"No." Sarah smiled and shook her head. "Thank you. All I want is the coffee."

"You're a cheap date," he murmured, his eyes dancing with a teasing gleam. "I'll keep that in mind when I make reservations for our dinner date."

"Dinner date?" Sarah blinked. "What dinner date?"

Jake was chomping away on his second dog. He washed it down with coffee before answering. "I owe you one."

"No, really, you don't," Sarah insisted, telling herself she absolutely could not see him again.

"A debt's a debt, Miss Cummings," Jake told her in a deep and serious tone. "You took me in when I was hungry. Took pity on me when I was alone and lonely." His somber expression warred with the sparkle in his eyes. "I do owe you one."

He was a police officer, Sarah reminded herself. A cop. She couldn't afford to see him, date him, be with him. He was too attractive, too charming, too damned nice.

"How about this evening?"

"All right." Shocked by the acceptance that blurted from her mouth, Sarah sat staring at him in self-amazement. Where was her mind? Her sense of self-preservation? Jake's steady regard held promise, and an answer. Lost, all lost in the depths of his warm, smiling eyes.

"Good." Jake's satisfied murmur flowed over her like a benediction. "Do you have a food preference? Italian? Chinese? Mexican? Steak and potatoes?"

Decisions, decisions. Sarah felt unequal to the task of choosing. It was a new sensation for her; as a rule, she was decisive, certain, prepared to meet any challenge. Except the one posed by those three male students—and now Jake.

In desperation, Sarah made the only decision she felt capable of making—no decision at all.

"I like all of the above, so I'll leave it to you. You choose the restaurant and the cuisine, please."

"Anyplace?" he asked, as innocent as a soft spring rain.

"Anyplace," she agreed, without thinking.

He pounced. "Okay, my place."

Anyplace but *there*. Sarah opened her mouth to decline, but Jake was quicker to the draw.

"I'll return the favor and cook for you this time."

No. Sarah slowly moved her head from side to side. Being with him in a public restaurant was one thing. Being alone with him, in his place, was out of the question. Again she opened her mouth to decline; again he was quicker.

"I'm a pretty good cook," Jake assured her. "And I promise you won't be disappointed."

That was what Sarah was afraid of, being alone with him, and not being disappointed. Yet, even as she told herself she could not allow the attraction she felt for him to lead her astray, her mind chose to have a mind of its own.

"What time?"

Jake's smile could have melted a polar ice cap. "I go off duty at five. What time are you through for the day?"

"I'm usually finished by three," Sarah replied, unable to believe she was voluntarily falling in line with his plans. Nevertheless, she continued to explain. "But today's Friday, and the head of the history department has a standing end-of-the-week wrap-up meeting every Friday afternoon. I seldom get home before four-thirty."

"Suppose I pick you up at six-thirty?"

"Six-thirty will be fine." Well, she was committed now, Sarah thought—or was it that she *should* be committed? "But it isn't necessary for you to pick me up," she went on, keeping her doubts and uncertainties to herself. "Just give me your address, I can find my way there."

"Uh-uh." Jake shook his head. "I'll come for you, and I'll bring you back home." His voice was edged with hard finality. "This is a quiet town, but I'm not about to take any chances with your safety."

It was a bit ridiculous, maybe even dumb, but Jake's adamant determination instilled in Sarah a pleasant feeling of being cared for and protected. Not that she needed protecting, she hastened to assure herself. She was quite capable of taking care of herself. And yet having Jake so obviously concerned for her well-being gave her a sense of security unlike anything she had ever before experienced. Sarah was touched, and she didn't know quite how to respond.

"Well, all right," she finally said, fully aware she had once again caved in to him. "If you insist."

"I do." Jake's voice was soft; his eyes were softer. "Would you like more coffee?"

"No, thank you. I haven't even fin—" Sarah broke off, her eyes widening as she caught sight of his large watch, and the position of the hands on its face. "Good grief, will you look at the time!" she cried, fumbling for her purse and books. "I've got a class in twenty minutes." Scooping up her things, she slid out of the booth.

"Hey, relax." Jake tossed some bills on the table and followed after her. "I'll run you over to the campus."

"No!" When she heard the note of panic in her voice, Sarah drew a deep, calming breath. "I, ah...I mean, really, I can get there as fast by cutting across the campus."

"Are you sure?" Jake frowned, watching her warily, as if she had suddenly flipped out or something.

Sarah could hardly blame him, but she couldn't explain her seemingly strange behavior. And there was no way she was going to be seen getting out of a patrol car anywhere near the campus. She might be attracted to Jake, but she wasn't stupid.

"Yes," she answered, starting for the door.

"The money for the check is on the table, Dave." Jake called, trailing after her. "See you tomorrow."

"I'll be here," Dave drawled.

"Bye, Dave," Sarah called over her shoulder, pausing to stack her books on one arm as Jake skirted around her to open the door for her.

"Have a good one, folks." Dave's laconic voice drifted to them from the kitchen.

Surely Jake wouldn't use his official vehicle this evening. The dismaying thought occurred to Sarah as she stepped outside and saw the black-and-white police car parked along the curb. No, of course not, she reassured herself. At least she hoped he wouldn't.

"Something wrong?"

"What?" Sarah swung around to stare at him, and nearly dropped the stack of books in the process.

"I asked if there was something wrong." Jake's expression said reams about her odd behavior. "You're looking at the car as if you're afraid it'll attack you."

"That's silly," she said, in what she hoped sounded like a tone of amusement. "I'm distracted, that's all, and I really must rush now." She strode across the pavement.

"Sarah."

Jake's urgent call brought her up short, and she teetered on the curb as she twisted around to face him. "Yes?"

"Careful of the curb," he cautioned. His lips twitched into a smile. "Maybe you should put on your glasses."

As nervous and edgy as she was, Sarah still could not suppress a smile in return. "I can see just fine," she said, loftily. "I only need the glasses for reading."

"Hmm..."

She turned back to the street at the skeptical sound of his murmured response. "Now I really must go."

"Sarah." Jake's lowered voice had the strength to pull her around to face him again.

"Yes?"

"Six-thirty," he said softly. "I can't wait."

The blunt honesty of his admission went directly to her senses, warming her from the inside out. The glow of anticipation in his eyes intensified the warmth, melting the last lingering shreds of her resistance.

"I'll be ready," she whispered, held motionless, as if mesmerized, by the promise in his eyes.

"Get cracking, or you'll be late for class."

Jake's low-voiced command jolted Sarah into awareness, of the time, of where she was, of the depth and power of the effect he had on her senses.

"I'm off," Sarah said, quickly scanning the street before dashing across it. And in more ways than one, she told herself, making a beeline for the campus.

Sarah was panting from her headlong rush by the time she was trotting past the library, two buildings away from her own. Intent on reaching her destination on time, she almost missed seeing the three young men huddled together at the corner of the brick structure.

But something about them drew her attention. Shifting a quick glance at them, she caught her breath. Even without her glasses, Sarah could see that all three of the students had a furtive, highly charged look.

*Silence is golden,* the tallest of the young men had told her, yet he was anything but silent at that moment. His voice low, his expression strained, Andrew Hollings appeared to be giving orders to the other two students.

"...and your mouths shut this time," Sarah heard him snarl. Feeling a premonitory shiver of dread, she averted her face and rushed by at an outright run.

What in heaven's name were they involved in? Sarah wondered, not for the first, or even the fifty-first, time. The three had done something, committed some crime, and, judging by the snippet of conversation she had unfortunately overheard last week, it had been some kind of robbery.

But why? The question of motive had nagged at Sarah all week. It didn't make sense. The three young men were all seniors. They were close friends, had been friends for years, long before deciding to attend the same college. They were all from upper-upper-middle-class families, and they shared similar backgrounds. They had all attended excellent schools, and had maintained high scholastic averages throughout their first three years of college.

Dashing into the lecture hall, Sarah was unaware of the greetings called to her by the gathering class. Her thoughts were centered not on her presentation, but on the mystery of the three young men, and their apparent foray into the dangerous territory outside the law.

Sarah addressed the class as usual. "Good morning, ladies and gentleman. Shall we begin?"

While guiding the class through the intricacies of ancient Chinese history, Sarah managed to push her concerns for the three young men to the back of her mind. But the minute the class ended, speculation and worry surged forward into her consciousness again. During her lunch period, her mind gnawed on the mystery as thoroughly as her teeth chewed the food she didn't want or taste.

That the three of them had taken at least one step outside the law was patently evident. Sarah had little doubt on that score. She had heard only bits and pieces of their muttered discussion, but what she had heard was more than enough to convince her and condemn them.

Her memory of the shocking bits and pieces she had heard was clear, sharp, frightening. Most of the comments had been made by two of them, who appeared, paradoxically, both nervous and some-what cocky.

*We pulled it off.*

*What if we were seen?*

*Do you believe what they paid us?*

*I wasn't sure we could do it.*

*The police...*

That was the extent of the bits and pieces from the two young men. The comments were suspect, but not conclusive out of context. But it was the harsh, biting remark from Andrew Hollings that had convinced Sarah of their complicity.

*If you hang on to your nerve, and keep your mouths shut, we'll be safe from the police.*

It was then that Andrew had noticed Sarah, standing in the shadows inside the doors of the lecture hall. He had glared at her with dark, threatening eyes and whispered the warning that continued to revolve inside her mind.

*Silence is golden, Miss Cummings.*

# Three

Jake was beginning to feel like he had been waiting for ever for quitting time to come, and for the damn light to turn green at the intersection.

Heaving an impatient sigh, he drummed his blunt fingertips on the steering wheel and shot a glance at his watch. He still had an hour to go. The two-way squawked just as the light finally changed color.

The instructions coming through were for Jake to investigate a reported theft. Responding to directions, he turned at the next intersection and headed out of town.

The scene of the alleged crime was on a property located on the very fringes of his jurisdiction. The house Jake arrived at was set some distance back from the blacktop country road. An expensive bi-level, constructed mainly of wood and natural stone, the place was private, hidden by a stand of screening trees. The man who answered the door-bell was in his early forties, trim, fit and mad as hell.

"I damn well don't believe this," the man raved, glaring at Jake as though he were personally responsible for the situation. "Lord, do you have any idea what it cost me?"

"No, sir," Jake answered, in a professionally calm and soothing tone. "I don't even know what *it* is."

"My car, damn it!" the man shouted, spearing stiff fingers through already ruffled hair. "Come look," he went on, charging past Jake.

Jake dutifully loped after the irate man, nearly crashing into him when he came to an abrupt halt at the open door of a two-car garage.

"Will you just look at that mess?" the man said, in tones of outraged disgust. "Over forty thousand dollars, and they stripped it bare."

They sure had, whoever they were, Jake silently agreed as he stepped inside the garage to view the remains of what had probably once been an im-pressive-looking luxury car.

Amateurs, he concluded. Professional car thieves wouldn't have taken the time to strip the vehicle, thereby losing the resale value of the left-over parts. Professionals would simply have swiped the car, most likely by running it onto the back of a truck.

"Almost sacrilegious," Jake murmured, in sympathy and understanding of the man's shock and fury. "And the sad part is, the thief or thieves will probably get upwards of fifty, sixty, seventy thousand for the parts."

"Lord!" the man growled. "I could throw up."

No doubt, Jake thought. "I hope you don't," he said in all seriousness. "The sight will make me queasy."

"No kidding?" The man shifted his gaze to Jake, obviously distracted by his admission. "But you're a cop."

"What does that have to do with the price of fish?" Jake asked dryly, stepping into the dim interior of the garage to get a closer look at the pile of debris.

"Well, you know..." The man flicked a hand, as if trying to pluck the answer out of the air. "People like you, cops, firemen, paramedics, you see all kinds of gory stuff—murder victims, people all mangled in highway collisions and such."

"Uh-huh," Jake grunted, kneeling beside the hulk of what had once been an automobile.

"Do those sights make you queasy?"

"Yeah." Jake cocked his head to grin at the man. "Sad, but regrettably true."

"I could never be a cop," the man confessed, grimacing. "I mean, with all the crap you people have to put up with from hoods and badasses— besides all that gory stuff. I guess it takes a certain type of person."

Like stupid? Jake hid a wry smile and kept the observation to himself.

"So, what do you think the chances are of me ever seeing my car parts again?"

Rising, Jake turned to look the man straight in the eyes. "You want an acceptable answer, or the truth, Mr.—" He paused and raised his eyebrows questioningly.

"Hawkins," the man supplied. "Robert Hawkins. And I'm a big boy—I can handle the truth."

"Okay, Mr. Hawkins, from my experience, I'd say your chances are slim to none."

Robert Hawkins sighed and allowed his shoulders to droop. "I suspected as much." He expelled a short humorless laugh. "Boy, the insurance company's gonna love me."

In spades, Jake thought. And higher premiums. But that wasn't his concern, or part of his job description. Get to work, Wolfe, he advised himself, taking a quick look at his watch. *Tempus fugit* and all that.

Sarah.

Excitement coiled deep in Jake's gut, playing hell with his libido, as well as his thought processes. Dragging his thoughts into line, and his notebook from his back pocket, he proceeded with the drill of getting the facts together for his official report.

"When did you discover the theft?"

"Right before I called the station. Three-thirty, quarter to four, somewhere around then," Mr. Hawkins said, shrugging. "Not long after I woke up."

"You work the late shift?"

"Hell, no." Hawkins sounded mildly offended, as if he believed himself too good for anything as plebeian as the graveyard shift. "I'm the personnel manager for the Franklin Container Company in Norristown."

"I see." Jake jotted down the information. "You were home sick from work today?"

"No, no," Hawkins snapped angrily. "What does that have to do with my car being ripped off, anyway?"

"I'm not just being inquisitive, sir." Jake employed a soothing tone. "I'm attempting to ascertain an approximate time when the robbery took place."

"Oh, sorry." Hawkins flushed. "I took a vacation day today."

If one was taking a day, Friday was a good one. Jake kept that opinion to himself, as well. Of course, the information given wasn't a whole lot of help in ascertaining the approximate time of the robbery.

Jake frowned.

Robert Hawkins got the unstated hint, and launched into an explanation. "My lady friend and I left early last evening for Atlantic City, and we didn't get back till around five this morning."

"You have a run of luck?" Jake asked, prepared to offer his congratulations.

"Not really." Hawkins shrugged. "Oh, I won a little, but that wasn't why we stayed so late."

"Hmm..." Jake murmured noncommittally. Hell, it wasn't any of his business. Besides, he never gambled, not anymore. He had lost the urge after gorging himself in Vegas during his rebellious, wandering years. He had been to the seaside resort only once, out of curiosity. Still, it sure seemed to him to be a lot of hours to spend in a casino.

"We had tickets for an early show," Hawkins said, apparently reading Jake's expression. "Then we gambled a little. Then we had dinner in one of the swank hotel restaurants. Then we gambled a little more. Then we took in a late show." He shrugged again. "You know how it goes."

"Well, no..." Jake admitted. "But I'll take your

word for it. Five o'clock, huh?'' he mused aloud, bringing the conversation back to the subject. ''That leaves eleven or so hours open....''

''And the door,'' Hawkins inserted, making a face.

Jake arched his brows. ''The door?''

''The garage door.'' Hawkins sighed. ''I was beat, all I wanted to do was hit the bed. I forgot to close the garage door.''

''It's your property,'' Jake observed.

''Yeah, damn it!'' Hawkins's anger was aroused again. ''Just because I forgot to shut the damn door, that doesn't give any two-bit thief the right to waltz in and strip my car, does it?''

''No, sir,'' Jake said, once again trying for a calming tone. ''You'll have to come down to the station to...''

''I know, I know,'' Hawkins cut in impatiently. ''Formality, red tape, and I'll bet you a dollar against a slug I'll never see those parts again.''

Jake shook his head. ''No, sir. No bet. Sorry.'' He glanced around the area. ''It'd be my guess the thief or thieves did the job somewhere in the couple of hours between the time you arrived home and dawn. You're pretty secluded here, but you do have neighbors, and stripping a car isn't the kind of crime usually committed in full daylight.''

''I suppose you're right.'' Hawkins stared at what had been his car less than twelve hours before and heaved a long sigh. "Does that help you at all?"

"Not much," Jake confessed. "But we'll get on it, put it out on the wire."

"Thanks."

Although Robert Hawkins didn't add "for nothing," Jake heard the implied phrase in the man's voice—and the despair. While he sympathized with the man, there wasn't much he could do about it, aside from the routine of asking questions and looking around for possible clues, such as tire tracks left by the vehicle the thief or thieves had used.

There were none. Other than the heap of what was now junk on the garage floor, there was nothing, except Jake's educated guess that the thieves were very likely amateurs—which really wasn't a lot of help, either.

It was past five by the time Jake got to the station, past quitting time, and he still had reports to complete. By the time he got home, it was creeping up on six. He still had to shower, dress and... Jake sighed as he glanced around the living room. He had to straighten up the place.

What in hell was he going to throw together for dinner? The thought struck him, stopped him cold in the process of plumping the throw pillows on the sofa.

Dashing into the kitchen, Jake peered into the

freezer. Fate smiled upon him; there were two thick Delmonico steaks, a package of frozen Idaho baked potatoes, and a frozen warm-and-serve apple pie—almost like homemade.

The liquor cabinet revealed a bottle of cabernet sauvignon, which he slid onto a rack in the fridge. At least the sink wasn't cluttered with dishes, since he hadn't bothered preparing breakfast that morning.

Jake shot a look at his watch, cursed and took off for the bathroom. He nearly scalded himself by stepping under the shower before adjusting the water temperature, and he nicked himself three times while scraping the beard shadow from his face. In between pulling on blue socks, darker blue pants and a lighter-blue-and-white striped shirt, and hop-stepping into black leather slip-ons, he tugged the covers neatly into place on the still-rumpled unmade bed.

Sarah.

A sensuous thrill arrowed through Jake's body.

A man could always dream.

Jake smiled in self-mockery as he shrugged into a navy Windbreaker, took another quick, longing look at the bed, then loped out of the apartment at six-twenty.

There was no law on the books against wishful thinking.

A man was entitled to his fantasies.

* * *

Was she completely crazy, or what?

Sarah tugged the brush through her hair and grimaced, both at the sharp pain in her scalp and at the question repeating itself inside her head.

Had she actually agreed to have dinner alone with a man in his apartment?

Yes, she had.

Crazy, or dumb or both.

Even now, hours later, Sarah couldn't believe she had capitulated so easily. And it wasn't just that Jake Wolfe was a virtual stranger to her, an unknown quantity... *He was a police officer, for heaven's sake.*

But he was such a nice police officer, Sarah defended herself. And, with his tall, long-muscled body, he did look fantastic in that uniform, she allowed, turning away from the dresser mirror to cross the bedroom to the clothes closet. And he was so strikingly good-looking, she reflected, staring dejectedly at the selection of garments draped on satin hangers looped over the metal rod.

And she had nothing glamorous to wear.

That errant, wailing thought startled Sarah out of her moody introspection.

Glamorous? Sarah frowned. The word *glamorous* connoted romance and excitement. She certainly was not looking for either of those things.

Who was she kidding? Sarah pulled a sand-washed silk dress in a forest-green, rust-and-gold pattern from the rod. All Jake had to do was glance at her with his deep, dark blue eyes and she got excited.

And mush-minded with thoughts of romance.

Her sigh whispered in the quiet room. A sigh born of dismay and anxiety. She couldn't take a chance on getting involved with Jake, or even be too friendly with him. She had seen the threat in Andrew Hollings's eyes when he had warned her to keep silent. His threat had not been an empty one. If she was seen in public with Jake, if her name was linked with his, Andrew would soon hear about it, and act on it.

Sarah shivered. Andrew had never appeared sinister or capable of violence. Nor had either one of the other two young men. They were all so bright, always well-mannered and pleasant.

What had they gotten themselves into to cause such a radical change in their personalities?

That their recent extracurricular activities had been illegal, Sarah had little doubt. She had heard enough of their discussion to convince her of their complicity, and some inner sense told her that none of them would hesitate to silence her if she gave any indication of voicing her suspicions—and most especially Andrew of the threatening tone and eyes.

Sarah sighed again, feeling trapped and frustrated. Jake looked to be the best thing to come her way in— Damn, she had never in her adult life met any man halfway as interesting and exciting as Jake. Why had she met him now? she thought in protest against the lousy timing of destiny. At any other time, in any other place...

Yet another, heavier sigh broke the silence.

Dragging her thoughts away from the edge of depression, Sarah slipped her feet into rust-colored suede heels and turned to leave the bedroom.

It was not another time or place, and she would have to deal with that fact. Jake was now and here and—

The doorbell rang.

Sarah froze in the bedroom doorway.

Jake was *here*.

A stab of sheer panic immobilized her for a moment, but then she raised her chin, squared her shoulders and crossed the living room to open the door. Her breath caught, lodged in her throat, at the sight of him.

Jake Wolfe looked devastating in navy blue.

"Hi."

His smile didn't exactly lack impact, either. She felt the blow to the tips of her tingling toes.

"Hi." Sarah could barely articulate the tiny word.

"You look beautiful." His bone-melting eyes made a slow survey of her body.

Sarah's bones dutifully melted. "Thank you."

Lord, did that reedy little voice belong to her?
"You...you're looking rather terrific yourself."

Jake's eyes softened.

Sarah's insides liquified.

"Ready?"

For anything you might suggest. Hearing the
yearning note in her silent reply, Sarah snapped
herself back to reality. There was no longer any
doubt in her mind; she *was* crazy.

"Yes," she said, reluctantly taking her gaze
from him to turn away. "Let me get my purse and
coat."

Jake moved into the room to help her with her
coat. Sarah immediately wished he hadn't played
the gentleman. The touch of his long, strong fingers on her shoulders, at her nape, sent a fiery
shower of sensations cascading throughout her being, and ignited a smoldering spark in the core of
her femininity. Feeling seared all over, she stepped
away from temptation.

"What's for dinner?" she asked, too brightly.
"I'm starving." She smiled, too brilliantly.

"Er...well..." Jake followed her into the hallway and stood to one side as she shut and locked
the door. "I wanted to cook one of my special
dishes for you, but I was running late and..." He
paused to give her a self-deprecating, and thoroughly captivating, smile. "How do you feel about
steak and baked potatoes?"

"I love steak and baked potatoes." Sarah frowned, and concentrated on descending the narrow, rather steep stairs. "Why? I mean, since I had a vegetable dish yesterday, and didn't want a hot dog this morning, were you thinking I was a confirmed vegetarian?" She tossed a quizzical glance at him.

"Something like that," Jake admitted, obviously relieved. He stepped around her to open the door. "I'm glad to hear you're not antimeat, especially red meat."

"Not anti, at least, not entirely," Sarah said as she walked past him. "But, in reaction to all the adverse publicity on it, I have cut down on my consumption of meat in the last few years."

"You know," Jake mused, trailing her outside and down the three shallow steps to the pavement. "I sometimes question the benefits of all the instant media communications we are bombarded with today."

"Are you implying that ignorance is bliss?" Sarah asked teasingly, while absorbing a wave of relief at the absence of a black-and-white police car along the quiet street.

"Yeah, I suppose I am." Grinning at her, Jake crossed the sidewalk to a smart-looking silver-and-gray sedan. "But, to use another old saying, maybe a little knowledge is a dangerous thing."

Ignorance is bliss. A little knowledge is a dangerous thing. Sarah felt chilled, struck by the truth of the maxims as they related to her own situation with regard to Andrew Hollings and the other two men.

A little knowledge concerning their apparently nefarious activities had robbed her of her own blissful ignorance, and placed her in danger.

Murmuring an absent "Thank you," Sarah slid into the car, then sat staring through the windshield, contemplating her precarious position, as Jake shut the door and circled around to the driver's side.

"Buckle up."

His soft command defused the flash of panic flaring to life inside Sarah. With breathtaking suddenness, she was struck by the realization that just knowing Jake was there, close by, gave her an intense feeling of security and protection.

But was it the presence of the man, or the police officer? Obeying orders, Sarah fastened the belt, and slanted a sidelong look and a tentative smile at him.

"What?" Jake's hands stilled in the act of connecting his own seat belt, a curious smile kicking up the corners of his well-defined mouth.

Should she take a chance and confide in him? Staring into his puzzled eyes, barely aware that he had spoken, Sarah toyed with the idea of dumping her worries, her fears, onto his broad, powerful-looking shoulders.

"Sarah?"

Ensnared in the morass of her own thoughts, Sarah continued to stare at him, weighing the pros and cons of revealing to him her suspicions about the three students.

On the pro side was Jake himself, tall, strong, exuding a palpable aura of capability and confidence. While on the side of the cons was the irrefutable fact that Sarah had no real evidence to present to him. There were the disjointed bits and pieces of conversation she had overheard, and her intuitive certainty, but she possessed no proof at all.

*Silence is golden, Miss Cummings.*

What, she wondered, would Jake make of Andrew's threatening advice to her? Then again, what *could* he make of it, when for all intents and purposes Andrew had merely cited yet another tried and true axiom?

"Sarah, honey, what's wrong?" Jake's voice wore a sharp edge of concern that cut through the gridlock of her converging thoughts.

"Nothing...I..." Sarah paused to gather her wits and find a plausible excuse for her distraction; unconsciously her decision had been reached. Rather than involve Jake, and possibly place him in danger, too, she would adhere to Andrew's dictum and remain silent.

Jake's eyes narrowed. "There's something. You look so...strained, almost frightened." He released the belt, and it snapped back into position, forgotten as he leaned across to stare deep into her eyes. "You're not afraid of being alone with me in my apartment, are you?"

"Oh, no," Sarah said at once, at that moment realizing she spoke the truth. "I was just thinking..." she began, searching for an explanation for her odd behavior. Then her eyes flickered and grew wide as another, equally compelling realization sank in. "You called me honey."

The tension around Jake's eyes and mouth eased visibly. His lips quirked in amusement. "Yes, I did."

"Why?" Sarah asked ingenuously.

The quirk on his lips grew into a beguiling smile. "Because you are one," he said with quiet simplicity. "A real honey of a woman."

"Oh." Sarah was nonplussed. For a woman who disdained the current free-and-easy use of endearments, she felt an inordinate sense of pleasure.

Stretching his long body, Jake leaned closer to her. "Do you mind?" His warm breath caressed her cheek, sending ripples of response through her in ever-widening circles.

Sarah shivered; the feeling was delicious.

"N—no..." She shook her head, and stopped breathing. Her action brought her lips to within a wish of his.

"May I taste?" Jake's voice was low, uneven.

Sarah's draining mind grappled with his request for a second, and then understanding spawned excitement. "Here?"

"Just a taste," he murmured, bathing her mouth and her senses with his breath. "An appetizer."

Sarah couldn't speak, couldn't think. All she was capable of was feeling—and, boy, was she feeling. Wild sensations skittered through her body and danced on the surface of her flesh. Her lips burned, her tongue tingled, her meager defenses collapsed.

"Yes, an appetizer, please."

Jake sighed; Sarah felt it in the depths of her being. His mouth brushed hers; she parted her lips. Accepting the silent invitation, he fused his mouth to hers.

Contact. Instant electricity. Sarah felt the charge in every cell and atom in her body. Jake didn't deepen the kiss; he didn't need to apply pressure to fuel the spark. The flame leaped higher and higher.

It was too hot, too combustible, too soon.

Cursing under his breath, Jake pulled back, all the way back to the driver's side, behind the wheel.

Stunned by the magnitude of the unique experience, still quivering in reaction, Sarah stared at him in mute wonder, and slowly raised her fingertips to her sensitized and trembling lips.

"We've got to get out of here." His voice was harsh, raw. "Lord, if Cal had cruised past the car just then, he'd have probably hauled us in and booked us for inflammatory and indecent public behavior."

"Cal?" Sarah blinked and let her hand drop unnoticed into her lap.

Jake drew a deep breath. "Cal Parker, the officer on second-shift patrol." He reached over his shoulder, yanked the seat belt across his body and fumbled with the lock, the fine tremor in his fingers forcing him to make three stabs with the prong before securing it.

"I see." Sarah swallowed; it wasn't easy.

He fired the engine and shot her a piercing look. "Are you all right, honey?"

"Yes." She managed a convincing smile.

"Ready for bland old steak and potatoes?"

"I'll be satisfied with a bland dinner." A teasing imp invaded her mind, and laughed at him out of her eyes. "Because you do serve up one spicy appetizer."

The rich sound of his delighted laughter filled the car, and every nook and cranny of Sarah's heart.

# Four

---

A kiss, just a kiss, and not even a very long or deep or intense kiss, at that. There had been no hot possession, no urgent pressure, no dueling tongues.

Just a kiss.

Uh-huh. It was just a kiss, all right, Sarah reflected. Just a kiss that registered 9.5 on her personal quake-measuring scale.

Heavens, over two hours had elapsed since that kiss, and she still felt the inner shocks and tremors. Two hours. Sarah flicked a quick glance at the man seated opposite her at the glass-topped dining table.

Surprisingly, the seconds and minutes of the previous two hours had flowed together smoothly, despite a strong, if unacknowledged, undercurrent of tension.

Sarah and Jake had worked together in outward compatibility and congeniality, chatting and laughing while preparing the meal and setting the table in the cozy dining alcove set off the kitchen. Yet, beneath their surface camaraderie, the tension had remained constant—not a sizzling, frizz-your-hair charge, but more a humming portent of promise.

There had been moments, moments fraught with inherent danger, moments when their arms had brushed, their fingers had touched, their eyes had met and clung.

The signs indicated the potential for another emotional quake—the big one. Sarah sensed it building in the shivery feeling inside her.

She was hiding it well, though, she assured herself, sighing in repletion as she placed her napkin on the table next to her plate.

"For a makeshift, rushed-together meal," she said, smiling across the table at Jake, "that was delicious."

"The pie didn't live up to its claim." Returning her smile, he picked up the wine bottle and topped off their glasses, champagne flutes he had produced for the occasion. "It didn't taste homemade to me—at least, not anywhere near my mother's apple pie.''

''I wouldn't know the difference,'' Sarah admitted, laughing. ''My mother is a disaster in the kitchen. My father always teased her by maintaining that she was the only cook he knew who could burn water.''

Laughing along with her, Jake slid back his chair and stood. ''Let's go into the living room and get comfortable,'' he said, picking up both glasses.

''After I clear the table,'' she said, standing and immediately reaching for the empty plates.

Jake stopped her by curling his fingers around her wrist. ''That'll wait.'' He dismissed the clutter with a shrug. ''After you.'' Releasing her wrist, he indicated the living room with a sweeping wave of his arm. ''I want to hear more.''

''About my mother's cooking?'' Unobtrusively rubbing the tingling skin where his fingers had circled her wrist, Sarah preceded him into the living room. ''What's to tell?'' she asked, grinning, as she settled into the corner of a long sofa. ''It's lousy.''

''Okay.'' Jake handed a glass to her, then settled himself on the plump cushion next to hers. ''Then I guess I'll have to be content with your life story.''

''My entire life story?'' Sarah blinked in feigned surprise. ''From day one?''

"Every detail," Jake insisted. "From day one, up to yesterday morning."

When we met. He didn't say it; he didn't have to. Sarah instinctively felt the importance he attached to the occasion of their first meeting.

"You're tired?" she asked, with an ease she was light years away from feeling.

"Tired?" Jake frowned. "No. Why?"

"My life story is boring fare," she explained. "Put you to sleep in no time."

"Boring, huh?" Jake's casual tone concealed the baited snare. "Even the steamy, sexy parts?"

Sarah walked into his trap without a thought. "There are no steamy, sexy parts."

A lazy smile sauntered across his lips. "Too bad." His voice held purring satisfaction. He raised his glass to take a sip of the wine, then raised his eyes to gaze into hers. "You want to add some? I'm willing to oblige."

He was teasing her, Sarah assured herself, taking a quick sip of her own wine to wet her suddenly parched mouth and throat. Well, two could play at that game.

"What did you have in mind?" she asked, in tones she hoped sounded blasé and world-weary.

"Getting naked in a tub filled with champagne," he suggested in a sexy drawl.

"Expensive." Sarah managed to maintain her cool composure, despite the bubble of laughter tickling the back of her throat. "Or do you have the wine on hand?"

"No." Jake appeared crestfallen.

"Well, then, I guess you'll have to settle for my life story, dull as it may be."

"Would you consider a bubble bath instead?" he asked hopefully. "I think I have some of that."

"No." Sarah shook her head. "Sorry, it's champagne or nothing."

Jake exhaled a long sigh. "You're a hard woman, Sarah." He paused. "Well, you're not physically hard. Your skin is soft and smooth and—"

Sarah interrupted him ruthlessly. "Do you want to hear my story or not?"

"Lay it on me." Jake flashed her a grin.

Fighting the dazzling effects of it, of him, on her uncertain senses, Sarah launched into a rapid-fire account of her existence prior to their first meeting.

"As I said previously, I'm from Baltimore. I was born and raised there, twenty-seven years ago. My father was and still is a structural engineer, in an upper-management position. My mother is a high school guidance counselor. I was always bookish, living in the historical past, keeping to myself, rather than joining in outside activities." Sarah paused in her narrative to take a sip of wine.

"No siblings...brothers, sisters?" Jake inserted into the lull.

Sarah shook her head. "No, I wish I did. I'd have loved a sister or an older brother, but..." She shrugged.

"That's a shame," he said in commiseration. "I have three—brothers." He laughed softly in reminiscence. "It got wild at times, but never dull."

"I envy you," she said wistfully. "Our house was always quiet. I got lonesome at times."

"No friends?" Jake raised his eyebrows.

"Of course I had friends." Sarah laughed. "Every one as bookish as I, a cadre of overachievers."

"Boyfriends?" he asked pointedly.

"A few," she admitted. "But nothing serious, until..." Catching herself, she let her voice fade away to nothing.

"Until?" Jake probed with intent.

Sarah hesitated, loath to talk about the single most uncomfortable and humiliating experience of her otherwise prosaic, uneventful life.

"That bad, huh?" Jake had the look of a dog with a bone firmly clamped in his teeth, a bone he would not relinquish without a struggle.

Stalling for time, Sarah took another long sip of her wine. In retrospect, and from a more mature perspective, the incident, though traumatic at the time, had diminished in significance. She had played the fool, but then, playing the fool was part of the rite of passage into maturity.

Jake decided the issue for her. "You fell in love?" he guessed, accurately.

"Yes," Sarah admitted with a wry smile. "And proceeded to make a fool of myself over the man."

"Big hunk on campus?"

"Oh, no. No half measures for me." Sarah grimaced. "I went the whole nine yards, falling for a professor—the head of the history department, no less."

"Who else?" Jake murmured. "And he made it known that he wasn't interested?"

"He was *very* interested. He was also very married. He let slip enticing little tidbits of information, such as how unhappy and lonely he was, hinting at a pending divorce." She sighed. "I lapped up every word."

"You...er, got involved?"

"Involved?" Sarah laughed; it had more the sound of a derisive snort. "*Involved* hardly describes it. For all intents and purposes, I literally worshiped him. He was willing to take anything I offered him. And, in my innocence—or stupidity— I eagerly gave him everything."

Except for a slight tightening of his lips, Jake betrayed no reaction to her blunt recount. His expression remained attentive, but seemingly unaffected. "And when you realized he was using you, you crept away to lick your wounds," he murmured, not in question, but in speculation.

"Oh, no." Sarah bit down on her lip before producing a patently false, overbright smile. "Not I, Miss All-Brains-and-No-Sense. I clung like a limpet." She blinked, glanced away, then turned to look directly at him. "It took a visit from his wife before I finally got the message."

"You loved him?"

"Yes," Sarah whispered. "With all the dramatic fervor only the very young can agonize over."

Jake gazed at her in contemplation for several long moments. "You're still hurting from the experience," he finally said, in a musing tone of voice, as if he were thinking out loud. "And still in love with him. Aren't you?"

His observation startled her. It shouldn't have, Sarah acknowledged. The pain, the humiliation, the self-condemnation she believed she had put behind her still festered deep inside her, hidden, but there. The realization, while enlightening, cast a sobering, unflattering light on her self-image.

"You don't have to answer," Jake said, setting his glass on the floor, then raising his hand to weave his long fingers through hers. "I had no right to ask."

Strangely comforted by the strength of his hand curled around hers, Sarah gave him a weak smile and a quick shake of her head. "It's all right. It was the logical next question. But your conclusion was wrong. Although I must admit to still feeling a residue of the pain and humiliation I inflicted upon myself, I am not still in love with him." She moved her shoulders in a parody of a careless shrug. "In fact, now, from a distance of several years, I realize I never was in love with him."

"Or any other man," Jake concluded.

"Or any other man," she concurred.

"Do you now hate all men?" His voice was low, intense, with a fine edge of concern.

"Hate?" Sarah echoed in surprise. "No, of course not. I'm not so simpleminded as to blame the entire male species for what, in effect, I did to myself. Besides, hate is such a debilitating, pointless emotion, isn't it?"

"Pretty much so," Jake agreed, stroking his fingers down the length of hers. "But," he went on, "I'm certain that there are some, maybe many, who would have taken refuge from self-condemnation by blaming and hating the entire world." He released her fingers to glide his hand up her arm.

Sarah suppressed a responsive gasp, but lost the battle against a receptive shiver. "You—" She had to pause to catch her breath and swallow. "You are very wise," she told him, in a small, trembly voice.

Jake smiled, and trailed his fingers along her shoulder to the side of her neck. "I've been around the block a few times." His index finger stroked the skin above her collar.

Sarah was finding it extremely difficult to breathe. "In...in connection with your police work?" Her voice had been reduced to a reedy murmur.

"Mmm-hmm..." Jake nodded, and shifted from the center cushion to the edge of hers. He leaned into her, so close she could feel his taut muscles, the heat from his body. "The police work," he murmured, prickling her ear and her senses with his warm breath. "And the rawness of life I experienced during my footloose years wandering around the country."

Rawness defined the sensation inside her. The fleeting thought flashed in Sarah's mind, then was gone. Feelings took over, feelings caused by the feather-light touch of Jake's lips against the sensitized skin behind her ear, feelings generated by the glide of his tongue from her ear to her jaw, feelings heightened by the movement of his mouth from her jaw to her trembling lips, and deeper feelings, hot and intense, ignited by the way her mouth was captured beneath the pressure of his lips.

Clinging to her last vestiges of lucidity, Sarah pressed her head back against the sofa, freeing her lips. "I...ah...Jake," she panted, tearing her gaze from the alluring flame flaring in his blue eyes to stare numbly at the tremor in the glass in her hand. "I'm afraid my wine's sloshing onto the floor."

"Easily remedied." Levering his torso over hers, he plucked the glass from her hand and set it on the end table next to the sofa. "There." Instead of moving back, beside her, he stretched out his long body the full length of hers.

He was lying on top of her! Sarah felt the weight of his broad chest against her breasts, the nudge of his hips against her pelvis, the bunched-muscle pressure of his long legs against her thighs, and the hard urgency of his...

Sarah shuddered in response to the flare of moist heat radiating throughout her being from the core of her femininity. Then his mouth brushed hers, and the heat expanded, flowing like molten lava through her veins.

"Now, where were we?" Jake murmured against her lips, filling her mouth, her senses, with his warm, intoxicating, wine-scented breath.

En route to mindlessness? Sarah couldn't articulate the reply that zapped through her surrendering consciousness. It didn't matter; Jake knew precisely where they were, where they were heading and exactly how to get there.

His lips settled on hers. Close, they were getting close. He slanted his mouth, moving his lips to part hers. Closer. The tip of his tongue made a tentative probe. Closer still. Then his tongue speared into her mouth at the same instant his hand covered her breast.

Destination attained.

Sarah's mind shut down. Sensations ruled. And the sensations were all-consuming. The inner heat intensified, sending a shivering thrill up her spine, then down again, back into the depths of her feminine being. Jake's mouth was hard, his searching tongue insistent, demanding a response from her, a response she was beyond denying him. While his tongue engaged hers in rough, erotic play, she raised her arms and coiled them around his taut neck, arching herself up, into him. An exciting, low groan rumbled in his throat. His hand flexed around her breast; his fingers were gentle, teasing, tormenting the tip of her breast into tight arousal, enticing a muffled gasp from her throat.

Sarah's stomach quaked.

The big one?

The fearful thought fought its way through the sensuous fog clouding her gray matter. Too soon, too soon, a faint inner voice warned. Understanding struggled to be born.

*Stop him.* Sarah heard the shrill inner command and forced her languid limbs to obey. With her dwindling resources of strength, she slid her hands down and pressed against his chest, moving him back, away from her.

"Jake…please…" she pleaded between gasps for breath. "You're moving too fast for me."

To his credit, Jake didn't persist. His chest heaving, his eyes dark and glittery, mirroring the extent of his passion, he flung himself back, away from physical contact with her. Half reclining, the rigidity of his body blatantly displayed the power and potency of his arousal.

As if pulled by an irresistible magnetic force field, Sarah's eyes were drawn to his sprawling figure. Her stomach muscles contracted at the sight of the fiery desire blazing from his eyes, the tightness of his clenched jaw, the lines of strain bracketing his compressed mouth, the quiver in the taut muscles in his legs, and the bulge at the apex of…

Sarah dragged her gaze away from temptation, and propelled herself forcefully from the sofa. "It's…uh, getting late," she said, in a squeaky, breathless voice. "I'll…er…I'll clear the table," she offered, making a beeline for the comparative safety of the dining alcove.

Jake didn't make a move to follow Sarah. In truth, he seriously doubted his ability to pursue her at that moment. He hurt, in the most vulnerable part of his body; the pain was not altogether unpleasant.

Drawing deep, calming breaths into his tight chest, he gazed down the length of his body, following the route Sarah's widened eyes had traversed moments ago.

A wry smile twitched his lips as his gaze came to rest on the full and obvious evidence of the cause of her precipitate flight.

He was hard as cast iron. Jake expelled a rueful chuckle at his apt comparison. He wanted to cast his iron, longed to cast his iron, was damn near perishing from the need to cast his iron, but his target had fled, leaving in her wake a very hard and very uncomfortable man.

He didn't blame her for fleeing. Her protest was valid; he had moved on her too soon, too fast.

At any other time, with any other woman, Jake might have rationalized his impetuous, unconsidered actions. He might have excused himself by citing the temptations Sarah presented—the allure of her body, so excitingly concealed, yet revealed, by that clinging silk dress, the sweet, moist appeal of her soft, full lips, the power of her initial melting response. But none of the excuses were valid, and he knew it. Sarah had not teased or deliberately tempted him. He knew that, as well.

It was hardly Sarah's fault that he couldn't seem to keep his hands, his body, his mind, off her, he admitted, still tingling, aching from the touch and taste of her.

On reflection, the swiftness and the uncommon strength of his arousal gave Jake pause. The experience was unique, he mused, a benchmark in his personal experience. Not even during his hot and overeager teenage years had his body risen to the occasion so quickly, so to speak.

Of course, he had been enduring a long dry spell lately, he reminded himself. It had been some months since he had been with a woman in an intimate way—ever since he had returned to Sprucewood, as a matter of fact. But he had gone through dry spells before, periods lasting even longer than this current span, and yet when offered the opportunity to end the dry spell, he had never sprung to full, throbbing life as rapidly, as urgently, as he had moments ago with Sarah.

Passing strange, Jake decided, frowning as he contemplated his pulsating state of disappointment. Even now, when the wind called Sarah had changed course and was blowing in the direction of the dining alcove, the sails of his libido remained in unfurled and bursting fullness.

Jake's rueful chuckle erupted in soft laughter. Damned if he wasn't thinking in allegorical terms, when he should be applying deductive reasoning to the mystery. He was a cop, wasn't he? he chided himself, sighing in relief as his body finally began to relax. So do your cop thing, he thought—examine the evidence and draw a conclusion.

Jake cocked his head as the sound of rattling dishes and cutlery assailed his ears. While he waited out the slow descent from an unprecedented sexual high, Sarah was keeping busy, working off her reactions to it by clearing the table of the remains of their meal.

Sarah.

Jake sighed and surged to his feet. The answer to his physical dilemma didn't require the deductive reasoning of a master sleuth, after all. Bending, he picked up his wineglass from the floor, then collected Sarah's glass from the end table. The answer was contained within her name.

Jake knew with sudden clarity that his instantaneous arousal had been fired by the woman Sarah, and not by a need for transient release with just any woman.

It was a scary concept. A self-confident smile playing over his lips, Jake sauntered across the living room. Lucky for him that he was a cop, a bona fide officer of the law, trained to deal with scary concepts.

The table was cleared, and the dining room was empty. Following the sound of running water, Jake continued on to the archway that led into the kitchen. Sarah stood at the sink, her back to him, her arms submerged in soapy water.

"You shouldn't be doing that," he said, hesitating in the archway. "You had kitchen duty last night."

"I don't mind." Her shoulders moved in a slight

shrug. "I'm used to it." Her hands stilled in the act of rinsing a plate. "Are you all right?" Her voice was low, so soft that he could barely hear it over the running water.

"I think I'll live."

Sarah slanted a quick look at him over her shoulder. "Jake, I'm sorry, but I…"

"I know," he inserted, trying to make it easier for her. "Not your fault, anyway," he admitted. "I pushed, and I deserved to be shoved back." He waited, and when she didn't reply, he crossed the room to stand next to her, close, but not too close. "I brought your wine." He held the glass up for her to see, then set it on the counter alongside the draining rack.

Sarah gave him a tentative smile. "I think I've had enough wine…more than enough."

"It wasn't the wine, Sarah," Jake said decisively, setting his glass next to hers before turning to face her fully. "And you know it as well as I do."

"No, it wasn't the wine," she whispered, lowering her eyes to avoid his piercing stare.

"Look at me, Sarah." Though he kept his voice soft, even, he injected a hint of command into his tone.

Sarah's head snapped up, as if yanked by a cord. She sank her teeth into her lower lip, but held his steady regard.

"There's a strong attraction at play here, physical and emotional. I know it, and you know it." He kept her pinned with his eyes. "Don't you?"

Sarah sighed, "Yes."

"Yes." Jake nodded. "I like being with you, and I believe you like being with me. Am I right?"

"Yes."

"Okay." Jake drew a breath, then threw caution to the winds. "I'll level with you. I want to go to bed with you." He shook his head, sharply, decisively. "No, I don't just want to go to bed with you, I want to submerge myself in you. I want it so damn bad my back teeth ache." He drew another, deeper breath. "But I swear I won't push you again. I'll wait until you tell me, openly, honestly, that you want it, too." He gave her a crooked grin. "It won't be easy...but I'll wait."

"Jake...I..." Her beautiful eyes grew misty with tears; they were nearly his undoing.

"Damn it, Sarah, don't cry, or I'll have to take you in my arms again, hold you close, feel your sexy body beneath that silky material and—" He broke off, stepped back and, turning, pulled a cabinet drawer open and groped inside for a tea towel. "Er...you finish washing. I'll dry."

"All right." Sarah laughed, and sniffed. "And while you're at it, you can tell me *your* life story."

# Five

"**I** came into this world as the clock struck midnight in the clapboard shack on the wrong side of the Reading Railroad tracks."

Struck midnight? Clapboard shack! Sopping dishrag in hand, Sarah forgot the glass she was in the process of washing and turned to frown at the storyteller.

Jake's expression was bland, innocent...deceptively innocent. His eyes, though, looked guilty as hell.

"Go on," she urged, giving him a wry, if not patently disbelieving, smile.

"It was a dark and stormy night…"

Sarah rolled her eyes.

"Well, it was." The twitch of Jake's lips belied his injured tone. "Cold, too."

"Uh-huh." Sarah fought back a giggle. "Continue."

"Outside the wind vas blowing…a pushcart filled mit snow?" Jake went on, in a heavily laid-on Pennsylvania Dutch accent, quoting a bit from *Dangerous Dan McGrew,* out of context and, she suspected, incorrectly.

Sarah lost it. Unmindful of the sodden rag she held, she brought her hand up to her mouth to muffle a burst of laughter, and proceeded to go into a fit of choking and gasping at the taste of dish detergent on her tongue.

"Serves you right," Jake said smugly, nevertheless nudging her aside to pour a glass of water for her to cleanse her mouth with. "It's what you get for doubting me."

"I do humbly beg your pardon," Sarah replied, grimacing at the aftertaste of detergent-tainted water.

"And rightly so," Jake retorted reprovingly. Then he ruined the effect by asking, anxiously, "Are you okay?"

"Yes," she assured him with a smile. "But how about something to wash away this awful taste?"

"Your wine?" Jake started to turn toward where he had set the glasses.

Sarah halted his movement by grasping his arm. "No, no more wine. Really, I've had enough."

"A soft drink?" he suggested, turning back to her. "Juice? Tea? Coffee?"

"Do you have decaffeinated coffee?"

"Sure." Jake was moving to the automatic drip machine as he answered. "I'll get it started."

"And while it drips through, I'll finish up here," Sarah offered, plunging her hands into the sink once more.

Fifteen minutes later, the kitchen chores completed, Sarah and Jake were back in the living room, this time seated in separate chairs flanking the window facing the street.

"Okay, you had your fun, and you eased the tense situation with your comedy routine," Sarah said, letting him know she was aware of his earlier intent. She blew on the steaming liquid in the cup cradled in her hands and arched her eyebrows. "Now, are you ready to tell me a little about yourself?"

"You really want to hear about it?" Jake managed to look skeptical and hopeful at one and the same time.

"Yeth, I weally weally do," Sarah insisted, in an impassioned Elmer Fudd impression.

This time Jake lost it, erupting with a roar of

appreciative laughter. "As I believe I might have mentioned, I like being with you, Sarah Cummings," he said after the bout of laughter subsided. "I also do believe you show signs of possessing a sense of humor as off-the-wall as my own."

"Do tell," she drawled, concealing the jolt of surprise dealt to her by the startling truth of his observation. Though quiet in appearance and demeanor, she always had possessed an appreciation for the ridiculous. Perhaps it derived from her study of the human foibles history was peppered with. Whatever, along with a strong physical attraction, and a genuine liking for each other, they shared a similar sense of humor.

"I just did," Jake replied, effectively ending her flit into introspection.

"Did what?" Sarah asked, having lost the conversational thread.

"Tell." Jake grinned.

Sarah heaved an exaggerated sigh. "Why do I have this sensation of going in circles?" Since the question was rhetorical, she didn't wait for a response, but plowed on, "Will you get on with it?"

"You're a har—" Jake broke off to shake his head. "I already said that, didn't I?" She nodded; he laughed. "Okay, I'll make it brief."

Sarah glanced at her watch. "Good. Time and tide...and all that jazz."

Jake laughed again. "God, we are trite, if nothing else." He frowned, collecting himself. "Now, where was I?"

"In a shack by the railroad tracks."

"Yeah, well," he grinned. "Actually, I was born right here in Sprucewood, thirty years ago this past summer. I was the youngest of four sons...and spoiled rotten."

"You were a terror?"

Jake grimaced and nodded. "And rebellious." He shrugged. "Being the last, and with three older brothers who excelled, most especially the eldest brother, I guess I felt that I had to make my own statement, be different."

"In what way?" Sarah frowned. "Different from whom—or from what?"

"The family tradition," Jake intoned in a deep voice. "You see, I come from a family of law-enforcement officers, stretching back over a hundred years." He chuckled. "I'm about convinced that the dedication to the law must be in the Wolfe genes or something. Hell, we've had sheriffs, deputies, U.S. marshals—you name it, we've had at least one."

"That's incredible." Sarah was genuinely fascinated by the idea, both as a person and as a historian. "Over a hundred years, and the tradition is ongoing?"

"Yeah. Anyway, my father was a member of the Philadelphia police force."

"But he lived here, in Sprucewood?"

"Mmm-hmm..." A faint, sad smile shadowed his lips. "He was originally from Philly. My mother was from Sprucewood. They met, fell in love and got married. They lived in an apartment in the city until my mother got pregnant, and then they decided to settle here to raise a family."

"And your brothers?" Sarah asked. "They're also in law enforcement?"

"Yes, but not here." Jake smiled. "The third son, Eric, is thirty-three. He followed my father into the Philadelphia police force. Right now he's assigned to the narcotics division, working undercover."

"Sounds dangerous."

"It is." Jake made a face. "But then, just being alive in today's world is dangerous."

Considering her own present precarious situation, Sarah had to agree. "Yes, it is. Then again," she elaborated, from a position of some acquired knowledge, "living in this less-than-perfect world has always been dangerous."

"I suppose so." Jake shrugged, as if to say "that's how it goes." "Which is why this old world needs people like the Wolfe clan."

"Yes. And the next brother?" she nudged.

"That would be Royce. He's thirty-six, and a sergeant in the Pennsylvania State Police, stationed up north, near the state lines bordering Pennsylvania, New York and New Jersey. That brings us to number one son, my brother Cameron.'' He paused, his expression mirroring open admiration. ''Cameron was and is the shining example the rest of us strive to emulate. While I was growing up, I adored him.'' He smiled derisively. ''And, in my rebellious years, I resented him, simply because he made me adore him.'' He laughed. ''Boy, a shrink would probably have a field day with that one.''

''Not necessarily,'' Sarah observed. ''I think it makes perfect sense. It's easy to resent someone you greatly admire, but feel you can never equal.'' Her smile was gentle with understanding. ''Easy, and probably quite normal.''

''Glad to hear it.'' Jake grinned at her. ''So scratch the shrink.''

''And what form of law enforcement is the estimable Cameron in?'' she asked, bringing him back to the subject.

''He's a federal government special agent—a sort of troubleshooter, I gather. He doesn't discuss it.'' Jake gave a short laugh. ''Hell, he doesn't talk about much of anything. The word on the street is that Cameron is referred to, by both friend and foe, as the Lone Wolfe.''

''A hero type?'' Sarah raised her eyebrows.

''From the top of his golden-haired head to the soles of his size twelves,'' Jake replied, dead serious. ''He's the type of man you trust immediately and explicitly. No questions asked. If Cameron says he'll do it—*any* it—you can go to bed and sleep tight in the assurance that he will not only do it, but do it with style.''

"Impressive.''

"Yeah.'' Jake grinned. "Daunting, too.''

"But necessary, in a historical sense,'' Sarah said, in the instructive tone she used in the lecture hall.

Jake frowned. "How so?''

"The hero type appears throughout history,'' she explained. "Heroes are the stuff of legend and myth. Where would civilization be without them? They define the ideal.'' She smiled. "The shining example you mentioned.''

"The ideal,'' Jake mused. "Yeah, that's Cameron, and, to a somewhat lesser degree, Eric and Royce, as well.''

"But not you?''

"The ideal? The shining example?'' Jake roared with laughter. "Not hardly, honey. I'm far from hero material. Ain't nobody dubbing me the Lone Wolfe.''

"A man apart,'' Sarah mused aloud.

"Exactly,'' Jake said. "Apart, detached, taking care of business, while directing all our lives from a distance.'' He chuckled. "At least he tries to direct. The rest of us give him his share of grief. At any rate, I know I do.''

"And how do your parents feel about him usurping their roles of authority?"

"Usurping? Are you kidding?" Jake laughed. "My mother and father set the example for the rest of us to follow in deferring to Cameron. I sometimes think my mother believes he can walk on water. And up until his death, my father began every other sentence with 'Cameron said.'"

"Your father's gone?"

"Yes." Jake sighed. "He was killed in the line of duty, almost two years ago."

"I'm sorry," she murmured, meaning it.

"So am I." His smile was bittersweet with self-knowledge. "His death was the catalyst that brought me home, made me reevaluate my lifestyle and priorities."

"And ended your rebellion?" she probed, softly.

"In spades," he confessed. "Suddenly it was grow-up time. It was time to put the toys away and get the rump in gear. I attended the police academy, then joined the force." His smile was devil-inspired. "And here I am, the model of conservative conformity you see before you."

"Uh-huh," Sarah said. I'll bet, she thought, reacting with an inner quiver to the unholy gleam in his eyes. In sheer defense against his attraction, she glanced away, and caught sight of the position of the hands on her watch. "My heavens!" she exclaimed in shocked surprise. "It's nearly midnight!"

"It happens every night at this time," Jake drawled, grimacing as he took a sip from his cup. "More importantly, the coffee's cold. How about a refill?"

"No, thank you." Sarah shook her head. "I have to get home. And don't you have to work early tomorrow?"

"No." That one small word held a wealth of satisfaction. "Tomorrow's my Saturday off." He arched his brows. "You want to do something... like dinner, a movie, or both?"

Sarah was tempted, sorely tempted. But memory slammed back, reminding her of the uncertainty of her position regarding Andrew Hollings and the other two students. For the past few hours, she had forgotten, relaxed her guard, enjoyed the time spent with Jake...in truth, even those hot and heavy moments...in real truth, maybe those moments most of all.

But, she reminded herself, they were all moments out of time, lovely moments, carefree moments, free of worry and stress, hidden away here in the privacy of Jake's apartment. But to go out in public with him...

"I, er, can't recall offhand if I have anything on for tomorrow night," she lied, putting him off. "Can you give me a call tomorrow?"

"Sure." Jake stood and, raising his arms above his head, stretched luxuriously.

Sarah's breath caught in her throat at the sight. His chest expanded, muscles rippling smoothly beneath his supple skin. Lord, he was one beautiful male animal. The aching observation sent her out of her chair.

"Whenever you're ready," she said, forcing herself to walk calmly to the table near the door where she had deposited her purse when they'd arrived. "I'm a little tired."

It wasn't until later, when she was curled up in her bed, that the realization struck Sarah that she had not just felt removed from her fears during those moments out of time in Jake's apartment. With Jake, she had felt more secure, protected, safer than she had ever felt in her life.

Jake not hero material?

A sleepy smile softened Sarah's worry tightened lips. Not a hero?

She'd be the judge of that.

Jake whistled softly as he loped along the flagstone path leading to the front door of a split-level home set on a small, well-kept lot on a quiet street.

Jake felt good, better than good, as good as the weather was beautiful. The day was a picture-perfect advertisement for a brilliant Pennsylvania autumn. The copper-hued sun sailed high across the deep blue sky, driving the temperature into the mid seventies. The air was clear, mild, invigorating.

Key in hand, Jake unlocked the door and stepped inside the quiet house. "Hey, Mom, you here?"

"I'm on the phone." Maddy Wolfe stuck her head around the archway into the kitchen and smiled at him. "Come say hello to your brother."

"Which one?" Jake drawled, descending the three steps into the living room and strolling through it to the large, spotlessly clean kitchen.

"Cameron," Maddy mouthed, handing him the receiver.

"Hi, big bro," Jake said. "Where are you?"

"None of your business," the familiar, cool, in-control voice retorted.

"Aha, playing secret agent man, are you?" Jake gibed, shooting a grin at his watching mother. She frowned her disapproval; his grin widened.

"Cute, sonny boy," Cameron gibed back. "When are you going to grow up?"

Jake was neither hurt nor offended by the crack, since it was a standard comeback of his brother's. In fact, he knew he'd be hurt if Cameron should cease his serious-sounding teasing, knew he'd be afraid his brother no longer cared. "All in good time. I'm young yet, remember?" he gave his usual rejoinder. "You're the one pushing forty, old man, not me."

"Smartass," Cameron muttered, drawing a chuckle from Jake. "How's Mother?"

"You were just talking to her," he said, glancing at Maddy. "Why didn't you ask her?"

"I did, Jake," Cameron replied on a long-suffering sigh. "But you know Mother. She'd tell me she was just fine if she was literally falling apart."

Jake ran a mock-serious look over his mother's healthy-looking, still lovely face and down the length of her shapely, well-preserved sixty-year-old body. "She looks good to me, big bro," he reported. "Fit, trim and sexy as hell."

"Jake Edward Wolfe!" Maddy admonished him sharply, turning her head to hide a smile.

"Having fun, sonny?" Cameron inquired, acerbically.

"I do my best," Jake answered dryly.

"Keep up the good work, Jake." Cameron's voice was laced with quiet approval. "You know Eric, Royce and I are proud of you, don't you?"

"Yeah, bro, I know," Jake said in an emotion-thickened voice; praise from Cameron was more precious than solid gold. "You want to talk to Mom again?"

"Yes…and, Jake?"

"Yeah?"

"Take care."

Jake swallowed. "I will. You too."

"Of course."

The supreme confidence in Cameron's voice banished the heavy emotion and brought the grin back to Jake's lips. Turning, he held the receiver out to his mother. "The feds' fair-haired agent wants to talk to you again."

Shaking her head as if to say he was a lost cause, Maddy took the phone and murmured to Jake, "I baked your favorite cookies yesterday. They're in the cookie jar."

"Gotcha. Any coffee?"

"No." She gave him a chiding smile. "Why don't you make some while I talk to your brother?"

A half-hour later, Jake sat opposite Maddy at the kitchen table, happily dunking his favorite apple-oatmeal cookies into his coffee. When a chunk of cookie broke off and plopped into the drink, Maddy raised her eyes but got up to get him a spoon to fish it out of the cup with.

"I hope you don't do that in public," she said, settling back onto her chair.

"Mother! I am crushed!" Jake cried in feigned protest. "Must I remind you that I am a municipal representative? An officer of the law, no less?"

"Yeah, yeah…" Maddy said, delighting him with her youthful, teasing slang.

"Speaking of officers of the law, you hear from Eric and Royce lately?"

"Yes." Maddy's lips curved in what Jake had always thought of as her proud-mother smile. "Royce called after he went off duty late yesterday afternoon, and Eric called this morning." Her eyes contained a suspicious sparkle. "My boys watch over me like concerned hawks. Your father would be pleased."

"With the youngest, too?" Jake asked, halfway afraid of her answer.

"Ah, Jake," she murmured. "I think your father would be pleased with you, most of all."

"Because I fell in line with the family tradition?"

"No." Maddy shook her head emphatically. "Because you left home a resentful boy and returned a man."

The emotion-tight feeling invaded Jake's throat again. Hell, for all that he had scoffed at the notion during those rebellious years, family acceptance was important, after all.

"Understand," Maddy continued when he didn't respond, "I know your father would have been twice as pleased, knowing you had joined the force."

"Yeah," he agreed. "I know it, too." He hesitated, then grinned to relieve the emotional tension. "And you know what? I like being a cop."

"I'd never have guessed," his mother drawled. "Which reminds me. I read in the morning paper that Officer Wolfe investigated a reported car-stripping yesterday."

"Yeah." Jake grimaced. "The choppers stripped the costly buggy clean, so don't go forgetting to keep the garage locked at all times."

"Really, Jake." She gave him a stern look. "I never forget to lock the garage—or anything else."

"Okay, okay," Jake said, laughing and holding his hands aloft in surrender. "Just a friendly reminder, is all."

"Hmm…" Maddy got up to clear and wipe the table. "I've got the makings for stuffed peppers," she said from the sink. "You want to come for supper?"

Jake loved stuffed peppers. Of course, Maddy knew he loved stuffed peppers. Jake suspected his mother feared he wasn't eating properly. "Can I let you know later?" he asked. "I might have a date for dinner."

"Might?" Maddy raised her eyebrows.

"I'm not sure yet," he explained. "I have to call her."

"Her?" Her eyebrows inched higher.

"A woman I met the other day," Jake explained. "Name's Sarah Cummings. She's a new associate professor of history over at Sprucewood College."

"Bright, is she?"

Her question sparked a memory flash; Jake could hear Sarah, so briefly, yet so succinctly, defining for him the role and purpose of the hero. "Oh, yeah," he answered in a decisive tone. "She's bright."

"Pretty?"

Jake could feel his features relaxing into soft, tender lines, revealing his thoughts and feelings to his astute mother. He didn't care; it wouldn't matter if he did. There was nothing he could do about it.

"Yes." Then he shrugged and shook his head. "No, she's not pretty. She's beautiful."

Maddy stared at him in open speculation for several long seconds. Then she gave a single sharp nod of her head. "Uh-huh. Like that, is it?"

"Like that?" Jake repeated. "Like what?"

"It appears to me like love at first sight," she observed seriously.

"Love at first sight!" Jake yelped. "Ah, c'mon, Mom. I just met the woman. Love at first sight." He snorted. "I think you've been watching too many television soaps."

Maddy favored him with her all-knowing-mother look. "I never watch the soaps, and you know it," she said haughtily. "But I've been around a spell, and I recognize the symptoms. You, my boy, appear to have every one of them."

"Showing symptoms does not necessarily confirm the disease," Jake retorted. "And you know that, as well."

"We'll see," she said serenely, her lips twitching. "So, are you going to call her, or what?"

Tickled once again by her use of common terminology, Jake's lips mirrored the twitch in hers. "Yes, I'm going to call her," he said in a tone of exaggerated exasperation, feeling his gut muscles clench in anticipation and excitement. "But I'm certainly not going to make the call with my mother hovering, all dewy-eyed and breathless, at my shoulder."

"Well, excuse me." Maddy sniffed disdainfully. "Go ahead," she ordered, indicating the wall phone with a flick of her hand. "Don't let me bother you. I'll go watch the Saturday-morning cartoons on the tube." She started for the living room, but paused in the archway to glance back at him, her eyes bright with the devilish, teasing light he had inherited from her. "Good luck, Jake. I'll keep my fingers crossed for you."

Thanking the universe at large for the blessing of having been born into the Wolfe family, Jake blew a kiss to his mother and reached for the phone.

# Six

The telephone rang at ten forty-five.

An intense thrill shot up Sarah's spine, instantly instilling within her a memory essence of Jake. She could see him, feel him, taste him. The image warmed and chilled her at the same time; her breath became reedy, her breasts ached, her lips burned.

Jake.

Sarah froze in position, on her hands and knees, on the kitchen floor. Half the floor covering sparkled with a just-washed cleanliness. The other half was dull and dry.

The kitchen phone was mounted on the wall on the wet side of the room.

Gloved palms flat on the floor, Sarah raised her head to stare at the white phone. Her teeth sank into her lower lip; her plastic-encased fingers flexed around the cleaning rag beneath her right hand.

The phone trilled a second summons.

She had been expecting the call, dreading it, anticipating it, all morning.

What to do? she asked herself, digging her teeth deeper into her lower lip. Answer it? Ignore it? Tear the persistent instrument from the wall?

Rebellion flared to life inside Sarah. Damn fate and circumstances. She wanted to see him, be with him, get lost inside the wonder of his laughter, his embrace, his touch, his hungry mouth.

Jake.

The phone rang a third time.

Maybe it wasn't even Jake. It could be anyone, Sarah reasoned…a colleague, her mother, a disembodied someone selling replacement windows, an official from a magazine distribution company, calling to inform her happily that she had won the sweepstakes grand prize of a zillion dollars.

Yeah, right.

The phone pealed for the fourth time.

Sarah gnawed on the abused lip.

Fool, she upbraided herself, dismissing the

twinges of strain streaking up her arms from the pressure on her flattened palms. Why hadn't she followed her first inclination this morning and by-passed the paper to get an early start on the weekly cleaning chore? Sarah asked herself, pushing her body upright. If she had left the news for later, she wouldn't have read the account that had set her mental wheels spinning in speculation and suppo-sition.

The fifth ring shrilled.

Sarah made a low, moaning sound deep in her throat. She hated having a phone ring on and on unanswered at any time, but she hated it even more now, when she felt certain the caller was Jake. She took one step, then hesitated, her right foot raised slightly, teetering on the edge of indecision.

If only she hadn't read that article in the paper. Her foot came down, in place. But, of course, after Jake's name jumped off the page at her, it had been impossible for her not to read it.

The phone rang for the seventh time.

Sarah shivered. Damn it! Why, why, why, had she immediately felt, sensed, a connection between Andrew Hollings and his friends and the account of a local resident's car being stripped? She had nothing to base such a suspicion upon, and yet…and yet, Sarah knew, inside, that there had to be a connection between the theft and the students' odd behavior.

The eighth trill beat against her eardrums.

Jake.

The intense desire to hear his voice simmered to a roiling boil inside Sarah, stirring up doubts and denials.

Pure speculation, she told herself, taking another two steps toward the phone. In truth, she knew nothing. She was spooked, that was all, spooked into drawing conclusions from sheer speculation and supposition.

The ninth ring seared her nervous system like an electric shock.

Sarah longed to dismiss her speculative notions and run to the phone. She had reached the point of yearning to hear Jake's voice at the other end of the line. She desperately wanted to accept his invitation for dinner and a movie, and yes, anything else he might suggest. Damn it, she wanted so badly to see him, be with him...touch him...in every way. Her body felt like an empty vessel, needing the strength and fullness of his to make her complete. It made no difference whether she had known him two days or two hundred years. She wanted Jake. It was as basic and honest as that. She took the three necessary steps to the phone and raised her hand.

But what if her instinctive reaction to that article was correct? Sarah asked herself, letting her hand hover over the receiver. Suppose her suppositions had validity. The article had said the police theorized that the theft had occurred sometime in the predawn hours yesterday morning. She had seen Andrew and his friends not many hours later, had noted their furtive nervousness. But, more importantly, she had heard the sibilant, whispery tenor of Andrew's voice, reiterating his innocent-sounding advice.

*Silence is golden, Miss Cummings.*

A chill of dread shuddered through Sarah.

The phone rang for the tenth time.

Coincidence? Sarah wanted to believe it, needed to believe it. She just couldn't. Call it intuition, gut instinct, whatever, but she just *knew*. Somehow, in some way, Andrew and his friends had been involved in stripping that car. And if her screaming intuition was right, she could not afford to be seen in public in the company of the police officer who had investigated the reported theft.

Sarah didn't become aware of holding her breath until the realization registered that the phone was not going to jangle an eleventh command.

The sudden silence felt as if the earth and every living thing on it had stopped breathing.

*Silence is golden, Miss Cummings.*

Golden? Sarah challenged the memory echo. No, silence was not golden, it was brass, and it carried the bitter, coppery taste of fear and despair.

"Jake." Whispering his name, Sarah lowered her forehead to the receiver.

Sheer determination and concentrated physical activity got Sarah through the rest of the morning and into midafternoon. The apartment had probably never received such a thorough cleaning. Even the windows sparkled in the autumn sunlight.

Throughout the intervening hours, Sarah had engaged in a running dialogue with herself, dissecting the situation. On one hand, she argued against the probability of Andrew and his friends being involved in anything illegal. Why would they be? she asked herself. She had made a point of checking their school records. All three young men came from well-off families; they wanted for nothing financially. Why, then, for what earthly reason, would any one of the three even dream of committing an act of thievery?

It didn't make sense.

Sarah conceded the point, then turned to examining the question from another perspective—her own. She had heard the snatches of conversation between them, and although they were suspicious in content, they were not conclusive proof of guilt, not by a long shot. Except for the added factor of Andrew's muttered warning to her.

The threatening sound of his voice, along with the frightening intensity of his narrow-eyed stare, clinched the matter for Sarah. They were up to no good, and she knew it.

So then, where did that leave the associate professor? Sarah asked herself, wielding the vacuum cleaner for all she was worth. Right behind the eight ball, she answered herself, shoving a chair to one side.

Naturally, during the course of her cleaning frenzy, Sarah did consider options other than remaining silent. She could present her suspicions to the police, or the college dean, or even ask the advice of the head of her own department. Of course she could, she derided herself. And afterward she could slink away with the sound of their collective laughter ringing inside her head.

Proof. Proof. Proof. A necessary factor, proof, if one set about pointing the finger of blame. And the bottom line was inescapable: she had no concrete proof.

Giving the bedroom windows what for, Sarah industriously applied the cloth to the pane...and her mind to her personal dilemma.

Another bottom line. Sarah wanted to spend time with Jake, a lot of time. She liked him, more than liked him. And, even with the crackling physical attraction that sizzled between them, she felt comfortable with him, as one would feel with an old friend, rather than a person one had so recently met—which, to her way of thinking, was somewhat amazing in itself. Just by being himself, Jake amused her, delighted her, excited her.

Had it really only been two days since they met?

Incredible. But there it was, plain as that streak down the center of the window. The streak posed no problem; one careful swipe of the cloth and it was gone. Sarah's feelings for Jake were not as easily dealt with.

Jake was a cop, and therefore a potential threat to Andrew and his friends.

And Sarah was getting pretty tired of bottom lines. The bedroom windows finished, she headed grimly into the living room to attack the two windows there.

Perhaps she was just being silly, or perhaps she was the biggest coward going, but to Sarah's way of thinking, there was simply no getting around it—by continuing to see Jake, and be seen with him, she would be placing herself in jeopardy...herself, and possibly Jake, as well.

Jake didn't have a clue about her suspicions, and so he'd be vulnerable, exposed to unforeseen danger.

Sarah's hand stilled on the windowpane. Would they hurt Jake, strike against him when he was unaware, unprepared? The thought sent a spear of panic skittering through her. They? she shook her head. Maybe not them, collectively—but Andrew? Sarah had a combined mental image and echo of

Andrew as he had looked, sounded, while issuing his warning to her. Conviction settled on her like a heavy burden.

Andrew would not hesitate in implementing any measure he deemed necessary to protect himself.

Shoulders drooping, Sarah stepped back from the partially cleaned window. Despite her personal opinion regarding Jake as a hero, there was no way she could knowingly place him in the position of sitting duck.

When Jake called, if he called, she had no choice but to tell him she could not see him...not tonight, and not in the foreseeable future.

The phone rang at exactly 3:26. Sarah knew the time because she had been glancing at the clock every ten or twelve seconds since around two. Squaring her shoulders, she lifted the receiver on the second ring.

"Hello?"

"Hi." Jake's voice, soft and sensuous, flowed through the line like warm honey. "How are you?"

"I'm fine," she lied. I'm miserable, she said in despairing silence. "And you?"

"Anxious."

She knew. Of course she knew. Still, she had to ask, "Anxious about what?"

"Sa-rah, hon-ey..." He drew her name, and the endearment, out, like a long, slow caress. "You know darn well that I'm anxious about hearing your answer."

Sarah inhaled, determined to say no.

"Will you come out with me tonight?" he asked, in that same honeyed, coaxing voice.

"Yes." Sarah's hand flew up to cover her traitorous mouth. So much for determination.

"Thank you." Jake's soft tone contained a wealth of relief. "I promise you won't regret it."

Sarah stifled a sigh; she already regretted it. The warm honey of his voice must have flowed into her ear and directly to her brain, smothering it. "Did you have anything in particular in mind?" A loaded question if she had ever heard one, Sarah upbraided herself. His low laughter confirmed her opinion, but, to his credit, Jake didn't stoop to sexual innuendo.

"What do you think of the idea of running into Philly for dinner and a show?"

Sarah brightened at his suggestion; if they skipped out of town, it would lessen their chances of being seen together by any of the three students.

"A show?" she repeated. "Do you mean a movie?"

"No, a Broadway show." Jake went on to mention a road-company group currently doing a run at a center-city theater of a smash musical that was still playing to near-capacity audiences in New York City.

"Oh, I'd love to see that show," Sarah said, with unbridled enthusiasm. "I've heard it's wonderful, but isn't it too late to get tickets for tonight?"

"I've got them," he reported, a note of satisfaction in his voice. "I called the theater and got the last two seats available. They're in the nosebleed section of the balcony," he warned her, "but the guy in the ticket office assured me the location of the seats affords an unobstructed view." He chuckled. "And we can take my binoculars."

"I can bring my opera glasses," Sarah offered eagerly, feeling giddy with relief and anticipation.

"There you go—we're set," Jake said, laughing.

"What time, Jake?" she asked, slanting a quick look at the wall clock.

"That depends on whether you prefer to have dinner before or after the show," Jake replied. "I know of several restaurants close by to the theater. You tell me your preference, and I'll call and make reservations."

"It doesn't matter to me," Sarah assured him, falling back on the traditional female response. "Which one would you prefer, before or after?"

Fortunately, Jake appeared unwilling to engage in that traditional man-woman stalemate. "Both," he replied at once.

"Both?" Sarah blinked. "I don't understand."

"Simple. The solution, that is, not you." Jake laughed. "We can have an early dinner before the show, and a snack after the show. How does that sound?"

"As wonderful *as* the show," Sarah admitted, joining in on his laughter. "So, what time, Jake?"

"Well, the curtain's at eight, and we don't want to rush through dinner," he mused aloud. "So suppose I make the reservations for six?" He didn't wait for a response from her, but continued on in the same musing tone, "Considering the Saturday-evening traffic, I'd suggest we leave a little after five. That'll give us ample time to park the car and walk to the restaurant. Okay?"

"Okay, I'll be ready," she said, not even bothering to conceal the eagerness bubbling over in her voice.

Sarah glanced at the clock again as she replaced the receiver. It was 3:40. Yikes! she thought, spinning around and dashing for the bathroom. That gave her only an hour and a half to get ready. She had to take a shower, shampoo her hair, do her nails and find something to wear.

The something to wear that she finally decided would have to do was another sand-washed silk confection in blending shades of green and brown. It was a filmy two-piece ensemble consisting of a blouse with a scooped neckline and sleeves tapering to loose, cuffed sleeves, and a full skirt that swirled enticingly around her ankles.

With sure and practiced fingers, Sarah piled her thick hair into a loose knot at the back of her head, allowing strategically placed tendrils to escape at her temples and nape. Her sole adornments were a pair of large gold hoop earrings.

Since her color was already heightened by excitement, Sarah merely enhanced the glow with a quick pat of translucent foundation, a brush of earth-tone blusher, a swish of muted olive eye shadow and a glide of terra-cotta lipstick. She was waving her hands in the air, drying the second application of polish on her nails—a vibrant golden-bronze shade that matched her sling-backed heels and evening bag—when the doorbell rang at precisely ten after five.

If Sarah had thought that Jake looked terrific dressed in a navy blue Windbreaker and a blue-and-white striped shirt—and she had—the impact he made on her senses when she opened the door for him carried double the breath-stealing effect.

Attired for an evening out in a charcoal brown suit, a pale yellow silk shirt and a yellow, brown and gold patterned silk tie, Jake looked like he had just finished filming a television commercial for a new, sexy cologne for the ''in'' man.

His freshly washed toast-colored hair glinted with golden highlights. The burnished skin stretched tautly over his strong features gleamed from a recent shave. His deep blue eyes sparkled with expectation.

"Hi." His low voice had acquired another coat of honeyed enticement. The soft, delectable sound of it went to her head like potent wine.

"Hi." Sarah stared at him in unabashed admiration, fighting to maintain a semblance of normalcy while trying to breathe, think, act, like a rational person.

"You're beautiful," Jake murmured, devouring her with a slow, encompassing look, the blue of his eyes darkening with flaring passion.

"Th—thank you..." Sarah could barely speak; she couldn't think at all, which freed her tongue to blurt out the truth. "You're beautiful, too."

Jake's burst of delighted laughter rumbled through the narrow apartment hallway. "Men aren't beautiful," he told her teasingly when his laughter had dwindled to a smile.

"You are," Sarah maintained, repaying his complimentary appraisal by running an assessing glance over his tall, angular, tightly knit body. "Handsome, too."

The glow of humor fled from his fantastic eyes, replaced by a leaping flame so hot in appearance that it seared Sarah to the depths of her being. "Be careful, honey," he advised her in a raspy whisper. "I've just discovered that I'm susceptible to flattery from you. Much more of it, and we might find ourselves right here, making a meal of each other and putting on a showstopping performance of our own.''

The realization that his warning held infinite appeal jolted Sarah into awareness of where they were. Good grief! Jake was standing in the hallway, and she was hanging on to the doorknob as if it were a lifeline!

''Ah...well, in that case...'' Sarah rushed on, painfully aware that she was babbling, ''I think we'd better go.''

''Coward.'' Jake's smile taunted her, and the lights dancing in his eyes excited her.

Releasing her death grip on the doorknob, Sarah silently endorsed his opinion, gulping as she spun away to grab the soft caramel-colored soft wool cape and bronze bag she had tossed on the chair just inside the door.

''I'm ready,'' she announced, swinging the cape about her shoulders before he had a chance to step forward to assist her and send her excitement level soaring with his feather-light touch, as he had last evening.

Jake didn't say anything; he didn't have to say a word. His laughing eyes said volumes about the amusement she afforded him with her show of skittishness and trepidation.

The atmosphere inside the car was charged with

sexual tension. Sarah imagined she could feel the shimmering electricity skipping over her sensitized nerves and her responsively quivering flesh.

Her trembling fingers fumbled with the simple process of inserting the prong of the safety belt into the buckle. Muttering a curse of frustration and self-disgust, she made another stab with the prong—and missed again. A shudder of intense awareness shot through her at the touch of Jake's warm flesh as he brushed her hands away to attach the belt for her.

"I know how you feel," he murmured, staring deeply into her widened eyes, while setting off tiny explosions deep inside her with the brief contact of the back of his long fingers against the contracting muscles of her lower abdomen. "I feel like I just might fly off in seventeen directions, too."

"You...you do?" Sarah asked, in a parched little voice, staring at him in helpless wonder.

"Of course." A wry smile slanted his tempting mouth. "As I told you last night, I want you, and since last night the wanting has grown even—" his smile curved derisively "—harder than before."

Words of protest, shock, denial, jumped from Sarah's mind to her tongue. Lies, all lies. She refused the words passage from her dry lips. One small word escaped her guard, the word she had repeated in silence, like a litany, throughout the day.

"Jake."

His eyes flickered. He shuddered, moved closer, then pulled back, shaking his head. A taut silence held sway for a moment. He broke it with a sound that was half laugh, half sigh.

"What is it with this car?" Jake mused aloud, slanting a twinkling sidelong look at her. "I'm beginning to suspect that the last time I had it washed, one of the attendants gave it a shot of deodorant spray bought from a company called Aphrodisiacs R Us."

His droll observation achieved its intended purpose. Sarah burst out laughing, relieving the strain and tension humming between them.

"Will you get this car moving?" she ordered, swallowing another rising tide of mirth. "I didn't take time for lunch, and I'm hungry." Narrowing her eyes in warning, she quickly added, "And don't you dare do a double entendre on that last word. Just let it remain the last word."

"Would I do that?" Jake murmured, more to himself than to her. His lips twitched. "Probably," he admitted, flipping the ignition switch to fire the engine. "So then it's a good thing she warned me against doing that," he went on, still talking to himself, as he eased the car away from the curb and into the late-Saturday afternoon traffic. "Keeps me on my best behavior...I guess."

"And it's my guess that your wrappings are getting a mite frayed around the edges," Sarah observed, relaxing with a sigh against the cradling seat back.

Jake kept up a nonsensical running commentary throughout the drive into the city, and by the time he pulled the car into the parking garage they were laughing easily together, like two teenagers out on a lark.

The restaurant Jake had chosen was really a pub, with an Irish ambience and a hail-fellow-well-met atmosphere. The hostess was pretty and friendly, chattering away as if they were old and valued friends as she led them to a high-backed corner booth that afforded conversational privacy. The indirect lighting was diffuse, dim, the primary glow stemming from amber bulbs fixed near to the ceiling. The amber-globed oil lamps placed on each table gave little additional illumination.

The menus the hostess gave them turned out to offer another source of amusement for Jake, simply because Sarah had to dig her glasses out of her bag to read it.

"What's so funny?" she asked, frowning as she squinted at the selections, which were printed in a small typeface.

"Nothing," Jake said, continuing to grin at her.

"It's just, well, the day I first noticed you sitting in that back booth at Dave's place, I thought you resembled an owl in those big round glasses." He held up a hand when she opened her mouth to protest. "A very attractive and interesting-looking owl," he said cajolingly. Then he ruined the effect by adding, "But an owl just the same."

Though Sarah gave him a fierce frown, she couldn't suppress the laughter bubbling up in her throat.

The food was delicious, accompanied by mutual teasing and bouts of laughter from Jake and Sarah. They lingered over the wine. Jake had allowed himself just one glass.

"I'm driving," he said. "But you may have as many as you like."

Recalling how quickly the wine had gone to her head just last night, Sarah, too, declined a second drink.

Nursing the excellent dry white, they lost track of the time, and they might have missed the curtain for the show if the hostess hadn't stopped by their booth to give them a gentle reminder.

The show turned out to be every bit as wonderful as Sarah had heard it was, and they left the theater humming snatches of one of the catchy musical numbers.

The tiring effects of Sarah's hell-bent industriousness in her cleaning frenzy earlier in the day caught up with her while she and Jake were having a snack in the same pub where they had eaten dinner. Even the coffee she had was unequal to the need for sleep that was weighing down her eyelids.

"Tired?" Jake asked, after her third smothered yawn.

"Yes," Sarah admitted with a rueful smile; she really hated to see the evening end. "I'm sorry, but I was up early and cleaning the apartment most of the day, and I can hardly keep my eyes open."

"Nothing to be sorry for," Jake said, motioning to the waiter for their check. "But now I'm confused about something."

"Confused?" Sarah frowned. "About what?"

"You did say you were up early?"

"Yes." Sarah felt so sleepy, she actually didn't get the drift of where he was heading. "So?"

Jake shrugged. "I called, in the morning. I thought that maybe you'd gone shopping or something."

"Oh." Sarah felt like a fool...a deceitful fool. "Yes, I mean, no, I didn't go out. I must have been cleaning the bathroom, running the water, and didn't hear the phone."

"Probably." Jake accepted her excuse without question, making her feel even more deceptive.

"Sorry," Sarah murmured, meaning it.

"No matter. We're together." Jake's smile chased the guilt from her mind, if not the sleepiness; she yawned again. "Come along, sleepy-head," he urged, polishing off his second cup of coffee in one gulp before sliding from the bench seat. "Time to head for home."

With her head settled against the seat's headrest, Sarah had slipped into a doze before they were out of the city. Not quite asleep, yet not fully awake, she floated on a lovely cloud, dreamy and secure with Jake at the wheel beside her. In her misty dream, she and Jake danced to the haunting strains of the love ballad from the show.

When they arrived at Sarah's apartment, Jake helped her from the car and steered her up the steps and to her door.

"Oh, Jake," Sarah whispered, rummaging in her bag for her key. "I had a lovely time. Thank you."

"Thank you," he whispered in return. "I had a lovely time, too."

The door swung open; Sarah stood still, captured by the expression in Jake's dark blue eyes. A thrill shot through her as he took a step, closing the distance between them. Suddenly she was wide-awake, alert, all her senses alive and aware.

"Can we make it even more lovely with a good-night kiss, honey?" His voice was low, enticing.

Sarah knew, with irrevocable certainty, that if she allowed the kiss, it wouldn't end there. She knew, and yet she didn't hesitate. Instantly she made a conscious decision to spend the night with Jake...in her bed.

"Yes," she answered, moving away from him to step into her living room. "But not out in the hall." Reaching out, she grasped his hand and gave it a light tug. "Come in, Jake."

# Seven

Jake's eyes flickered in surprise, but he didn't hesitate. Without uttering a word, he crossed the threshold, shut and locked the door and, turning, drew her very gently, very carefully to him.

"You're sure, honey?" he asked, in a dry, not-quite-steady murmur. His gaze delved into hers, a laser-blue light seeking the truth.

"Yes, Jake." Sarah slid her tongue over her excitement-dried lips, and shivered as his glittering gaze fastened onto her mouth. "I'm sure."

His hands moved across her shoulders to her cape, then under it. The soft wool garment slid unnoticed to the floor. His suit jacket followed a moment later.

Sarah didn't move. She couldn't. All she could do was watch as, slowly, maddeningly, Jake lowered his head. Quivering in anticipation, Sarah parted her lips. His mouth touched hers in a feather-light caress.

"Sarah," Jake groaned into her mouth. The sound of her name echoed inside her spinning head.

"Kiss me." Sarah heard the raw, pleading note in her voice. She didn't care; it didn't matter. All that mattered in the world, her world, was his mouth.

He answered her plea. Slanting his head, Jake touched her lips with his, and made them his own. They were chaste, sweet, and for an infinitely long, frustrating moment he maintained a light, delicate touch.

The very delicacy of his kiss was an inducement to madness and abandon. Moaning a protest low in her throat, Sarah raised her hands to grasp his head, urging him, his mouth, into fuller contact with hers.

Obeying her silent command, Jake took her mouth in a kiss so fiery that she felt the scorching brand in the depths of her femininity. His tongue caressed, tormented, the tender inner skin of her lower lip, making her frantic for more of him, and still more. Growing desperate, Sarah plied her own tongue, luring him inside.

A low grunt of satisfaction rumbled in Jake's throat, and then he plunged in, his tongue filling the moist cavern of her mouth, igniting a singeing spark in her body that had her clinging to him, her curling fingers anchoring in the crisp strands of his thick hair.

It was like coming home.

The vague thought flitted through Sarah's mind as she settled into his crushing embrace, conforming the round softness of her body to the angular hardness of his.

And Jake's body was hard, from his plundering lips to the solid width of his shoulders and chest to the taut muscles of his thighs, and every inch in between. His hands pressed against her spine, urging her closer and closer still, until Sarah felt fused to him, mouth to mouth, breasts to chest, hipbone to hipbone, womanhood to manhood.

Raking the sweetness of her mouth with his tongue, Jake curved his body over hers, bowing her spine, arching her up, into him, his heat, his hardness.

Sarah's world, narrowed down to the small space their fused bodies occupied, burst into flame. It was a beautiful blaze, breathtaking, exhilarating, life-giving.

Like the fabled phoenix rising from the ashes,

Sarah's spirit soared on the wings of a consuming passion unlike anything she had ever before experienced.

She burned, outside, inside, to be one with Jake, to be filled by Jake, to belong to Jake.

Conveying her desire, her burning need, Sarah scored his scalp with her fingernails and moved her body sinuously against his aroused flesh.

Jake growled and pulled his mouth from hers to blaze a fiery trail of stinging kisses and gentle bites down the arched column of her neck. His tongue unerringly found the erratically beating pulse at the base of her throat, and teased it into a thundering that thrummed against her eardrums.

Murmuring his name, Sarah glided her lips along the curved edge of his ear and dipped the tip of her tongue into the small hollow. His body jerked at her delicate touch, thrusting his pelvis forward. Sarah felt the expanding strength of his need, and gloried in it.

She skimmed her palms over his shoulders, down his arched back, to clasp him by the hips, pulling him, his hardness, more tightly to her yielding softness.

"Sarah, Sarah, Sarah..." As he murmured her name, Jake lowered his hands to grasp her waist, and as if his legs would no longer support him, he dropped to his knees on the floor in front of her and buried his face in the silky material pooling in the valley between her breasts.

Sarah went weak, her knees threatening to buckle, toppling her to the floor before him. Clutching his shoulders, she remained upright, shuddering in response to the sensations streaking through her body at the wet, hungry touch of his lips closing around the tip of one breast.

It was heaven. It was hell. It was beautiful. It was unbearable. It was too much. It was not enough.

Not nearly enough.

Sarah wanted, wanted, wanted. The wanting enveloped her mind, driving out conscious thought and reason.

''Jake.'' Her voice had been reduced to a mere whisper, barely a sound at all, a sighing murmur screaming to him of her need, her desire, her unleashed passion.

As nearly nonexistent as it was, Jake heard her cry, and the supplication entwined with it. He drew his head back, leaving the hard tip of her breast pushing against the moist spot on the silky material. Raising his head, he again stared with probing intent into her eyes. A moment, two, and then he tightened his grasp on her waist and pulled her to him to slowly drag her body down the length of his.

Sarah felt the carpet fibers scrape her knees, and

then her body being lowered to the floor. Jake followed her down, flattening her breasts with his chest, crushing her lips beneath his greedy mouth.

*At least the carpet's clean.*

The irrelevant consideration zinged through her mind, to her sense of humor and out her throat on a breathless gurgle of laughter.

Jake pulled back to gaze at her, a puzzled frown scoring his brow. "Something's funny?"

Sarah bit her lip and shook her head, creating a crackling static with the friction of her hair against the carpet. "I...I just had a dumb thought," she explained.

He looked skeptical. "What dumb thought?"

The sudden release of the sensual tension of the previous minutes took its toll in a bout of the giggles. "I...I just thought that—" Sarah paused to draw a controlling breath "—at least the carpet's clean."

Looking stunned, Jake stared at her for heart-stopping seconds. Then a twitch tilted up the corners of his compressed lips, and his shoulders began to shake. "You sure do know how to bring a man down to earth," he told her accusingly, nearly choking on the laughter he was obviously suppressing. His smile took a crooked turn. "And to his knees," he muttered wryly.

"Oh, Jake, I'm sorry." Contrite, Sarah stroked her fingers down his smooth cheek to the muscle kicking along his squared jaw. "I didn't mean to spoil the moment."

Now his smile curved at a sensuous angle. "Spoiled?" He dipped his head to administer a quick, hard kiss to her ruefully set mouth, and gave a low grunt of satisfaction when she shivered in response. "Nothing's spoiled, honey." His smile grew wickedly daring. "Or even deflated, for that matter." He rotated his hips against her to prove his assertion.

Gasping at the sensations his movement sent rioting through her, Sarah arched her spine reflexively and tightened her grip on his shoulders. Her senses swam, drowning once more in a molten flow of sensuality. Straining up, she sought his smiling mouth with her tingling lips.

"More?" he murmured, teasing her with tiny hit-and-run touches of his lips against hers.

"Yes, yes," Sarah pleaded, digging her nails into the silky material covering his shoulders. "And I don't care if the carpet's clean or filthy."

"But I do." Jake drew back. "Not about the carpet," he continued, moving into a kneeling position next to her. "I care about you." He slid one arm under her shoulders, the other under her knees.

Anticipating his intent, Sarah held her breath and curled her arms tightly around his neck.

"I lost my head for a moment there," he confessed. Taking a deep breath, he lifted her up, close to his chest, and surged to his feet. When he was standing, he remained still for a moment, his chest heaving from the exertion.

Her senses stabilizing, Sarah eased the pent-up breath from her emotion-tightened throat and gazed up at him in enthralled silence.

"I'm damn near exploding with wanting you, honey, but not like that, rolling around on a hard floor." His blue eyes darkened to the deepest sapphire. "Oh, no, not like that," he whispered, bending his head to brush his mouth over her parted lips. "I want to savor each and every nuance along the way from excitement to explosion."

"Oh, Jake." She sighed and pressed her lips to the side of his throat. "So do I."

Her admission set him moving, through the living room and into the bedroom. Clinging to him, Sarah closed her eyes, deciding she rather enjoyed the sensation of being literally swept off her feet by her hero, rendered breathless and eager, like a heroine straight out of history or a movie or a romance novel.

And Jake *was* a hero, she mused dreamily, sighing as he set her upright next to the bed. Her hero…whether he saw himself in the role or not. A secret smile curving her lips, Sarah raised her head and parted her lips in excited expectation of his kiss.

Jake didn't disappoint her. Murmuring her

name, he fitted his mouth to hers, instantly submerging her once more in a sensuous realm of glittering sensations.

Sarah responded without hesitation. Her defenses were not only down, they were utterly demolished. It had been so very long since she had felt the passionate demands of the flesh, and even then the demands had been as weak as water in comparison to the wine-heady clamor she experienced each time Jake kissed her, touched her, as he was at this moment.

His hands stroked her shoulders, her arms, her back, bringing her flesh to glorious life with each successive caress. Sarah reciprocated in turn, gliding her palms from the back of his neck to his shoulders and down his chest. In a well-choreographed dance of love, they moved in unison, her fingers working on the buttons of his shirt as his hands tugged her blouse from the waistband of her skirt.

There was no fumbling, no groping. Between heated, ever-deepening kisses and warm, soft murmurs, they removed the material barriers of convention between their two separate beings, which were raging to blend into one.

When at last the final wisps of cloth were tossed aside, they sank onto the bed as one. Eager hands reached to touch, to know, trembling fingers explored quivering flesh.

Jake drew the tips of his fingers along the curve of her breast. "So soft, so beautiful."

"You taste salty," Sarah murmured, gliding the tip of her tongue along the curve of his shoulder.

He gave a shuddering response, then drew one from her by gently lashing the crest of her breast with his tongue. Gasping, she arched her back, and carefully sank her teeth into his supple skin in a delicate love bite.

Grunting his enjoyment and appreciation of her gentle aggression, Jake drew the tight tip of her breast into his mouth. Sensations splintered inside Sarah at the pleasure inflicted by his suckling lips.

Tension spiraled, building higher and higher. Shuddering, moaning, she skimmed her hands down his torso. Sarah's palms tingled at the feel of his warm, passion-moistened skin, the muscles clenching beneath her hands.

"Yes, yes..." Jake's voice was little more than a hoarse, ragged groan. "Sarah, touch me, please..."

She hesitated a moment, but then, crying out in reaction to the pull of his lips on her breast, she slid her palms lower, over the flat tautness of his belly, and lower still, to the apex of his thighs.

Jake drew a harsh breath and went still, as if arrested by the feelings instilled by her skin gliding over his, waiting, waiting for a more intimate caress.

Quivering, barely breathing herself, Sarah reached down and cradled him with her trembling fingers.

Jake's pent-up breath whooshed from his throat, bathing her breast in warm moisture, tightening the tension inside her, emboldening her to further exploration. Marveling at his silky hardness, she curled her fingers around him.

"Sarah." His voice had been reduced to a raspy whisper. "Oh, Sarah, that feels so good." Deserting her other breast, his hand slid to her waist, to her hip, to her—

*"Jake."*

Sarah didn't recognize the voice that cried from her throat. Her mind spinning, her senses rioting out of control, she arched her body, high, into the pleasure-giving probe of his caressing, stroking fingers.

The tension spiral compressed, radiating shards of fiery desire into the core of her femininity. Sarah couldn't bear it, and yet she craved more.

"Jake, Jake, please," she sobbed, writhing in response to the deepening intimacy of his searing touch. Not fully aware of reciprocating his caress, she wrenched a groan from the depths of his throat with the movement of her fingers caging his smooth, heated flesh.

"Yes, now," Jake muttered, as if through teeth clenched against loss of control. Grasping her by the hips, he raised her from the bed, moved into position between her thighs, and stared down at her hands, still cradling his quivering flesh. A shudder ripped through him as she slowly withdrew her hands in a lingering caress.

"Yes, Jake!" she cried. "Now!"

"A moment," he murmured, reaching for the small square packet he had placed on the nightstand. The tremor in his fingers betrayed his heightened passion as he swiftly adjusted the sheathing protection.

"Now." He moved to the very portal, paused for a tormenting heartbeat, then thrust forward, filling the aching emptiness inside her.

The tension spiral went crazy, and Sarah went crazy with it. Clinging to him, afraid she'd fly apart if she let go, she moved in time with the ever-accelerating, hard-thrusting rhythm of his body. His mouth captured hers, his tongue reflecting the possession of his pounding body.

The tension spiral tightened, tightened, tightened, and then it snapped, shattering into a million lights, sparkling throughout Sarah's entire being, erupting from her passion-dried lips in the cry of his name into his mouth.

*"Jake!"*

Her muted scream seemingly lashing him on, Jake thrust deeper and deeper. Then, shudders cascading the length of his body, he tore his mouth from hers, calling her name, over and over, in a harsh, exultant cry of intense release.

A chill permeating the air brought Jake to the edge of consciousness. Not fully awake, yet no longer asleep, he felt confused by the conflicting sensations of cold and warmth, and by a deep inner sense of well-being. He lay on his left side, which was warm, but his right side, exposed to the air, felt chilled to the bone.

Had he tossed off the covers sometime during the night? he wondered, yawning. A movement beside him brought a question to his sleep-clouded mind.

Movement?

Fighting his way out of the lingering fog of slumber, Jake pried his eyes open. Memory rushed back, clear and exciting, at the sight that met his startled gaze.

The woman snuggled against him was the direct cause of his partial warmth, and his complete well-being.

*Sarah.*

A smile, soft and tender, curved Jake's lips, lips that could taste the distinctive flavor of Sarah. He whispered a long sigh of utter satisfaction.

Never, never, throughout all his years of wandering, or even before, with any of the girls and women he had known, had Jake felt anything even remotely akin to the shattering and glorious joy he had experienced with Sarah.

She murmured, shivered and snuggled closer, dispelling his bemusement. Sarah was obviously feeling the cold in her sleep. Chastising himself for falling asleep so soon after attaining what he believed was the nearest he would ever get to paradise, Jake reached across Sarah to grasp a corner of the coverlet and pulled it over them, cocooning them within its warmth-giving comfort.

The warmth enveloping him, Jake set about easing his cramped muscles. Sarah's head was pillowed on his left arm, and it was sending out warning signals of complaint. Moving slowly, carefully, so as not to disturb her, he slid his arm from beneath her and slid a real pillow under her head to take its place. Sarah slept on. Encouraged, Jake shifted his hips and stretched out his long legs, laying the right one over hers. Sarah was still out for the count. Fearless now, he curled his right arm around her waist and gently drew her closer to the rapidly increasing heat of his naked body. A victorious smile sashayed across his mouth at the silky feel of her skin gliding against his hair-roughened, quickening body.

He was sorely tempted to wake her.

Sarah sighed contentedly in her sleep.

Jake felt her sigh in the depths of his soul.

How was it possible, he mused, ruthlessly tamping down his passion, that this particular woman possessed the singular power to affect him so deeply, so completely?

Pondering the question, Jake drew distracting pleasure from the simple exercise of detailing her delicate features. Sarah *was* lovely, with her satiny skin, her mass of auburn hair and her soft brown eyes. But surely the strength of her attraction went deeper than facial beauty. Of course, she had a delectable body that could drive him, and probably dozens of other men, straight to distraction, if not perdition. But he had known other women equally beautiful, even more so in form, as well as facial features.

Dismissing mere good looks as a consideration, Jake delved deeper for an answer. On numerous occasions, Sarah had revealed to him a sharp intelligence, and Jake did appreciate a bright, if not necessarily savvy, woman. Also, in addition to her other attributes, she possessed a keen, often wry, sense of humor. Jake acknowledged that of all the factors in her favor, Sarah's sense of humor was very likely the most appealing and important to him.

In other words, Jake reflected, as far as he personally was concerned, Sarah had one hell of a lot going for her, more than enough to instill within him strong feelings of not only wildly elated hormones raging to merge, but of protection, tenderness, caring and...

*Love at first sight?*

Jake's thought process came to an abrupt halt as an echo of his mother's voice rang inside his head. Could it be possible? he wondered, staring, amazed, into Sarah's sleep-vulnerable countenance. Was it really possible to fall in love at first sight?

Jake's memory did an about-face, taking him back to his first sight of her at Dave's place. He was prepared to admit that from his first sight of Sarah, looking endearingly owlish in those big round glasses, he had been instantly attracted, instantly interested, almost as instantly aroused. But love?

Love was heavy, serious business, encompassing commitment and fidelity. The kind of stuff families were made of. Did his attraction, his interest, even his desire, run that deep?

"Jake." Sarah murmured his name in her sleep. A small, sweet smile curved her slightly parted lips.

Jake had the weird sensation of his insides turning to mush. Did his feelings run that deep? Jake mused, his own lips tilting in a smile of willing defeat.

Oh, yeah. Maybe even deeper.

# Eight

Sarah woke to a tickling brush and a prodding nudge from a very sexy man. Opening her eyes a fraction, she stared into Jake's passion-darkened eyes.

"I'm sorry," he murmured, offering her a heart-stopping morning-after smile. "Go back to sleep, honey. I didn't mean to wake you."

"Well, maybe *you* didn't," she said softly, "but a rather persistent part of your anatomy did."

Jake maintained a straight face for all of ten seconds, then burst out laughing. "I knew it. I knew it was your sense of humor that got to me," he crowed, managing to thoroughly confuse and amuse her.

"Really?" Sarah opened her eyes wide and fluttered her lashes. "And here I thought it was a part of *my* anatomy that got to you."

"That, too." Jake's grin was positively wolfish. He moved his hips, eliciting a gasp from her.

"You're incorrigible," she scolded him, unsuccessfully fighting a giggle.

"Insatiable, too," he drawled, slowly, tantalizingly raising the leg he had moments before slipped between her thighs.

Sarah shivered responsively to the arousing feel of his muscle-bunched thigh pressing against her. Melting, figuratively and literally, she let her eyes close, and, reacting reflexively, she moved her lower body slowly back and forth.

Jake inhaled sharply, then lowered his head to capture her parted lips in the heated snare of his hard, hungry mouth. His tongue raked across the edges of her teeth, then speared into the honeyed recess of her mouth.

Sarah was immediately caught within the senses-inflaming web of sensuality Jake's kiss, his touch, wove about her. Curling her arms around his hips, she rolled onto her back, bringing him with her, into position between her parted thighs.

"You set me on fire, honey," Jake murmured

as he lifted his mouth a hairbreadth from hers. "I have never, ever, become so hot, so hard, so fast."

Sarah made a soft sound, deep in her throat, and gently sank her teeth into his lower lip. "And I," she whispered, pausing to lave the spot with her tongue, "I have never, ever become so hot before...at all."

"Not even with your professor?" Jake asked, drawing his head back to gaze intently into her surprise-opened eyes.

Sarah blinked and shook her head. "No," she admitted, sinking her teeth into her own lower lip. "I, ah...you see, well, while I enjoyed being caressed and stroked, I..." She ran her tongue over her dry lips, then blurted out, "I never, ever had a... Ah, I never reached..." Her voice failed.

"You're kidding." Jake stared at her in astonishment. "Last night was your first—"

"Yes," Sarah interjected, feeling her cheeks growing warm. "My very first...with you."

"Hot damn!" Jake whooped, dipping his head to reward her with a quick, hard kiss. "And?" he demanded, raising his head to monitor her expression and her response.

"And?" Sarah frowned, uncomprehending.

Jake gave her a look of sheer disbelief. "And, what did you think, feel? Did you enjoy it?"

"*Enjoy* hardly describes it," Sarah answered, exhaling a deep sigh of satisfaction. "It was..."

She hesitated, searching for a definitive word. "Everything." She smiled dreamily. "Everything I had always heard it was, but didn't believe could ever really be possible."

"Oh, Sarah." Jake's tone was humble. His eyes were soft, and his kiss was a benediction. But his body betrayed the solemn moment by leaping with renewed life. Jake raised his head to look at her with eyes now glittering with devilish intent. "Wanna experience that *everything* again?"

"Would Dan...Quayle?" she asked, innocently.

"Sarah," he said in a smiling warning.

"Does Tom...Cruise?"

"Sarah." Jake's smile gave way to laughter.

"Can Gregory...Peck?"

*"That does it."* Growling his appreciation, Jake pounced on her mouth and on her willing, eager body.

This time their lovemaking was hot and fast, hard and deep, wild and erotic, infinitely, thrillingly satisfying, and mentally and physically exhausting.

Entwined, locked together in the most intimate of embraces, their bodies spent in ultimate depletion, Sarah and Jake caressed and stroked each other to sleep.

Jake woke to bright sunshine and the muzzy realization that it had to be near, if not already past, noon.

He had to go to work!

The startling thought banished the last clinging wisps of sleep, and brought another, even more jolting realization of where he was. And where Jake was, exactly, was buried deep within the moist, encasing warmth of Sarah.

His body stirred, beginning to expand to fill her alluring sheath. Again? Jake blinked and grinned, both amazed and amused by the virile prowess he hadn't been aware of possessing. He wanted, longed, ached to test that heretofore unknown ability, but time decreed he postpone his test until another day, unless, unless...

Jake shot a hopeful glance at the small clock on the nightstand and sighed in disappointment. He had no time to spare wallowing in bed...and in Sarah. Heaving another sigh, he slowly eased himself from her, careful not to awaken her. A soft, loving expression crept over his face.

Sarah looked so peaceful, so vulnerable, in her slumber. Peaceful, vulnerable and... A streak of male pride lit a gleam in his eyes. Sarah looked so relaxed, so replete, so utterly, beautifully satisfied.

Lord, he hated to leave her. But leave her he must, he told himself. Sliding from the bed, he padded barefoot into the bathroom. After taking care of that business, he returned as silently to the bedroom to gather his clothes from the floor and get dressed.

Sarah woke, tossing the coverlet aside, stretching and yawning and testing the limits of his endurance and resolve. Catching sight of him, frozen in the act of shoving his arm into the sleeve of his jacket, she sat bolt upright. Frowning, she raked her fingers through her wildly tangled hair and asked, "Where are you going?"

Out of my head if you don't cover your tempting self, Jake thought in silent despair. "I have to go to work," he said, shrugging into the jacket.

"It's Sunday," Sarah protested. Then her frown darkened in consternation. "Isn't it?"

"Yes," Jake replied, in a voice strained by his inner battle to withdraw his avid gaze from the tantalizing allure of her luscious, naked body, her moist, parted, pouting lips. "But I still have to work."

"Oh." Sarah's lips turned down in a disappointed curve. "But you only had one day off."

Jake lost the inner battle, and made a visual feast of her. "I know." He smiled, inordinately pleased by the disappointment she wasn't even trying to conceal. "It's the way our schedule works. I get two days next week. Sunday and Monday."

She glanced at the clock. "What time do you start?"

"Three." Jake dragged his eyes from her form

to the clock. The hands stood at 12:52. "I go off duty at midnight." He shifted his gaze back to her...face, and arched one eyebrow questioningly. "Will you miss me?"

Sarah tossed him a droll look. "Would a fish miss wa—?"

He cut her off, shaking his head and grinning. "Not again. Answer me, damn it. Will you miss me?"

Her fantastic eyes took on that pansy-velvet softness. "Yes, Jake." Her voice was just as soft. "I'll miss you." She shrugged. "But I have plenty of work to keep my mind occupied. I've got a pile of assigned essays on the Zhou dynasty to read and grade." Her lips took on the downward curve that so tugged at his heart. "Still, I'll miss you like hell."

His throat suddenly tight, Jake took a step toward her, then backed up again. Damn, he didn't want to go, he railed, adoring her with his eyes. "Er..." He cleared his throat. "What time do you take lunch tomorrow?"

Sarah gave him a distracted look.

"Was the question too difficult?" He clenched his hands into fists in an effort to keep himself from crossing the room to her.

"Cute," she muttered. "I get a break between classes at one on Mondays."

"Will you meet me at Dave's place for lunch?"

he asked, keeping his eyes fastened on her face while edging back, toward the door.

"Will you kiss me goodbye?"

"I'm afraid to."

"Afraid!" Sarah cried. "Why?"

Jake snorted in a rueful, derisive way. "I'm afraid that if I kiss you, I'll never get out of here."

Sarah actually appeared to glow from his compliment. A mischievous smile tilted her lips. "Okay." She drove him wild by heaving her chest and breasts in a sigh. "Sorry, but, no kiss, no lunch."

"Sarah," Jake groaned, struggling to control a smile. "You're a hard woman."

"So I've been told," she retorted. "Now get your rump over here and give me a kiss."

"Man, oh, man," he groused. "The things a guy has to do to get a lousy lunch date." His dancing eyes belying the complaint, grateful for the excuse to do what he desperately wanted to do, Jake crossed to the bed, slid his arms under hers and hauled her up, crushing her breasts against his chest.

"Yes," Sarah said, raising her mouth for his kiss. "But remember what *I* had to do for a lousy dinner."

"You are definitely asking for it, honey," Jake said in warning, again losing the battle against laughter.

Her expression brightened with delighted surprise. "Yes, I am, aren't I? How wonderfully... freeing!"

Loving her like mad in that instant, sharing her delight, Jake took her mouth in a soul-enslaving, emotion-sealing, hair-curling kiss.

His body reacted to the kiss, the tentative touch of her tongue, in a normal, healthy, painful way, sending warning signals from his groin to his mind.

He *had* to get out of there.

Hearing the sharp inner command, Jake released her and beat a hasty retreat to the door.

"Tomorrow. Lunch. Be there," he panted.

Sarah had the nerve to taunt him. "Or?"

"Or I'll come looking for you," he threatened, yanking open the door and striding out of the room.

The exciting sound of Sarah's throaty laughter brought him up short, two strides beyond the doorway. Acting on sheer impulse, he spun and strode back to the doorway.

Sarah's eyes lit up at the sight of him, their revealing sparkle showing her approval of his impulse. "Jake?" She gave a tentative smile. "You look so odd, disturbed. Is...is something wrong?"

"No, honey." Jake shook his head and gulped a courage-gathering breath. "It's...er, I just thought you should know that..." He paused, then plunged ahead. "I love you. I love you like hell."

"Oh, Jake!" Sarah cried, moving to scramble from the bed. "I love you, too."

*Go. Now. Or you'll never go.*

"Tomorrow, love," Jake said, obeying the inner voice of reason by spinning away and literally running for the entrance door to the apartment.

The plaintive sound of Sarah's voice calling to him followed Jake from the apartment and down the stairs and echoed in his head inside the car. Motionless, he waited for the expected sinking reaction to his impetuous admission; it didn't materialize. What he felt was an expanding joy inside him in response to Sarah's reciprocal confession.

How could he leave her? Jake railed, staring sightlessly through the windshield. How could he force himself to go, now, after hearing her say she loved him? He ached to hold her, caress her, laugh with her, love her, make love to her, with her, all day, all night, forever.

His hand grasped the door handle; sheer willpower kept him from releasing the catch. Jake had to leave Sarah, and he knew it. He had a job, responsibilities, that he could not in good conscience simply ignore. And yet, missing her already, and greatly tempted to chuck the job, if only for the day, Jake gave a sharp shake of his head in self-denial. Then he fired the engine and switched on the citizens band radio, which was always set to the police frequency.

He'd call her during his dinner break, he promised himself, using the treat as a means to get himself in gear. The car moved forward into the deserted Sunday street. Jake handled the car smoothly but automatically.

His thoughts entangled with memories of the night and morning spent with Sarah, and the multifaceted, supremely satisfying results derived from it, Jake paid scant notice to the crackle issuing from the CB, until the voice of the day patrol officer sputtered from it, snaring his full attention.

Officer Jorge Luis was reporting in on his initial response to yet another car-stripping investigation.

Another? Jake shot a frowning glance at the CB just as Jorge reported the modus operandi of the theft. From what Jorge was saying, it was apparent that it was the second such crime he had investigated since Friday.

The second? Jake wondered when the other theft had occurred. Hell, he'd only been off one day— but somebody had been busy.

The MO was exactly the same as that of the theft Jake had investigated two days ago. Both cars, late-model luxury sedans, had been stripped down to the bare bones.

Amateurs. Jake again defined the thieves, an uneasy feeling curling in his gut. Damned if it wasn't shaping up as if they might be dealing with a local ring here.

Jake heaved a sigh and applied the brakes as he approached the red light at the intersection near his apartment. That was all they needed, he thought, tapping his fingertips on the steering wheel. A blasted ring of amateur parts thieves, looking to become professionals.

The light flicked from red to amber to green, and within that tiny pause, Jake got a hunch, and acted on it. Instead of turning right, onto the street where his apartment was located, he drove straight ahead, heading out of town.

Jake's destination was a junkyard situated on the fringe of the Sprucewood town limits, but within the town's police jurisdiction.

Maybe his hunch would prove groundless, Jake reflected. But, then again, it couldn't hurt to have a look-see, he figured, since doubt about the place already existed.

Not only Jake, but every other member of the department, had at one time or another expressed suspicions about the junkyard, and the irascible old coot who owned and operated it. The prevailing theory being that the place was used at times as an intermediary drop-off for stolen cars and parts ultimately headed for a chop shop in one of the larger nearby cities, like Norristown, Wilmington, Camden or—most likely—Philadelphia.

Acting on their suspicions, every member of the force, the chief included, had made a point of visiting the establishment off and on, and had come away empty. So, for that matter, had various officers of the state police.

But, what the hey, Jake mused, it still couldn't hurt to have a look around. Coming to another highway intersection, he made the turn onto an old, less traveled route that went right by the eyesore.

Jake slowed the car's speed as he approached the junkyard and began rubbernecking, checking out the fenced area, which was littered with mangled, rusting old heaps and spare parts. Nothing appeared unusual. In fact, it was as quiet as a church—an abandoned church. But then, he reminded himself, it was Sunday.

The car was barely moving, just creeping along, by the time he drove past the entrance to the yard. Risking a longer, more intensive look, Jake noticed three young men giving the once-over to the banged-up heaps parked at the very front of the junkyard, all of which had For Sale stickers plastered on their mostly cracked windshields.

Kids, Jake decided, probably from the college, looking for a jalopy with which to haunt the streets and hunt the girls. A smile twitched the corners of his mouth. Jake liked kids, all kids. Although, even from a distance, Jake could see that these were not really kids, but young men, likely college seniors, in their early twenties. It didn't matter. To Jake, as long as they were in school, from prekindergarten through college graduation, they were kids.

Wishing the trio luck in their hunt—for a car and for the girls—Jake eased his foot down on the accelerator, increasing the car's speed. A short distance farther along the highway, he pulled onto the lot of a deserted gas station, made a turn and drove off again, heading back to town.

Telling himself to get a move on or he'd be late for work, Jake slanted a cursory glance at the junkyard on his way by, and eased his foot off the gas pedal.

Now that's odd, he thought, frowning. The three young men he had noticed before were climbing into a gleaming new—and wildly expensive—black-and-silver van, customized with all the luxury extras, like miniblinds and curtains at the windows.

Both puzzled and curious, Jake took a hard, quick but comprehensive look at the man preparing to get into the driver's side of the sleek vehicle. From habit, he stored the man's vital statistics in his memory file: above medium height, slender, slightly muscular build, good-looking, long nose, strong jawline, dark hair and eyebrows, fading summer tan, no visible scars or identifying marks.

Got it. Now get moving, Jake advised himself, catching sight of the time on the dashboard clock. It was past one-thirty. He still had to shower, shave, get into uniform and... Jake's stomach emitted a low growl. He had better rustle up something to eat. It was time to get kicking.

Jake indulged himself reminiscing about Sarah during the drive back into town; he really had no choice, for she filled his mind to the exclusion of any other concerns.

It was incredible, he marveled, counting the number of days since he had first spotted her sitting in that corner booth at Dave's place, looking so studious and owlish, and so very appealing, in those oversize glasses.

Four days. Jake shook his head in wonder. Who'd have thought it? He grinned as he made the turn onto the street. Incredible? Ha! He laughed aloud. It was more like pretty damned amazing.

Who'd have thought it, indeed? he wondered, taking the steps to his apartment two at a time. Jake Wolfe, footloose and fancy-free, taking the leap from heart-whole to crazy in love in one giant bound.

Sarah. Lord, he did love her, Jake thought, tearing his clothes off as he strode from his front door to the bedroom.

Love at first sight? Well, perhaps not at *first* sight, Jake hedged, heading for the bathroom. Maybe not even at first dinner together. The second dinner, here at his place? Jake pondered the possibility as he adjusted the water temperature before stepping under the shower.

A vision filled his mind, sharp and clear, of those heated moments he'd had with her on the sofa after dinner Friday night. She had responded so sweetly, before breaking free to escape into the kitchen.

Yeah, he decided. It had probably begun on Friday.

Either way, his mother was going to be very smug about being proved correct, once she knew. Jake grimaced as he lathered shampoo into his hair. And his brothers... He groaned. His brothers were going to have a field day with it—and with him. Their baby brother, snared in love's trap, so to speak.

Oh, well... Jake shrugged and rinsed the mound of spring-rain-scented lather from his head. They'd change their tune in a hurry after they met Sarah.

Sarah.

The vision in his mind shifted to the night and the morning he had spent with her. Sarah was so...so magnificent in surrender, giving of herself with every living particle of her mind and body.

The steaming water pulsating from the shower jets cascaded down the length of Jake's body, triggering memories and images and sensations. The sluicing water revitalized his flesh. The feel of it recalled to his mind the silky feel of Sarah's satiny legs, sliding along his thighs, tautening his muscles, causing a quiver in the lightly sprinkled short hairs.

Lost in a dream of her, of the exquisite moments in her encircling embrace, his body joined with hers, his heart pounding, his pulse racing, Jake closed his eyes and reexperienced the wonder that was Sarah.

Love her? Jake drew a shuddering breath. No, he didn't love Sarah; he adored her.

His body responded predictably to his memories. He wanted her, here, now, with him, a part of him. Hurting from the intensity of his need for her, Jake arched his body and threw back his head. The pulsating water beat against his flesh, and poured into his open mouth, effectively swamping the memory flow.

"Damn fool!" Choking, coughing and laughing at himself, Jake turned off the water and stepped, dripping wet, onto the bath mat.

Boy, you've got a real case, he told himself, rubbing the water from his body with a large towel. You are definitely down for the count.

Shrugging, Jake tossed the towel in the direction of the hamper and sauntered into the bedroom. It didn't matter. Nothing mattered except Sarah.

Sarah.

A thought, a startling consideration, made Jake pause, his hand thrust inside his underwear drawer.

Recalling her remark of earlier that morning about feeling wonderfully free, Jake mused that maybe, just maybe, you had to be willing to surrender your freedom to achieve the real meaning of being free.

Frowning over the concept, Jake glanced around the room, as if seeking truth. What he found was the face of the clock, just as the hands positioned themselves at 2:15.

Lord! He had no time to indulge in philosophical meanderings. He had to go to work!

# Nine

She was in love.

Sarah spent the majority of the afternoon in a euphoric haze, marveling over the wonder of it all.

How was it possible? How had it happened? The questions arose to confront her; Sarah sidestepped them by telling herself that, even though she had never believed in the concept of love at first sight, it had happened, therefore it was possible.

End of questions. Besides, she felt too good, too well loved and satisfied to tax her brain and her emotions. In her estimation, Jake Wolfe epitomized everything that mattered to her. His senses-stirring attractiveness aside, Jake was kind, gentle, strong, honest, a joy to be with, to laugh with, and a veritable powerhouse of a lover.

The thought was arousing, and sent delicious shivers skipping up Sarah's spine and down her legs. Not again! Laughing silently at herself and the weakness the mere consideration of Jake could instill inside her, Sarah polished off a lunch of scrambled eggs and toast while telling herself to get busy.

Sarah had yet to as much as glance at the pile of essays waiting for her attention.

After Jake's precipitate flight, she had dawdled for nearly an hour, luxuriating in a tub filled to the rim with hot water and topped by a mound of perfumed bubbles. The heated water had soothed the tight achiness in her thigh muscles and the tenderness at their apex.

Jake was one masterful lover, Sarah had reflected, closing her eyes, floating in the tub of sensual recall. Beneath the waterline, the tips of her breasts had hardened into tight buds of pleasure aroused by the thrilling memories performing an erotic dance in her mind.

Sarah's sensitized flesh remembered the feel of Jake's hands, exploring every inch of her quivering body, his mouth, suckling greedily before moving on, seeking to know her, all of her, her deepest secrets.

The perfumed scent of the bath salts wafted on the steam, filling her senses. Sighing, Sarah moved slowly, sinuously, unconsciously reveling in the flow of silky water caressing her skin. Her thighs parted, her breathing grew shallow, quickening with the images playing inside her head, images of Jake, stroking her, loving her, possessing her, with his hot kisses, his thrusting tongue, his hard, powerful body.

A moan, low, needful, whispered through Sarah's parted tingling lips. The whimpering sound scattered the images, bringing her to her senses.

Memory melt. The realization of the hot moisture gathering in the depths of her femininity brought a self-conscious flush to Sarah's cheeks. She was ready for him, wanting him so much, she was shocking herself. Slamming her thighs together, she jolted upright, her movement so abrupt that she set the water lapping, splashing out over the rim of the tub.

Enough of the fantasizing, Sarah told herself, proceeding with her bath, and the subsequent mopping of the floor, with brisk, no-nonsense efficiency.

After her bath, she spent another half hour shampooing, conditioning and blow-drying her hair.

Then, her body not only replete, but clean and glowing with health and well-being, Sarah trailed into the kitchen to start a pot of coffee. While the aromatic brew dripped into the pot, she stared into space, a soft smile curving her lips, drifting in a dream of Jake.

Her first cup of coffee did revitalize Sarah somewhat, enough for her to wander to the front door and collect the Sunday paper from the hallway. But, although she carried the paper to the table by the window in the tiny dining area, she didn't so much as glance at the headlines. Secure and protected within a cocoon of exciting love, Sarah had no interest whatever in the machinations of the outside world.

Hugging her happiness close, she mooned about the apartment, absently touching things, plumping throw pillows, gazing out the window at the sparkling autumn afternoon until hunger drew her out of herself and into the kitchen.

Her meager meal consumed, Sarah carried her dishes to the sink, refilled her coffee cup and, picking up the paper as she passed the table, settled herself on the couch in the living room. The very first article to catch her eye burst her euphoric bubble of well-being and happiness.

The article gave an account of another car-stripping, which had occurred sometime Saturday night—last night, while she and Jake had been together.

Andrew.

The young man's name and image filled Sarah's

mind and chilled her soul. Had Andrew and his two friends——? Her thought splintered as she shook her head.

It didn't make sense. Neither Andrew nor the other two men had any conceivable reason for stealing anything—let alone car parts, for goodness' sake.

And yet, and yet... Sarah shuddered at the memory of Andrew's threatening tone of voice, the expression of menace that had tightened his visage.

She knew, she just knew, there was a connection between the theft of the parts and the furtive look about the three friends, and Andrew's subsequent warning to her to be silent.

*Jake.*

Shoving the paper aside, Sarah jumped up to pace the length and width of the room, distractedly raking her hands through her neatly brushed hair.

She had agreed to meet Jake for lunch tomorrow but... Sarah bit her lip. Dave's place was so close to the campus, too close. Suppose Andrew were to see her with Jake? He might even recognize Jake as the police officer who patrolled the perimeters of the college grounds.

Sarah came to a dead stop, her mind shrieking a warning. She would have to contact Jake, tell him she couldn't meet him. She could not take the risk of placing him in danger.

*He's a cop. The risk of danger is part of his job.*

The inner voice of reason broke through the paralyzing mist of panic seeping into Sarah's mind, calming her frantic fears. Drawing a deep breath, she examined the inner assurance from a rational perspective.

Jake was a law-enforcement officer, a professional, trained and prepared to deal with criminals of all kinds. She herself had considered his qualities, his strengths, and decided that Jake was definitely hero material. What he and his brother officers did for a living might be scary for the women who loved them, but that was their problem...her problem....

Jake was tough and self-confident, supremely capable of taking care of himself, Sarah told herself sternly. And, instead of hanging back, avoiding him, she should risk the possibility of him ridiculing her intuition about the three men and tell Jake about her suspicions.

Really, Sarah chided herself, heaving a sigh of relief—what could Andrew do to her, anyway?

Her decision made, she left the papers scattered on the couch, collected her briefcase and returned to the table in the small corner near the window. She had work to do, and the day wasn't getting any younger.

Sarah had read and graded over half of the assigned essays, and was feeling pleased about the quality of most of them, when the phone rang, a little after seven.

Jake? Bright expectation sent her flying from her chair to the phone on the kitchen wall.

"Hello?" Her voice held a breathless, hopeful note.

"Hi." Jake's voice was low, sexy, hinting at remembered intimacy. "I couldn't wait until tomorrow," he murmured, robbing her of the little breath she possessed. "I had to at least talk to you before then."

"I...I'm glad," Sarah admitted, way beyond ingenuousness and game-playing.

"How are you?"

"Missing you."

Jake drew a sharp, audible breath. "I'm hurting," he confessed, exhaling a derisive chuckle. "Hell of a state for a man who's supposed to be working."

Sarah had a sudden, clear image of Jake as he had appeared earlier that morning, naked and gloriously aroused, and knew the state he was referring to. "Ah...where are you calling from?" she asked, in the hope of diverting the distracting, sensuous trend of her thoughts.

"The diner out on the highway. I'm on my supper break," he replied, in a more normal, less enticing tone. "Are you getting anywhere with your work?"

"I'm over halfway through the essays," she answered on a sigh of gratitude. "For the most part, they are really well written and quite good."

"The students must have a good teacher," Jake asserted, offering her a blatantly biased compliment.

Not nearly as good as the teacher the *teacher* had, Sarah reflected with arousing recall, while voicing a murmured "Thank you, I do my best."

"If memory serves," Jake drawled, "your best far surpasses excellence."

Sarah grew warm all over, warm and mush-minded. Her fingers plucked at the worn, soft jeans encasing her legs, and her misty-eyed gaze strayed, around the kitchen and through the archway, to collide with the papers strewn on the couch. The sight jolted her back to reality.

"Jake, stop," she protested, tearing her riveted stare from the papers.

"Stop what?" he asked with feigned innocence.

"You know what."

His soft laughter held the allure of forbidden delights. "Okay," he agreed. "What do you want to talk about?"

"Well..." Sarah hesitated, and an inner voice shouted, *Tell him. Now.* "Er...I read in the paper about the reports of two cars being stripped. Are you working on those?"

"Not at the moment," Jake's voice was dry as

a rainless August, indicating his belief that she was merely trying to change the subject. "Why?"

"Well, I mean, two car-strippings in as many days…" she said, slowly leading up to the moment of disclosure.

"Three," he inserted.

"What?" Sarah blinked.

"There was another this morning," Jake explained. "I heard the day officer call in his report over my car CB on my way home from your place."

A glimmer of hope sprang into Sarah's mind. Maybe her intuition about the students was wrong. Maybe… Another consideration, this one for Jake's safety, sent a chill down her spine. She had to know, had to ask. "Do you believe you are dealing with professional thieves here?"

"Possibly." Jake sounded coolly unperturbed, almost nonchalant. "But I seriously doubt it."

"Why?" Sarah asked, feeling juxtaposed between the conflicting emotions of relief and renewed fear.

Jake chuckled tolerantly at her persistence. "Because all three of the thefts had all the earmarks of having been committed by rank amateurs."

Sarah frowned. "How would you know that?"

"Honey, they stripped the damn things," he answered patiently. "Real professionals would simply have swiped the entire car."

"Really?" Sarah was intrigued. "Why?"

"Easier," Jake replied, laughing softly. "Mere seconds are required for a professional to steal a car, locked or not. It can take minutes—a few or a lot, depending on the adeptness of the thief, or thieves—to strip a car down."

"Oh" was all Sarah could think of to say, because her mind was busy repeating the word *amateurs*. Her intuition had been correct—she now felt positive about it. She drew a long breath, preparing to lay her concerns on Jake's broad shoulders, but she didn't get a word out of her mouth.

"Oh, honey, I've got to hang up," Jake said. "The waitress just set my dinner on the counter."

"Oh…okay," Sarah said, feeling and sounding deflated.

Jake obviously attributed her tone to disappointment over having to disconnect, for he murmured, "I'll see you tomorrow at Dave's place."

"Yes." Resolve now colored her tone; she would definitely talk to him tomorrow.

"Good night, honey." Jake's voice indicated his reluctance to hang up.

"Good night," Sarah said on a sigh, sharing his reluctance. "You'd better go. Your meal will get cold."

"Not as cold as I feel at this moment." Jake's voice went low, intimate. "I need you to hold me, make love with me, warm me up, set me on fire."

"Oh, Jake," she whispered on a sigh.

"Oh, hell," he growled in return. "Good night, love."

Sarah heard a soft click, and then a dial tone. She closed her eyes, fumbled the receiver onto the cradle and sighed again. "Good night, love."

Nearly two hours later, Sarah's resolve was in shreds, and her fear was renewed and running rampant. She had just finished reading Andrew's essay. In and of itself, as a completed assignment, the essay was not merely good, it was brilliant—comprehensive, well written, and deserving of an A+. It was the central theme of the work that terrified Sarah.

Andrew's theme was power. Personal power. With the skill of a master weaver, he had woven that theme through the essay. The finished product could be likened to a written tapestry depicting the machinations of the feudal nobles who, by cleverly using their own power, had so weakened the power of the Zhou dynasty that China had declined into a confused mass of separate and contentious states.

In any other situation, with any other student, Sarah would have happily praised Andrew's accomplishment. But, having read between the lines, as well as the actual typewritten words, Sarah had garnered insight into Andrew's character. It was not a pretty or a reassuring sight.

To Sarah's mind, the picture of Andrew that

emerged was that of a bright, confident, emotionally cold young man, playing mind games by testing his intelligence and sharpening his wits against the grindstone power of the status quo.

The last hopeful vestiges of lingering doubt in Sarah's mind were swept away by one reading of Andrew's essay. She also knew without a doubt that he was the driving force of the three students, directing and controlling the activities.

Sarah had repeatedly questioned her own intuition, her instincts, simply because there appeared to be no obvious reason for the men to engage in unlawful pursuits. Now she knew better. Andrew wasn't in it for the money, she theorized. In a strange way, he was gambling, betting he could outthink and outwit the authorities.

Sarah's theory scared the hell out of her. But she no longer gave thought to the possible danger to herself. Her primary concern was for Jake.

*She could not tell him.*

After gingerly stuffing Andrew's essay into her briefcase, as if afraid it might attack if she didn't get it safely contained, Sarah sat, staring and immobile, while her mind proceeded to summon up, with perfect recall, her phone conversation with Jake.

Rank amateurs, he had called the thieves. But it wasn't Jake's phrasing that had made an impression on her, it was his tone of voice. He had sounded so unconcerned, almost casual in his attitude toward the amateurs.

And Sarah felt a sinking certainty that there wasn't a thing casual about Andrew.

Sarah drew a shuddering breath and conjured up the worst possible scenario. What if she told Jake of her suspicions about Andrew, and his veiled threat, and, instead of laughing, he gave some credence to her fears? Or even just decided to humor her? Sarah knew the answer. Jake would commence an investigation, and with his casual attitude, and fully aware that the suspects were students, still young men, he would be at a disadvantage from the outset. Jake would be in the position of believing he was hunting a tabby cat, when in truth he'd be stalking a tiger. Jake might be hurt, even...

*No.* Sarah shook her head sharply back and forth, rejecting the scene. It would not happen, because she refused to allow it to happen.

She would obey Andrew's dictum and remain silent, Sarah decided, her course set. For, although she had likened him to a hero, Sarah had no intention of putting Jake to the test. Quite the opposite. She would do anything she had to do to protect him.

Sarah had spent a restless night, intermittently wakeful and half sleeping, tormented by nightmares. The same terrifying dream kept recurring, a dream in which she saw Jake sprawled on the floor in a dark place, wounded and bleeding. Yet no matter how hard she fought, strained, to get to him, something held her back, and she could not move.

Around five, jerking awake for the third time, her skin cold and clammy with perspiration, her pulse racing, the sound of her voice screaming Jake's name reverberating in her head, Sarah flung the twisted covers from her and dragged her depleted body from the bed.

While drinking an entire pot of coffee, Sarah finished reading and grading the last of the essays. After Andrew's, they were blessedly bland. Forgoing food, which she was certain would choke her, she bathed, dressed and left for school, the acrid aftertaste of too much coffee stinging the back of her throat, the effects of too little rest pricking her eyes.

Sarah spent the morning alternately racking her brain to remember her classroom subject matter, and shooting increasingly nervous glances at her watch. Inner conflict tore at her feeble composure. She longed to see Jake, to be with him, to crawl inside the haven of his strong embrace and hide there. And at the same time she was afraid to see him, afraid of inadvertently letting something slip, revealing her fears to him.

By the time her lunch break came, Sarah felt fragile, close to unraveling. The sight of Andrew's van, pulled up at a traffic light at the intersection near Dave's place, stopped her in her tracks as she approached the street, once again preparing to jaywalk across to the luncheonette. The added shock of seeing Jake on the opposite sidewalk, in uniform, propped against his patrol car, his hand raised to her in greeting, had the breathtaking effect of a hard blow to the heart.

Indecisive, wanting to turn tail and run, Sarah hesitated, teetering on the curb.

"Come on, honey," Jake called, motioning her forward with a wave. "Before the light changes."

Reluctant, yet feeling caught, without recourse, Sarah slowly crossed to him. From the corner of her eye, she saw the light change to green, the van creep forward. Her stomach clenching, she stepped onto the sidewalk.

"Hi." Jake's smile was soul-destroying.

Sarah opened her mouth to respond, then gasped in disbelief as, stepping to her, Jake swept her into his arms and kissed her, hard, full on her surprise-parted lips—just as the van slowly cruised past.

Jake's kiss was shattering to Sarah's already riddled nervous system. The fact that Andrew had been a witness to Jake's embrace and kiss compounded the shock.

Unwilling even to contemplate what Andrew

thought, in what manner he might react, yet unable
to think of little else, Sarah moved like an autom-
aton when Jake steered her into the small restaurant.

"Have I outraged your sense of propriety?"
Jake asked in a teasing whisper, urging her into the
corner booth.

Grasping at the excuse he so innocently offered,
Sarah swallowed, nodded, and stuttered in agreement. "I, er—I'm not used to being—ah, you
know…"

"Affectionate in public?" Jake inserted, openly
laughing at her stammering.

"Y-yes." Telling herself to get her head together, Sarah gulped for a calming breath.

"I'm sorry." Jake's hand, warm and comforting, covered hers. "But it seems like forever since
I left you yesterday. I had to kiss you or explode."

"Oh, Jake." Wanting to bawl, Sarah forced her
lips into a smile. "I missed you, too."

The laughter fled from his face and his eyes,
replaced by an expression so intent, so loving, that
it brought a rush of hot tears to Sarah's eyes and
a wailing protest into her mind.

*Damn Andrew and his stupid power games.
Damn his threats. Damn him. Damn him.*

"Hiya, folks, what are you going to have today?"

Dave's cheery greeting broke the chain of

Sarah's angry, resentful thoughts. She looked up at him, then across the table at Jake. He grinned and handed the pasteboard menu to her. A frown knit her brow as she squinted, without her glasses, at the selections, which consisted mostly of sandwiches.

The very idea of food made Sarah's stomach roil. Still, knowing she had to make the effort, if only to stave off questions from Jake, she searched for the least digestion-offending item on the card.

"Sarah?"

"Ah…" Sarah swallowed the taste of bile. "I'm really not very hungry today." She managed a weak smile for Dave. "Do you have a soup of the day?"

"Yep." Dave nodded emphatically. "Split pea with ham. I made it myself this morning."

"I'll have that," she said, setting the menu aside.

"That's all?" Jake scowled. "A bowl of soup isn't enough to get you through the rest of the day."

"Yes, it is." Not looking at Jake, she smiled at Dave. "Just the soup, please. Oh, and a small glass of milk," she added, hoping to neutralize the coffee seemingly burning a hole in the floor of her stomach.

"Yes, ma'am." Dave smiled back at her before turning his attention to Jake. "What about you?"

"The usual."

Dave grinned. "Two Coney Island dogs and a chocolate shake. Right?"

"You got it."

Sarah suppressed a shudder, and the urge to comment on his less-than-nutritious choices.

"So, did you get through that pile of essays?" Jake asked the minute Dave turned away.

The essays. Andrew. Sarah was forced to suppress another, deeper shudder. "Yes," she replied, in that instant coming to a firm decision born of frustration and anger.

Andrew would have to be dealt with. And she, not Jake, was going to do the dealing.

"So?" Jake nudged at her wandering attention.

"So…what?" Sarah frowned and fingered her paper napkin, tearing it; her decision carried with it a boatload of anxiety-causing baggage.

"So…how were they?" Jake frowned and shifted his gaze from her picking fingers to her eyes.

Sarah shifted her gaze, fearful of betraying herself, her anxieties. "They were very good. I didn't give a grade under a B−."

"What's wrong, honey?"

Sarah felt her eyelashes flicker, and drew on every ounce of control she possessed to keep her voice even, natural. "Wrong? Nothing. Why?"

"You're acting strange, nervous." Jake frowned. "Almost as if I make you uneasy."

"You? That's ridiculous." She pulled off a strained laugh and a fairly reasonable shrug. "I didn't sleep too well, that's all. But other than that…" She let her voice trail away, and shrugged again. "I'm fine."

Although Jake's expression said clearly that he was unconvinced, to Sarah's heartfelt relief he didn't pursue the subject. But a strained tension lay between them all through the interminable meal. Through sheer application, Sarah managed to consume every drop of her soup and milk, and even one of the crackers from the packet Dave served with the soup. But she felt utterly exhausted when, at last, she slid another of many glances at her watch and saw with relief that it was time for her to return to the campus.

"I…er, I've got to go," she said, avoiding Jake's eyes as she collected her things. "I've got a class in less than half an hour."

"How about tomorrow, same time, same place?" Jake asked, tossing enough bills on the table to cover the check and a generous tip for Dave.

"I'm…not sure," Sarah hedged, scouring her mind for an excuse as she slid off the seat. "Ah, I seem to recall the department head saying something about a faculty meeting." She walked determinedly toward the door, talking to him over her shoulder. "Could I give you a call at home before I leave in the morning?"

"Sure." Both Jake's tone and his expression were strained. "Honey, hold up a minute," he said, reaching out to grasp her arm as she pushed through the doorway and started across the sidewalk.

"I've got to go, Jake." Sarah could hear the desperation in her voice. "I'll call you." Pulling away from his hand, she stepped into the street. She had taken four long steps when the loud sound of screeching tires drew her head around, and she saw the vehicle streak through the intersection.

*Andrew's van was aimed directly at her!*

"Sarah!"

# Ten

With the harsh sound of his shout ringing in his head, his heart racing in his chest and his throat closing around a lump of fear, Jake sprinted after Sarah.

It was over in seconds, yet it seemed to go on forever. Everything blurred, yet remained clearly defined within the depths of his subconscious.

Jake caught a flash of black and silver. The large vehicle was bearing down on Sarah. There was no time to think. Tasting stark and absolute terror for the first time in his life, Jake reacted. Dashing in front of her, he shoved Sarah back, out of harm's way, instantly taking a flying leap after her to gain his own safety.

The vehicle sped past, missing Jake by mere inches. A moment stretched into eternity. Sarah lay in a shuddering heap near his shoulder. Reactive tremors rippling through his body, he pushed himself to his knees, simultaneously reaching for Sarah with unsteady hands. Taking her with him, he stumbled, steadied himself, and stood up.

"Holy—"

"Jake, are you all right?" Sarah cried, running her hands over his shoulders and down his chest.

"Yeah, yeah, I'm okay," he assured her, clasping her head in his hands to peer into her face. "Are you hurt?"

"A scrape... My knee..." Sarah was gasping for breath. "Oh, Jake, I was so frightened. The way you were flung to the street...I thought he had struck you!"

Jake exhaled a shaky laugh. "I did the flinging. That driver must either be drunk or drugged out of his mind." He paused to grab a breath. "Did you happen to get a look at the licence number?"

"No," Sarah said tremulously. "Did you?"

"No." Jake heaved a sigh. "I didn't even get a make on the vehicle. It all happened too fast."

"Y—yes."

Sarah was white as a sheet, and her eyes were wide, owlish-looking—even without the big round glasses. Sliding his hands to her arms, Jake started toward the sidewalk. "Let's go back inside, honey. You need to sit down."

"No." Shaking her head, Sarah came to an abrupt halt. "I'm all right." She turned to face the street again.

"Sarah, wait." He held her still when she would have walked away.

"I can't." Her expression was set in adamant lines. "I'm okay, and I've got a class. I'll call you." Pulling her arm free, she scanned the street and hurried away.

Almost, Jake thought, staring after her, as if she were running away...from him.

But then, Sarah had appeared to be shying away from him since before, and during, lunch, Jake mused, watching her as she cut across the campus.

*What in hell?*

Rattled from the near miss by the careening vehicle, and confused by Sarah's odd behavior, Jake stood staring across the way for long seconds after Sarah disappeared from his sight. A strange something niggled at the edges of his consciousness, tapping, as if for his attention.

But at that moment all Jake's attention was centered on Sarah. What had happened within the last twenty-odd hours to so unnerve her? Because Sarah had been nervous. And the baffling part was, she had seemed to be nervous of him.

Jake shook his head, as though in the hope of clearing his mind. It didn't make sense. Not after the night and morning they had spent together, laughing, loving. And she had sounded fine, relaxed and affectionate, when he had talked to her on the phone last night.

But she had said she hadn't slept well, Jake recalled, feeling a sudden emptiness. Was Sarah suffering misgivings about their shared intimacy, their declaration of love for one another?

For a moment, a long moment, Jake felt physically sick. Then reason asserted itself, chasing the nausea. Sarah's reaction to that near miss had not been that of a woman having second thoughts about her lover.

But, if it wasn't their relationship, what was bugging Sarah? He knew that something sure as hell was.

The persistent niggling at the back of Jake's mind tapped harder, seeking recognition.

Jake frowned and shrugged the uneasy sensation aside. He didn't have time to probe the inner workings of his gray matter. His primary concern was for Sarah.

Heaving an impatient sigh, Jake raised his arm to massage the tension-taut muscles twanging at the back of his neck. His gaze glanced off, then returned to, the black material covering his arm.

The uniform. Jake's thoughts swirled back to the

morning he had first noticed Sarah sitting in the back booth inside the very restaurant he was standing in front of at that moment. An image formed of her behavior that morning when Dave introduced them. Sarah had appeared unnerved by him then, too. Memory nudged, and Jake recalled that he had pondered the possibility of Sarah being uneasy because of his uniform.

Of course, Jake had dismissed the idea as ridiculous. Now he wasn't so sure. But why would the sight of a police uniform unsettle someone—unless that someone had something to fear from the law?

But what, by any stretch of the imagination, could Sarah have to fear from the law…and therefore from him?

Though, admittedly, Jake had known Sarah a very short time, he felt he knew her very well. And the Sarah he felt he knew had nothing to fear from the law, or from him—most especially from him.

Why then did she appear so nervous while in his company when he was in uniform?

Damn strange, Jake mused, sparing a glance at his watch. There was still some time before he began his shift. Hoping to be able to spend more time with Sarah, he had dressed for work early, and had even picked up his patrol car before coming to meet her. He had time to ponder the puzzle.

Frustration eating at him, the niggling at the edge of his consciousness continuing to tap away,

Jake walked to the car, slid behind the wheel and
then sat, still as a stone, staring straight ahead, into
the middle distance.

Sarah.

It simply didn't make sense.

Jake had never been able to tolerate things that
didn't make sense. And so, in any instance, situation, happenstance, that made no sense, he would
mentally pick at it, poke it, turn it inside out until
it did make sense.

Perhaps that was why he enjoyed being a cop,
Jake theorized, unaware of the everyday movement
of people and traffic around him. Plodding though
it often was, he enjoyed the process of systematic
elimination to attain resolution of any given problem.

Okay, Mr. Law Officer, do your enjoyable thing,
Jake told himself. Eliminate. Take it apart. Then
put it back together. The beginning might be a
good place to start.

Sinking into a plodding mode, Jake mentally
ticked off the particulars.

Sarah, nervous and visibly uneasy on being introduced to him Thursday morning. Sarah, relaxed
and at ease with him when he invited himself to
dinner Thursday evening. Sarah, hesitant and uncertain Friday morning about accepting his invitation to have dinner with him. Sarah, relaxed and
at ease with him at his place Friday evening. Sarah,

vague and unsure about going out with him Saturday evening. Sarah, relaxed and at ease with him Saturday evening—and positively abandoned with him later, both Saturday night and Sunday morning. Then Sarah this morning, once again nervous and uneasy with him.

*Damn! It still didn't ma—*

It was at that split second that the niggling poked a hole in the veil of Jake's subconscious. He had a fleeting image of a large vehicle, saw a flash of black and silver, heard the echo of Sarah's cry.

*"I thought he had struck you!"*

He? Jake repeated in silent contemplation. He hadn't given any thought to the term at the time; it would be natural for her, or anyone, to speak of the driver as *he*. But, just for the sake of supposition, could Sarah have been referring to one particular he—a he she knew and possibly feared?

Farfetched? Way out? Sure, Jake conceded. But, on the other hand, what if— Jake blinked, and realized he was staring intently at the intersection. His subconscious replayed the scene for his conscious mind.

He could hear again the screech of tires as the van shot forward, see the flash of black and silver, feel the stark terror gripping him. A reactive shiver streaked up his spine, causing the short hairs at the back of his neck to quiver.

That driver had been neither drunk nor drugged

senseless. He had made a deliberate attempt to run
Sarah down!

Van? Jake frowned. Now, where...

Black and silver!

Jake's subconscious replayed another hidden
memory. He could see the black-and-silver van of
yesterday morning, and the young men getting into
it, young men he had immediately assumed were
college kids.

And Sarah taught at the college.

Coincidence? Jake made a snorting noise. Coincidence be damned! Now it was beginning to
make a little sense. But he needed to plod a little
further, probe a little deeper.

On first spotting the kids—the young men—at
the junkyard, Jake had thought they were looking
for some cruising wheels. And so it had struck him
as odd when, after turning around, he saw them
piling into that expensive van. Why, he'd reflected,
since they already had the use of that love boat on
wheels, would they be looking at wrecks in a junkyard?

Jake made a face. Just another thing that didn't
make— Jake jolted erect in the seat. The junkyard!
The very same junkyard that every local police officer suspected was being used to fence stolen cars
and parts! Could it possibly be that those college
kids were the amateurs committing the thefts?

Jake quivered, not unlike a bloodhound that has

picked up the scent of a fugitive. His instincts screamed that he was on to something. But wait, he cautioned himself. Even if those three young men were the thieves, where did Sarah fit into the picture? he asked himself. Nothing, no one, would ever convince him that Sarah was involved in the crimes.

A blank wall. Jake sighed, then went still as another possibility worked its way to the forefront of his mind. What if Sarah had inadvertently seen or heard something…something indicating the men's involvement or intent?

It was all supposition, of course, but…damn, Jake thought, grimacing at a seeming error in his deductions. Sarah had shown agitation and nervousness around him on Thursday morning, and the first of the thefts had been reported on Friday. Well, that killed that theory, he thought dejectedly. Unless…unless there had been other, previous thefts, outside the jurisdiction of the Sprucewood police force.

He needed to talk to Sarah.

Cursing the necessity of waiting until his supper break, Jake fired the engine, checked for oncoming traffic, then pulled the car into the street. Waiting would not be easy, but in the meantime, he had a job to do.

Before he spoke to Sarah, Jake decided to check

the wire for any reported thefts of car parts within a reasonable striking distance of Sprucewood.

It was late, close to twilight. Sarah's last class had ended hours ago, and still she sat in her small office, her insides and her hands shaking.

The tremors rippling through Sarah were no longer in direct relation to the terrifying incident of earlier that afternoon, although her brush with death had initiated the process. But as the day crept on, a subtle change had occurred within her, altering her fear, transforming it into anger.

Now, as evening approached, Sarah's anger had reached a level of sheer rage, rage at Andrew Hollings, the intelligent student who had out-smarted himself by attempting murder. And Sarah labored under no illusions concerning Andrew's motivations; he had coldly, deliberately tried to run her down.

Andrew's attempt on Sarah's life was damning enough in her eyes. But even more damning was the frightening realization that Andrew had come within inches of killing Jake—even if inadvertently.

Andrew's criminal and destructive activities had to be stopped, and Sarah had come to the conclusion that, since she was the only person aware of what he was up to, she was the only one who could stop him.

But first she needed proof, something concrete that she could present to the authorities, to Jake. It was her need for evidence, and a method of gathering it, that had kept Sarah sitting quietly in her darkening office ever since she had dismissed her last class for the day.

After examining, then rejecting, several ideas, Sarah settled on the one method she thought just might work. That method came to mind along with a memory of something Jake had said about one of his brothers being an undercover cop with the Philadelphia police.

Sarah reached for the phone on her desk and punched in the extension number for the college admissions office. Minutes later, she replaced the receiver, then jotted down Andrew Hollings's address on a notepad. A small, grim smile curling her lips, Sarah pushed out of her chair and strode from the office. She had to hurry home and get her car out of the garage; she had a job of surveillance to do.

Pay dirt—on two fronts. Satisfaction lightening his step, Jake loped from the police station and got back into his car. A check of the AP wire had given him information about two separate car-parts thefts, the first ten days ago in the nearby town of Valley View, the second in the Philadelphia bedroom community of Golf Acres, located some thirty miles west of Sprucewood.

Jake's second front had been the head of the Sprucewood College security force, who had provided Jake with the make, model and year of the black-and-silver van, in addition to the name and address of its owner.

Andrew Hollings. Jake rolled the name around in his head as he pulled the car into the lot at the diner. He had every intention of checking out the digs of one Mr. Andrew Hollings. But first, he needed to talk to Sarah.

It was dark, and cold, and kind of scary—too close to Halloween for comfort, Sarah reflected, even if she did appear dressed for the upcoming All Saints' Eve celebration, in boots, old jeans and a bomber jacket, a knit cap hugging her head, hiding her hair.

Perhaps she should have taken a few minutes to stop by the variety store to purchase a fright mask and gone the whole undercover route.

Laughing softly at the fanciful thought, Sarah drew her coat more closely around her shivering body and peered through the windshield at the large Victorian house that had been converted into student apartments.

Andrew shared one of those apartments with his

two friends. The black-and-silver van was parked at the curb in front of the building.

Was she on a fool's errand? Sarah asked herself, ignoring the grumble of hunger from her stomach and settling more comfortably in the driver's seat of her small car. Suppose she sat there all night and none of the men ever left the apartment? What would she do then?

Probably starve to death, Sarah thought wryly, rubbing her palm over her empty middle.

Where in hell was she? Jake fumed, listening to the twelfth ring of Sarah's phone. After the fifteenth ring, he slammed out of the diner and stormed back to the patrol car. It was after seven, and Sarah hadn't mentioned anything about having plans for the evening. Where could she be?

With a friend. At a meeting. Shopping. Get a grip, Wolfe, Jake told himself, tamping down an expanding sense of incipient panic. Sarah could have had any number of things to do. She was an adult, and fully capable of taking care of herself. Just because he loved her, he berated himself, that didn't mean she had to clear her plans with him. They weren't attached at the hip, for Pete's sake.

He'd have to wait until tomorrow morning, when she called him. As a rule, Jake could endure waiting for just about anything. But, damn, he railed, he hated waiting to hear from Sarah, especially tonight. The imposed wait caused a crawly sensation in Jake's gut. He didn't like the feeling. Cursing softly, he headed the car in the direction of the address passed on to him by campus security. It was a slow night, and the CB was quiet— for the moment. Jake was on his supper break. Maybe he'd spend the time checking out the place where Hollings lived.

Sarah was sorely tempted to turn on the engine, run the car heater, if only long enough to warm her cold-stiffened fingers and toes. Keeping her riveted stare fixed on the front entrance to the apartment, she reached for the ignition key. She froze in place, fingers gripping the key, as Andrew and his friends came out of the building and strode along the walkway to the sidewalk and the van parked alongside it.

Her breathing shallow, uneven, Sarah watched as the three men got into the van. The headlights flared on, and then the vehicle began to move. Sarah hesitated a moment, two and then, her fingers trembling, she fired the engine and, careful to keep at a safe distance, followed the van.

Jake had no sooner brought the car to a stop near the intersection closest to the apartment building when three men came striding out, piled into the black-and-silver van and drove away.

Interesting, he mused, giving the van the once-over as it cruised through the intersection. Deciding to tag along for a spell, Jake reached for the ignition, then paused as a small car fell into line behind the van.

Damned interesting. Starting the engine, Jake eased the patrol car into the street and around the corner, bringing up the rear of the curious procession.

The van led the way out of town, onto a secondary road, into the countryside. After passing a field of drying cornstalks, the van turned onto a dirt track. It glided to a stop beside a tumble down barn. The other, smaller car drove right on by, Jake noted with some satisfaction.

Jake was familiar with the property, and the structure, which was really only half a barn, since the other half had been destroyed by fire a couple of years ago.

Now, what business would three young men have poking around a deserted, burned-out barn? Jake asked himself, feeling certain he knew the answer. Hell, half a barn was better than nothing, when you needed a place to stash some hot car parts temporarily—wasn't it?

Sighing at the audacity of the young, Jake brought the car to a stop on the dirt shoulder of the road, got on the CB, gave a low-voiced report, then stepped out of the car. Moving with silent swiftness, he approached the closed, upright side of the barn, his hand dropping to unsnap the flap over the butt of his police revolver—just in case.

Sarah twisted her head around to mark where the van had turned, but continued on her way for about a quarter of a mile. Making a tight U-turn on the narrow road, she drove back, bringing the car to a stop near the dirt track. Her heart pounding inside her breath-constricted chest, she left the car, dashed across the road and crept along the track. Stopping midway to scoop up a stout stick—should she need to stand and defend herself, Sarah thought, a bit hysterically—she then resumed her creeping pace to the barn.

Jake could hear the low mutter of male voices from the other side of the barn wall. A yellowish-gold beam from a flashlight skipped over the cracks in the weathered boards. Standing in the pitch-blackness near the gaping, burned-out end of the wall, he eased his revolver from the holster, then stepped around the sagging wall.

"Police," Jake called out in a commanding voice, skimming a glance over the area to place the men. Though he spotted the cluttered heap of car parts, his nerves tightened when he realized he could pinpoint only two of the men. But the tightness didn't reveal itself in his stern expression or his hard voice. "Don't move. Don't even think about it."

Jake? Sarah's steps faltered at the sound of his voice. How—? What—? Rushing forward, she came up to the barn on the other side of the standing wall. Peering around the edge of the charred plank, she saw Jake standing in the opening opposite, his pistol drawn and leveled on Andrew's two friends.

But where was Andrew?

Even as the question filled her mind, Sarah caught sight of him, a tire iron in his raised hand, inching along the shadowed inside of the wall... heading for Jake.

Stifling a shocked gasp, and without pausing to think of her own safety, Sarah lifted the stick above her head and ran into the barn, directly at Andrew.

"Hey!" one young man exclaimed.

"What the—?" the other shouted.

Andrew screamed as the thick stick sliced through the air and struck the tire iron from his hand.

"Sarah!" Jake's voice wore a heavy coating of fear. "Get the hell over here, behind me!" While keeping his eyes fastened on the men, he reached out, clasped her by the wrist and literally swung her around and behind him.

"Jake...I..." Sarah began, only to be silenced by the harsh sound of his voice.

"You, Hollings, stop whining and get your ass over there beside your buddies." Jake smiled; the three young men blanched. "Just give me an excuse," he said, sounding not at all like a nice man. "If one of you moves, or even breathes heavy, I'll drop all three of you. *Then* I'll read you your rights."

The three men suddenly appeared to be cast in cement. Fighting a nervous giggle, Sarah leaned forward, to whisper over Jake's shoulder.

"My hero."

"Bag it, honey," Jake retorted in a murmur.

Stepping around to stand beside him, Sarah shot a glare at Andrew, and then asked Jake, "Can you manage all three of them by yourself?"

Jake slid a glittery look at her.

"Well, can you?" she persisted.

"Is Joel...Grey?"

At that precise instant, as if to punctuate Jake's dry-voiced query, the wail of a police car siren broke the silence of the autumn night.

"Lord, I'm hungry," Jake groused, draping an arm over Sarah's shoulders as he escorted her to her car.

It was over. Sarah felt as though she had been tumbled through a harvester, bundled and banded.

And she still had to explain the whole thing to Jake and the authorities. Apart from that, though, she felt pretty good...and hungry, too.

"And me," she said, tightening the arm she had slung around his waist. "I didn't have dinner."

"Me either." Jake sighed. "I decided to use my break time to do a bit of sleuthing."

"I'm glad you did." Sarah tilted her head to look at him. "I don't suppose Dave's is open at this time of night?"

"No, he closes at six," Jake said, coming to a halt next to the driver's side of her car. "But the diner's open."

"Can you take the time?"

"Well, sure," Jake said, grinning at her. "I'm entitled to a supper break."

"Good. I'll meet you there." Sarah pulled the door open and slid behind the wheel. "Last one there pays the check," she called, firing the engine as she shut the door.

"I'll get you for that," Jake shouted after her as she pulled away from him. "And you'll love every minute of it."

And Sarah most certainly did.

"I like your method of getting even." Sarah stretched with slow, deliberate sensuality, and smiled with revealing satisfaction and repletion.

Over forty-eight hours had elapsed since the

night of Andrew's and his friends' apprehension...and Jake's teasing promise to *get* her for tricking him.

And get her he had, in every way his fertile imagination could conceive of, all of which had excited Sarah to an unbelievable degree.

It was Jake's day off, and they had spent the hours, and themselves, in his bed.

Now, nearing midnight, his body still buried deep within hers, Jake raised his head from the satiny pillow of her breasts and grinned at her...looking both sleepy and rakish.

"And I like your sweet surrender to my methods." Lowering his head, Jake brushed his lips over hers, then groaning, captured her mouth in a searing kiss.

With a sense of disbelief and wonder, Sarah felt Jake's body quicken with hard renewal deep inside her, inciting an instant response from her.

"Again?" She stared at him in astonishment.

"Wild, huh?" Jake's expression revealed his own sense of amazement. "But I just can't seem to get enough of you." His gaze intent, watching for her reaction, he moved his hips. A satisfied smile tilted his lips when she arched into his gentle thrust.

"I...I can't seem to get enough of you, either," Sarah admitted, grasping his tight buttocks to draw him fully into her aching hunger.

His muscles growing taut with increasing desire, Jake thrust to the very core of her femininity. "Do you think we're simply insatiable?" he asked, in a voice rendered harsh by his constricting breath. "Or do you think there could be another reason for this unending need for each other?"

"What other reason?" Sarah asked, knowing the answer, but longing to hear it again.

"Love?" Stilling, Jake stared into her passion-bright eyes. "I do love you, Sarah. Not just your body, and the pleasure it gives me, but your heart, and your mind and everything else that makes up my Sarah."

Tears filmed Sarah's eyes, blurring the image of his adored face. "And I love you, Jake Wolfe, in every possible way there is to love a man. I want to be with you forever."

Holding desire at bay, Jake sealed her fate with a gentle kiss of promise. When he raised his head, his own eyes were suspiciously bright, even though a grin tugged at his lips.

"I hope forever takes a long time in coming. Loving you, the waiting for it will be heaven."

* * * * *

# WOLFE WATCHING

# One

She was a breath stopper.

Eric Wolfe inhaled and watched the young woman exit the house and stride along the flagged path to the sidewalk, hang a left, then head right toward where he was making a pretense of working on his bike in the driveway of the residence three properties down from her own.

The honey blonde wasn't very big; she was really quite petite, but every inch of her was packed with feminine dynamite.

Her delicate features fit perfectly in her heart-shaped face. Brown eyebrows gently arched over dark brown eyes fringed by incredibly long eyelashes, lending an overall appearance of wide-eyed innocence.

*Right.*

Eric's mouth slanted at a cynical angle.

Her name was Christina Marianna Kranas. Her friends called her Tina. She appeared to be something of a contradiction. She rarely, if ever, dated one-on-one, and yet she very obviously enjoyed her nights out and a good time. And she had lots of male, as well as female, friends.

Eric wasn't one of them. He was a neighbor, a relatively new and temporary neighbor. But Eric knew just about all there was to know about her.

Born and raised in Philadelphia, Christina Kranas was twenty-six years and four months old. She had married in haste at the advanced age of twenty-one. It hadn't worked. The man had a criminal record—he had been collared and booked numerous times—but he had never served time. There had never been enough hard evidence to prosecute with any hope of getting a conviction. Christina had claimed she didn't know about his scrapes with the law.

Eric was reserving judgment on her claim.

The marriage had quickly disintegrated, barely lasting eighteen months. The union had been childless. Christina had been granted a divorce almost four years ago.

Eric was less than impressed, since the man continued to pay periodic visits to her...and his best friend, who just happened to own and live in the house across the street, the house Eric had under observation.

Too convenient by far.

Her former husband was a good-looking guy named Glen Reber. Christina had assumed her maiden name upon receiving her divorce decree.

She had also assumed the responsibility for the mortgage on the small ranch-style house on the quiet street in the middle-income section located on the very edge of Philadelphia's city limits. She owned and operated a classy-looking florist shop in center city.

Christina stood exactly five-foot-two-and-three-quarter-inches tall. She maintained a weight of ninety-eight-and-one-half pounds—discounting nor mal monthly fluctuations. She wore a size 32B bra, size 5A shoes, and a size 3 petite dress, depending on the maker and quality of the garment. Her ring size was also a 5.

Eric knew all Christina's vital statistics because he had made it his business to know; committing to memory every factor gleaned about a possible suspect was part of his job.

He took his job very seriously; he always had, and even more so since the death of his father at the hands of a strung-out cocaine dealer during a drug bust three years ago.

At present, Christina was striding along in low-heeled size 5 shoes, making for the bus stop at the corner, because her car had been in a repair shop for three days to meet State inspection standards. And his presence in the driveway at this precise time of the morning was not a mere coincidence.

Eric ran an encompassing, if unobtrusive, glance over Christina's enticing form as she drew closer to him. Her outfit was both casual and smart looking. She had great taste. The observation was not a new one for him. He had reached the conclusion about her style at first sight of her, which had occurred nearly a week ago, on the very day he moved into the bachelor apartment above the garage attached to the three-bedroom house.

Eric had also concluded that watching Tina was the one pleasurable side benefit of the unpleasant business associated with being an undercover police officer.

Eric was good at his chosen profession; he knew he was, in all probability, good at it because he liked being a cop. It ran in the family. Generations of Wolfe men had served the law, in one form or another. The third of four sons, all in law enforcement, Eric was the only one who had followed his father into the force in Philadelphia.

He had volunteered for undercover work in the

narcotics division after his father was gunned down in the line of duty.

Only, in this instance, Eric was working under his own auspices; he was officially on vacation. He had requested leave time after receiving a tip from one of his informants, a tip that had fired his anger.

The informant had told Eric that the latest word on the street was that there were dealers—ostensibly an ordinary middle-class couple—doing business out of their home in this quiet community minutes away from center city.

While important, that information alone had not been the catalyst that motivated Eric. It was the informant's claim that the couple had been the suppliers to the man who had shot Eric's father that had been the factor in determining his actions.

Eric wanted vengeance—and he wasn't inclined toward having his methods questioned by the department. Fully aware that he could be summarily dismissed from the force if he screwed up, he had decided to take vacation leave in order to play a hunch.

Since the hunch and the subsequent idea of taking up residence in the neighborhood were his, to all intents and purposes he was on his own. Eric rather liked the idea.

Eric had been maintaining surveillance on Christina for a week now. He had been open in his movements, visible as he tinkered with his bike in the driveway, pleasant in response to greetings offered by passing residents, but he had yet to exchange a word with her.

*Today was the day.*

Pulling a rag from his back jeans pocket, Eric slowly straightened to his full six-foot-four-inch height. He flashed his most charming smile as he casually wiped his hands on the grimy cloth.

"'Morning," he said as she drew even with him.

Christina started, as if rudely jolted from introspection by the sound of his voice. Her smooth stride faltered.

Eric controlled the smile itching to become a grin.

"Ah...good morning..." she returned, her lips forming a tentative smile, while her eyebrows crept together in a frown.

"Beautiful day," Eric observed, keeping her from rushing on. "Unusually warm for November."

"Yes...er, it is..." she agreed, taking a step forward to resume her brisk pace.

"Want a lift?" His offer brought her up short once more. "I think I've finally solved the problem here." He waved a hand at the bike. "I'm going into town."

Christina shifted a leery look from her soft gray wool slacks and matching hip-length jacket to the Harley. "Ah...I don't think so, thank you."

"It's clean," he assured her, flicking the rag at a nonexistent speck of dust on the gleaming silver-and-black machine. "And I have an extra helmet."

"No, really, I..."

"There goes your bus." Eric indicated the corner intersection with a nod of his head and smiled ruefully. "I'm sorry. I'm afraid I made you miss it." He raised his eyebrows. "How long before the next bus?"

She sighed. "Half hour."

"My offer of a lift is still open," he said, in a tone designed to convey his eagerness to be of help.

Christina stood, silent and uncertain, for several seconds, and then she sighed again. "Okay, thank you."

Eric turned away to head for the garage—and to hide a smile of satisfaction. "I'll get the helmet...back in a sec."

A motorcycle. Suppressing yet another sigh, Christina stood staring at the shiny bike. A big, dangerous motorcyle, driven by a man she didn't know from Adam.

Not too bright, Tina, she told herself, even if the man did happen to look like a walking, talking twentieth-century version of a classic Greek god.

Only this particular Greek god had the formidable appearance of a modern-day Teutonic warrior.

Christina felt a delicate tingle skip up her spine. He was one attractive representative of the male species. Crystal blue eyes gazed out at the world from beneath a shock of wavy golden brown hair. His facial bone structure was chiseled, defined by high cheekbones, a straight, aristocratic nose, a strong, squared jawline and a mouth that held a promise of inflicting infinite pleasure...or pain.

The speculation intensified the tingle in Tina's now-stiffened spine. What had she let herself in for here? she wondered anxiously. She didn't even know this man's name, for pete's sake! And he literally towered over her.

Tina judged him to be at least six-three, possibly six-four, and without a visible ounce of excess flesh on that lean, flatly muscled frame.

And she had agreed to ride away with him on that monstrous machine. Was she nuts, or what? she asked herself, glancing around, as if for an avenue of escape. If she had any sense left at all, Tina thought, she'd take off at once and, if necessary, run all the way into center city.

"Name's Eric, by the way."

Tina's body jerked with mild shock at the sudden sound of his voice. But she managed to swallow the yelp of surprise that sprang to her throat at the sight of him standing beside the bike, his face concealed by a black-visored helmet. She drew a measure of reassurance from the fact that he didn't look anything like her preconceived notion of a leathered, chained, tattooed biker. But, on the other hand, he looked too appealing with his lean body clad in tight jeans, chest-caressing pullover sweater and expensive, if rather beat-up, running shoes.

"Eric...Wolfe."

What else? Tina squashed the nerve-jangling observation, along with her senses-stirring response to the low, attractive sound of his voice.

"I moved in a week ago."

"Ah...how do you do?" Great response, Tina, she chided herself, reluctantly extending her right hand. His hand, long, broad, slim fingered and strong, shot out to enclose hers, drawing the tingle from her spine to her fingertips—and every inch in between. "I'm Christina Kranas," she said, sliding her palm away from the too-warm, strangely intimate touch of his. "I live three houses down."

"I know."

Coming from behind that black visor, his simple reply had an ominous overtone that further intensified the tingle now jabbing throughout the entire length of Tina's body. "Really?" she said, infusing coolness into her usually low, somewhat throaty voice.

"Sure." His voice carried an unmistakable

smile. "Couldn't help but notice you...the times I've been out here, working on the bike, you know?"

"Oh." The stiffness eased a little inside Tina; his explanation did have a reasonable ring. "Ah, yes, I see." But why hadn't she noticed him? she mused, skimming a quick glance over his person. He was pretty hard to miss, and—

"Chris for short?"

His question derailed the train of her thoughts. "Chris?" She frowned, then shook her head when his meaning registered. "No. Tina."

"Umm. Makes sense." Now his voice contained a definite shade of muffled laughter. "Well, then, Tina..." He made a sweeping gesture with his arm. "Ready to go?"

*No.* Tina clamped her lips against the sharp refusal; she *had* agreed to the lift. "Yes...I suppose so." Even she could hear the lack of conviction in her voice.

"It's perfectly safe," he said reassuringly, holding the helmet out to her with one hand while lifting a windbreaker from the seat of the bike with the other.

"I...um, it looks so powerful," she said, her stomach clenching as she watched the play of shoulder and chest muscles as he shrugged into the windbreaker.

"It is." Raising a hand, he flipped up the visor

to grin at her, and dazzle her with his white teeth. "But I can handle the beast."

Despite her trepidation, Tina felt a smile tug at her lips; this man was not without charm. "Well...okay." Drawing a breath, she took the helmet and eased it over her head, careful not to dislodge the neat pleat she had folded her long hair into at the back. Fully expecting to have her vision curtailed by the dark visor, she was surprised by the range of visibility it afforded her. "How do I...er...mount?" she asked, eyeing the bike with suspicion from behind the dark cover.

"Like this." Still grinning, Eric swung his right leg up and over the bike, then stood straddling it. "Come on," he urged. "You're wearing pants."

Oh, what the hell. So thinking, Tina marched to the side of the bike and swung her own leg up and over. Although she completed the exercise, her effort did not bear comparison to his for smooth adroitness. When she was in position, he flipped down his visor and lowered his long torso onto the seat.

"Okay, settle in behind me," Eric directed, effortlessly holding the machine upright and steady. "Then grab on to my waist, my belt...or whatever, and hang on."

Tina bristled at the slight accent he had placed on the "whatever," but she followed his instructions, opting for his belt.

"By the way, where do you want to go?"

"Oh, you can drop me off anywhere close to Wannamaker's," she answered, distracted by his question.

Eric flipped a switch; the beast growled to life and an instant later roared out of the driveway and turned left onto the street, sounding beautifully tuned and in perfect running condition.

Exclaiming at the sudden burst of motion in a startled shriek, which went unheard over the roar of the bike, Tina tightened her grasp on his belt and hung on for dear life, shutting her eyes tight as Eric whipped in and out around the snaking lines of rush-hour traffic.

Every muscle in Tina's body was quivering by the time Eric glided the bike to a smooth stop along the curb opposite one of the wide showroom windows of Wannamaker's department store.

"Thank...thank you," Tina said, breathless and still quivering as she scrambled off the machine he thoughtfully tilted toward the pavement for her. Feet once more firmly on the ground, she removed the helmet and handed it to him.

Eric accepted the headgear with a shrug. "Anytime." He paused, then quickly qualified, "That is, anytime I'm off from work, like today."

Tina raised her brows. "Friday is your day off?"

"No." He shook his head. "Ah, I'm on vacation

leave.'' He arched a toast-colored eyebrow. ''You work nearby?''

''Yes. I own a flower shop on Chestnut Street.'' Tina gave him a smile of pure envy. ''I wish I could take a vacation but with the holidays coming up, I can't afford the time.'' She sighed. Then, reminded of work, she glanced at her watch. ''I have to go. Thanks again.''

''Sure.'' Eric sketched a wave, the bike growled, and then he roared away from the curb, leaving her standing there, inhaling exhaust fumes and staring after him.

Shaking her head, Tina took a tentative step, testing the steadiness of her legs. She was still feeling a little quivery and mildly shocked from the mad dash into town. And yet, at the same time, she felt wildly exhilarated, and more vibrantly alive than she had in ages.

All of which had absolutely nothing to do with the residue of warmth simmering in her thighs from being pressed tightly against Eric Wolfe's narrow buttocks, Tina bracingly assured herself as she joined the forward thrust of the pedestrian traffic hurrying along the sidewalk.

He could still feel the pressure of her legs clamped to his butt.

Weaving in and out of the crowded city traffic, Eric shifted in the saddle and grinned behind the visor. Felt good, too, he decided, savoring the physical sensation.

Due to the increasing demands of his work, very real and considerable current health concerns and a lack of time for much of a social life, it had been a while, a good long while, since Eric had enjoyed the pleasure derived from a woman's legs wrapped around him—for any reason.

So, in light of his self-imposed celibacy, Eric told himself, the reactions he was now experiencing were perfectly normal, if a bit intense. And they certainly were intense, with fiery strands of sensation coiling around the sides of his hips and converging in a most vulnerable section of his body.

Eric attempted to moisten his parched lips with a quick glide of his tongue; it didn't help much. His tongue was every bit as dry as his lips.

*Wild.*

Eric utilized an enforced wait for a traffic light to ponder these not-at-all-normal physical responses. All this heat from the feel of Tina's wool-covered legs clasped to his jeans-clad hips? he marveled, revving the motor impatiently. What in hell would it do to him, how would it feel, to be cradled by her silky thighs, naked flesh pressed to naked flesh?

It would feel good...maybe too damn good.

Keep your mind on the business at hand, Wolfe,

Eric advised himself, shifting once more in the bike's saddle to ease a gathering tightness in his body, and zooming through the intersection when the light blinked to green.

*Business.*

*Hell.*

Gripping the handlebars, Eric swooped around the slow-moving car of ancient vintage putt-putting in front of him. The business at hand concerned the illegal possession and sale of narcotics. A nasty business, and very likely conducted to the tune of millions of dollars.

And he was fairly certain that business was being conducted in that ordinary-looking middle-income house across the street and down a few properties from the garage apartment he had so recently moved into.

What Eric wasn't at all certain of was the possible involvement—or lack thereof—of one Christina Marianna Kranas in that nasty business.

The question mark stabbed at Eric's mind as persistently as the memory of her encasing legs stabbed at his body.


"Ouch!"

"You okay, Tina?" Susan Grant poked her head around the doorway into the workroom.

"Yeah." Tina's self-disgust was evident, even with the tip of her finger stuck in her mouth. "I

pricked my finger on a corsage pin,'' she explained
to her frowning assistant.

''You've been kind of not quite with it all morning,'' Susan said, stepping through the doorway
separating the workroom from the showroom.
''Something bothering you?''

*Not something, someone.*

Keeping the thought where it belonged, inside
her rattled mind, Tina shook her head. ''No, I
guess I'm just a little distracted today.''

Susan's frown dissolved into a teasing smile.
''Thinking about tonight…and Ted Saunders?''

''Well…perhaps.'' Tina forced a light-sounding
laugh and turned back to the worktable. Her answer had verged on an outright lie. No ''perhaps''
about it…she hadn't given a single thought to the
coming evening or her date with Ted. In fact, until
Susan mentioned it, Tina had completely forgotten
she had made a date for that evening. Why had she
made a date with Ted for this evening?

Tina frowned. Oh, yeah, her car was in the shop.
For that matter, she didn't really consider it a real
date…even though Ted had been after her to go
out with him for some weeks now. She had con-
sistently put him off.

She would have put him off again when he
called late yesterday afternoon, but Ted hadn't actually asked her for a date. Ted had asked her if
she planned to join their group of mutual friends

at their usual Friday-evening get-together at the tavern. Tina had told him she was. Knowing her car was in the shop for repairs, Ted had then offered to stop by her place and give her a lift to the tavern. Fully aware that he had his own agenda, that of convincing her to regard him in the role of prospective suitor, Tina had nevertheless accepted his offer with gratitude.

End of date business; she still had no intention of expanding their friendship into a more intimate relationship. She wasn't interested in any kind of male-female relationship other than friendship. She'd been that route; it had a lot of potholes and detours.

No, thoughts of the coming evening were not the cause of her state of mind, Tina acknowledged, jabbing the long, pearl-tipped pin through a stem on the elegant corsage—this time correctly. The root cause of her distraction stood six foot four, and possessed a lean, mean sexiness that wouldn't quit.

Wolfe.

Tina sighed.

What else?

Eric was bored. Bored and itchy. There wasn't a damn thing happening in the house across the street.

Deserting his position behind the lacy curtain at

the solitary window in the minuscule living room
of the bachelor flat, Eric prowled to the even tinier
kitchen and pulled open the door of the compact
apartment-size refrigerator.

"And when he got there, the fridge was bare,"
he paraphrased in a disgusted mutter.

Heaving a sigh, Eric inventoried the contents of
the small unit. A quarter of a loaf of bread, a week
past the sell-by date on the wrapper; one slice of
lunch meat, curl dried around the edges because he
hadn't rewrapped it properly; a small jar containing
two olives, sans pimentos; a carton of milk; and a
package of butterscotch Tastykakes.

Hardly the ingredients of a well-balanced dinner,
he allowed, sighing once more as he shut the door.
He really should have stopped at the supermarket
on his way back from the city this morning...but
then, Eric conceded, he really hadn't been concerned with his stomach this morning. His concern
had centered on a lower portion of his anatomy.

Tooling a powerful bike through a city the size
of Philly required concentration...plus the ability
to sit comfortably in the saddle. And, with Tina's
thighs pressed to his rump, Eric had lacked both
requirements.

Would she be going to the tavern tonight?

The question had skipped in and out of his mind
all through that boring day. From the detailed information he had received on her, compliments of

his older brother, Cameron, an FBI agent, Eric knew that Tina generally met her friends at a neighborhood tavern on Fridays, for an evening of fun and frivolity.

Eric likewise knew that the tavern served up a decent charbroiled steak with side orders of tossed salad and Texas fries. He had heard, as well, that the pizza was first-rate. He loved charbroiled steak and Texas fries. Good pizza, too, come to that.

Should he?

His stomach grumbled.

Eric's smile was slow and feral.

Why the hell not?

# Two

He stood out in the human crush like a fiery beacon on a fog-shrouded beach. The indirect amber lighting sparked bronze glints off his gold-streaked mane of tawny hair.

Tina spotted Eric Wolfe the instant she crossed the threshold into the dimly lit taproom. A frisson of shocked surprise rippled the length of her small frame; her step faltered; her thighs quivered with remembered warmth.

Appearing casual, as though her hesitation were deliberate, she studied him while making a show of glancing around the spacious room.

Eric stood propped against one end of the horse-shoe-curved bar, his back to the wall. He was dressed casually, quite the same as that morning, but in newer tight jeans and a different, brown-and-white patterned sweater. His right hand was wrapped around a long-necked bottle of beer, which he intermittently sipped as he lazily surveyed the laughing, chattering patrons crowded into the noisy, smoky tavern.

"Do you see them?"

Tina's body reacted with a slight jolt to the intrusive sound of Ted's voice too close behind her. Them? She frowned. Oh, *them!* Reminded of her friends, Tina dragged her riveted gaze from the alluring form at the end of the bar and transferred it to the far corner of the room, where she and her friends usually congregated at two tables shoved together.

They were there, in force, all eight of them. Two of the women and one of the men had arms raised, hands waving, to catch her attention.

"Yes," she finally answered. "There in the back, at the same old stand."

"Here, let me go ahead," he said, moving in front of her. "I'll clear the way."

Following in Ted's footsteps, weaving in and out and around tables and the press of bodies standing by, reminded Tina of the ride that morning, and the man in command of the bike. She slid a sidelong glance at the bar, blinked when she saw the empty spot at the end of it, then crashed into a beefy man who had just shoved his chair away from a table and was half in, half out of his seat.

Yelping, the man stumbled backward. His shoulder collided with Tina's chest, knocking the breath from her body and sending her reeling. Oblivious to the mishap behind him, Ted plowed on toward the corner and their friends. Backpedaling, Tina careered off another patron and emitted a muffled shriek as she felt herself begin to go down.

A hard arm snaked around her waist, breaking her fall, steadying her, shooting fingers of heat from her midsection to her thighs. She knew who her rescuer was an instant before his low voice caressed her ears.

"Don't panic, thistle toes." His voice was low; his arm was strong, firm. "You're all right."

Tina didn't know if she felt insulted or amused by Eric's drawled remark; she did know she felt suddenly overwarm within the circle of his arm— overwarm, yet strangely protected and completely safe.

"Thank…you," she said, between restorative gulps of breath. "A person could get trampled in this herd."

Eric's smile stole her renewed breath. The laughter gleaming in his crystal blue eyes played hell with her still-wobbly equilibrium. A muscle in his arm flexed, sending rivulets of sensation dancing up her spine.

"You're welcome." Keeping his arm firmly in place around her waist, he turned his head to make a swift perusal of the room. When his glance came back to her, he arched his eyebrows promptingly. "Where were you heading?"

"Over there," Tina answered, indicating the front corner with a vague hand motion.

"What happened to your escort?" Eric's voice conveyed censure for the man's dereliction of duty in caring for her. "Did he desert you in this zoo?"

"He was clearing the way for me." Tina's smile was both faint and wry. Looking at the table, she saw that most of her friends were now on their feet, their conversation animated as they stared back at her. Ted stood next to the table, his expression a study in confusion and consternation.

"Looks to me like your native friends are getting restless," Eric observed.

"Yes...er, I'd better join them." Tina took a step, fully expecting him to remove his arm; it not only remained in place, it tightened, like a steel coil anchoring her to his side. He began to move, drawing her with him.

"This time, *I'll* run interference."

Turned out there was no interference to run; Eric's intimidating size, coupled with his air of self-confidence and determination, had the patrons

clogging the spaces between the tables in their
haste to get out of his way.

"Tina, what happened?" Ted demanded, eying
Eric warily when they reached the table.

"It was nothing," she replied, trying to make
light of the embarrassing incident.

"She could have been injured."

Tina shivered at the hard condemnation in Eric's
tone, and saw Ted visibly flinch in reaction to the
piercing stare from the taller man's laser-bright
eyes. "But I wasn't," she quickly inserted. "So
let's forget it." Forcing a carefree-sounding laugh,
she swept her friends with an encompassing look
and rushed on, changing the subject. "I don't
know about anyone else, but I'm starving."

"Relief's on the way." The assurance came
from one of the men. "The pizza's been ordered
and should be coming any minute now."

"Good." Smile in place, Tina turned back to
Eric. "Thank you again. I..." she began, intending
to gently but decisively dismiss him.

"We ordered plenty," a female voice piped in.
"Would you care to join us, Mr.—?"

"Eric Wolfe," he supplied, extending a smile
and his right hand to the man closest to him.

"Bill Devine." Bill grasped Eric's hand and
jerked his head to indicate the woman next to him,
the one who had initiated the introductions. "This
is Nancy Wagner."

Nancy...supposedly her best friend! Tina fumed in silent frustration as the round-robin continued.

"Wayne Fritz."

"Georgine Cutler."

"Mike Konopelski."

"Vincent Forlini."

"Helen Elliot."

"Louise Parsons."

"Ted Saunders."

Eric's smile vanished as the circle was completed with Ted. His voice took on a hint of disdain; his handshake was insultingly brief. "Saunders."

A strained silence descended on the group around the table. A red tide rose from Ted's neck to his cheeks. Tina felt a stab of compassion at his obvious abashment, and a sense of astonishment at Eric's powerful effect on her friends. Eric had merely repeated Ted's name, and yet his tone, the look of him, had held the force of a hard body blow.

Tina's sense of compassion, and her underlying unease, lasted a moment, then dissolved into impatience and annoyance. With his attitude, by his very presence, Eric had thrown a pall over the congenial atmosphere, stifling the fun of the group's weekly get-together. Growing angry, determined to send him on his way, she opened her mouth to issue polite but pointed marching orders to him. The first word never cleared her lips.

"Heads up, folks!" The warning came from the waiter, who was bearing down on their combined tables, a large tray balanced on the fingertips of both upraised hands. "Pizza!"

The aroma wafting from the steam rising from the pies brought a wash of water into Tina's mouth. Her stomach rumbled, reminding her that she had skipped lunch. Tilting her head to look directly at Eric, she managed a parody of a smile, and attempted once more to send him packing.

"Ah...thanks again, I..." And once again she found herself unable to accomplish her goal.

"What do you say, Eric?" Mike—the rat—called from the far end of the table. "There's plenty of room, and pizza. Wanna join us?"

Apparently the moment of embarrassed silence was over.... Of course, Tina knew too well that her friends were never silenced for very long. They were too exuberant, bursting with youth and the joy of life. Staring into Eric's alert, watchful eyes, she narrowed her own in a bid to convey her reluctance to have him invade their clannish circle. Her empty stomach lurched at the smile that began in the depths of his eyes an instant before it was reflected in his lazy smile.

"Sure. Why not?" Eric shrugged, setting the muscles in his shoulders and chest into an impressive rippling motion beneath his sweater. "Thanks."

Ted moved forward to hold a chair for Tina.

Eric moved faster. With a casual-looking, smooth turn of his body, he blocked Ted's movement. Pulling one chair aside, he kept a firm hold on it while sliding another one out for Tina. The moment she was seated, he dropped into the one he was holding and drew it into the table next to hers. Ted was relegated to the only remaining chair...between Mike and Helen, at the far end of the other table.

"Hope you like your pizza loaded, Eric," Bill said, grinning. "We ordered the works on both."

"I like it any way I can get it," Eric drawled, slanting a hooded, sultry look at Tina that implied something other and much more intimate than pizza. "But I like it best spicy and sizzling hot."

Denying the flare of response that leapt to life deep inside her, Tina glared a warning at him before turning away.

"So what are we waiting for?" Helen wailed from the end of the table. "Serve it up!"

In between bursts of conversation and laughter, the pies were parceled out and demolished. When it became clear that appetites were still unsatisfied, more pizza and fresh drinks were ordered. It was a normal Friday night.

Not quite normal, Tina mused, squirming in the

allotted space afforded her between Eric on one side and Vincent on the other. On a normal Friday night, she could relax away the tensions of the workday, not have the tension increased by the sensations instilled by a hard thigh pressing against her leg, a muscled shoulder nudging her arm, a pair of crystalline blue eyes probing into her thoughts.

Tina's appetite for pizza deserted her, replaced by a different, sharper hunger below her stomach. Forcing herself to chew and swallow the food she no longer desired, and refusing to acknowledge the sensual craving, Tina managed to consume two slices of the pie without choking.

Next to her, Wolfe wolfed down half a dozen slices between pulls on another beer. Nothing wrong with his appetite, she thought, sliding a wry look at him.

Correctly interpreting her expression, Eric grinned, and once again set his shoulder and chest muscles into action with a careless shrug.

Tina shot an arched look back at him.

"I was hungry," he said, pressing his hard thigh more firmly against hers. "Still am," he went on, in a lower, breathy murmur. "But not for pizza."

Shock—or something—zigzagged through Tina. She went cold, stiff as a board, outside—and hot, soft as warmed satin, inside. The sensation of craving deep within her contracted into a tight mass of need, expanding the sense of shock to the farthest reaches of her body and mind.

What was happening to her? she marveled in confused silence. What kind of sensual power did Eric Wolfe possess to so effortlessly affect her in this manner? She hadn't experienced such a compelling carnal compulsion since—

Tina's mental process stalled, then raced forward, blurting the truth into her disbelieving consciousness. Never before in her life had she experienced such a depth of carnal compulsion. Not even with her husband. Not on his most potent night, or day, had Glen ever managed to arouse her in body or mind to the degree that Eric Wolfe had accomplished with smoldering glances, murmured innuendos and the relatively minor pressure of his thigh and shoulder against her own.

It was weird. It was scary. It was not to be tolerated, Tina decided, edging closer to Vincent. She didn't appreciate this hot-and-cold, hard-and-soft reaction to what, in fact, were the blandest of advances.

"Another drink?"

Tina's thoughts fractured. Blinking, she turned to face Eric, certain her expression was every bit as blank as her mind. "Ah...what?"

"Would you like another seltzer?" He inclined his head, indicating the tall glass in front of her, empty except for a wedge of lime and three half-melted ice cubes.

Feeling dull witted, Tina stared at the glass in bemusement, wondering when she had drunk the fizzy water...and why her throat still felt so dry.

"The waiter's waiting." Eric's droll drawl snagged her attention. "Would you like another?"

"No. Thank you." Tina shook her head. She felt suddenly tired, drained by the interior havoc created by this too-attractive, too-sexy, too-*close* man. "It's been a long day." Beginning with a short, wild ride, she added to herself. "I'd like to go home."

"I'll take you."

On that silver-and-black monster? Tina stifled the question, and shook her head again. "No, you won't," she said with tight asperity. "I came with Ted, I'll go home with him."

"Yes, but when?" Eric sent a pointed glance at Ted, then back to her.

Leaning forward, she gazed down the length of the tables to where Ted was engaged in a heated political discussion with Helen, Mike and Louise. At that moment, the waiter set a full mug of beer in front of him. Obviously Ted hadn't given a thought to leaving yet; it was still early, after all.

"Whenever." Tina lifted her shoulders in what she hoped conveyed an attitude of indifference she was far from feeling. "I think I will have another seltzer, after all."

*Cool. Christina Kranas was one cool cookie.*

Interesting, Eric mused, how the so-very-cool cookie called Tina could activate his personal heat button. Concealing a sardonic smile, he turned away and raised a hand to attract the waiter's attention.

After placing her drink order—seltzer? Eric grimaced—he shifted around to her again, only to find that Tina had turned her back to him to join in on a conversation in progress between Vincent and Bill.

Lazing in the chair, Eric monitored the discussion on the pros and cons of the current professional football season, and various teams, primarily the Philadelphia Eagles, while at the same time doing some professional work of his own, that of evaluating the members of Tina's close-knit group.

They appeared ordinary enough—all-American, clean-cut, ages running from the mid- to late twenties, upper-middle to middle class, well educated, motivated, career minded. Everyday, normal, innocent.

Maybe.

Then again, maybe not. Eric hadn't remained alive by relying on guesswork. He wasn't about to begin now. Although he regretted having to do so, he would have to go back to the well of information at the fingertips of one special agent for the FBI, his brother, Cameron Wolfe—referred to by his fellow agents as the Lone Wolfe.

Eric was prepared to endure the ribbing Cameron would most assuredly give him about a member of the force having to once again come begging for assistance from a federal agent. His brother's teasing was nothing new, and it was a price Eric was more than willing to pay.

Raising his arm, Eric took a small swig from the long-necked bottle, swishing the beer around inside his mouth before letting the brew trickle down his throat. The bottle was his second for the night…his second and his last.

Eric knew better than to overindulge at any time. A soused undercover cop had even less value than a soused anyone else, and was potentially a lot more dangerous…to himself, to the force and to bystanders, innocent or otherwise.

"Aren't you about ready for another beer, Eric?" Bill asked, almost as if he had tapped into the other man's thought process. "You've been nursing that one since right after you sat down. Hell, the rest of us are on our fourth."

No kidding? Eric mentally responded, lips curling into a rueful smile. "Two's my limit," he said truthfully. "I can't tolerate more than that, it goes to my head," he explained, lying without compunction.

"Bummer." The unsolicited opinion came from Vincent. "I can knock 'em back all night without getting woozy."

"Yeah, you just can't drive," Bill retorted.

Vincent shrugged. "I don't have to." He favored Tina with a sweet smile. "We have a non-drinker in the group."

Eric had known from the investigative report his brother had provided for him that Tina rarely indulged in any kind of alcoholic drinks, the exception being the occasional celebratory half glass of champagne at holidays, weddings and such. He hadn't known that she was the designated driver for the less prudent members of her circle of friends. He again arched a brow at her.

"You're the official D.C., huh?"

Tina frowned. "D.C.?"

"Drunk chauffeur," he explained, grinning to ease the sting from the expression.

"Hey, I resent that," Vincent protested, loud enough to be heard over Bill's eruption of laughter.

"Sorry, no offense meant." Though Eric offered the apology to Vincent, he kept his gaze steady on Tina.

"I don't mind." She was quick to the defense. "It doesn't happen too often...and they are my friends. And I prefer having them alive."

"Thatta girl, Tina," Vincent crowed, raising his frothy mug in salute to her, while leveling a smug look at Eric. "She doesn't want to see this handsome face and body all torn and mangled in a wreck of metal."

"Oh, brother." Bill rolled his eyes.

"No, it's true," Tina said, her smile soft, maternal. "I don't want to ever see any of my friends or anybody else for that matter torn and mangled."

Eric felt an odd little catch at the base of his throat at the softness of her smile, the caring sound of her voice. It was not the sound or look one would expect from a woman involved, even peripherally, with the pushing of narcotics.

Chill out, Wolfe, he advised himself, taking a sip of the now-warm beer to dislodge the catch. More than most, he knew how deceptive appearances could be.

Take this group, for example, he mused, shifting his eyes from Tina's tender expression to sweep the occupants of the two tables with a swift but encompassing glance.

They all appeared to be perfectly normal, average, law-abiding citizens. But were they? Ah, there's the question, Eric thought, appearing quite normal and average himself as he laughed at a quip from Bill. He was in a particularly good position to know that appearances quite often did not reflect reality.

From the bits and pieces he had picked up from the conversations around the table during the demolition of the pizza—which had actually exceeded its reputation—Eric had gleaned the information that the careers of the individuals were diverse, ranging from carpenter to corporate middle manager and several different job descriptions in between, including Tina's ownership of the florist shop. All quite normal, with such a varied assortment of individuals.

Perhaps. Keeping his expression free of his speculative thoughts, Eric skimmed the faces around him. But on the other hand, he reasoned, for all he and the world knew, this varied assortment of individuals with diverse career pursuits might well be in the business of supplementing their incomes with the profits garnered by dealing in illegal substances.

Of course, the world would continue to revolve in its ignorance. Eric fully intended to glean the necessary information, first thing in the morning, or as soon as Cameron could gather it for him.

The search might prove fruitless. Eric hoped it would; he was enjoying their company. Nevertheless, the investigation and follow-up would be done, whether the results were good, bad or merely indifferent.

Meanwhile, there was a question about Tina. A very big, very unsavory question.

*Was she mixed up in a narcotics mess?*

Her attractive peal of laughter drew Eric's attention—and his hooded eyes—to her profile. She was looking at Nancy at the end of the second table, laughing appreciatively at whatever the other woman had said. Once again he felt that odd catch in his throat.

Why did she have to be so damned appealing? Eric asked himself, studying her with an appearance of lazy disinterest. The problem was, there wasn't a thing lazy or disinterested about his perusal of her.

Merely looking at Tina reactivated the memory of her slender thighs banding his hips and posterior, driving a wedge of heat to the apex of his thighs.

Damn. He was hard. Eric drew a long, slow breath and shifted unobtrusively in the chair, easing his leg to the side, away from the too-enticing touch of hers.

What was it about this particular woman? he wondered, sketching his gaze over Tina, from the top of her shimmering blond hair to the slender ankles beneath the hem of her wool slacks, lingering on the gentle curves in between.

She was attractive.... Okay, she was more than attractive, he conceded. Her petite frame held infinite allure. Her face, though not classically beautiful, was delicately featured, lovely, with that mass of honey blond hair contrasted with dark brown eyes and brows and an abundance of long lashes above a small, straight nose and a delectable pair of lips made for crushing by a man's passion-hardened mouth.

Eric swallowed a groan and shifted again. What in hell was he doing to himself? Now he was not only hard, he was hot and uncomfortable, and he had completely lost the thread of the ongoing conversation.

Maybe it was time to cut out of here, he thought. Get some fresh air. Get some rest. *Get a grip.*

Lifting a hand to his mouth, Eric covered a manufactured yawn. "Well, I don't know about the rest of you folks," he announced, pushing his chair back away from the table, distancing himself from Tina. "But I'm ready for bed."

"Yeah, me too," Bill said, stifling a genuine yawn. "I've got to work tomorrow."

Three of the others agreed that it was time to leave, since they also had to work. The remaining members of the group protested. Tina stayed silent, but stared at Ted in mute supplication.

"But it's not that late," Helen pointed out.

"Only a little after twelve," Mike said, glancing at his watch.

"We can stay for a while," Ted insisted, seemingly unconscious of the appeal in Tina's eyes. "You're not ready, are you, Tina?"

"If you wouldn't mind, Ted." Though she smiled, she also sighed. "I'm tired, and I have a lot of orders to get out early tomorrow morning."

Ted frowned.

Figuring it was worth one more shot, Eric spoke up. "I can take Tina along with me, Ted, if you want to stay. I live right up the street from her."

"You do?"

Though Ted asked the question, all the others looked at Eric in surprise.

"Yes." Eric smiled. "I moved into the neighborhood a couple of days ago."

"Well…" Ted began uncertainly.

"No." Tina's smile was pleasant, but her tone was adamant. "We can stay for a little while, Ted."

Good-nights were exchanged, and Eric turned to leave. As he did, he caught the glow of triumph gleaming in the brown depths of Tina's eyes.

Think you've won, do you? A grin twitched Eric's lips as he strode for the exit. Tina, my sweet, all you've won is a minor skirmish, he told her in silent amusement.

*We'll see who wins the war.*

# Three

___

The city transit bus ran over a pothole. The resulting bump shuddered through the vehicle and the few remaining passengers still on board near the end of the line.

The jarring sensation rippled up Tina's spine to the back of her neck, aggravating the throbbing pain in her temples. The pain had been little more than an annoying ache when she awakened that morning. Not enough sleep, she had thought, dragging her tired body from the bed to the bathroom.

A stinging shower had not revived her lethargic body or relieved the ache in her head. Telling herself that she should have insisted Ted bring her home at a reasonable hour didn't help much, either. Tina hadn't insisted; Ted and the others who had remained in the tavern had lingered on long after the rest of their friends had called it a night, talking and drinking, until the bartender had shouted his nightly last-call-for-drinks warning. And even then she had not been able to go directly home, as she had assumed the responsibility of driving Ted and the others to their respective homes.

Then, with the prolonged goodbyes at each successive house or apartment, it had been very late when she finally crawled into bed.

When she left her house that morning, Ted's car was parked in her driveway. Although Ted had urged her to use it to get to work, Tina had flatly refused, unwilling to take on the added responsibility of driving his fairly new car in the morning and evening rush hours.

And so, in consequence, simply getting herself out of bed and together and to the corner bus stop was like pushing a rope uphill...with her nose.

The thought had sprung to mind, more than once, that perhaps she should have accepted the offer of a lift home last night from her new neighbor. Tina had pushed the thought aside every time it insinuated itself into her consciousness—for what she felt were excellent reasons.

Eric Wolfe was too good to look at, too charming, too…too masculine. The merest consideration of the tall, gorgeous, tawny-haired hunk sent Tina's pulses into overdrive and her breathing processes into decline, and set her thighs to tingling in remembrance of being pressed to his firm, jean-clad tush.

And it simply was not like her to react in such a manner to a man—any man. Her blatantly sensual response confused Tina; hadn't her former husband cruelly accused her of being cold, lacking normal sensuality?

Upon long consideration of her unresponsiveness to Glen's lovemaking, and the attempted advances made by other men since her divorce, hadn't she been forced to concede to the validity of his claim?

Sadly, Tina had to admit that in all honesty, the answer to her own questions had to be yes.

But then, if Glen's accusations, and her reluctant agreement with them were accurate, why did her mind persist in envisioning a man she hardly knew? Tina wondered, her headache made worse by the questions hammering at her.

Then, as if mentally dodging the tormenting images of one unmentionable man wasn't enough, business in the shop had been brisk, demanding her scattered attention. Consequently, her headache had steadily increased throughout the seemingly endless day. And now, past six-thirty in the evening, all she wanted to do was swallow two aspirins, lie down and hopefully escape from her unwelcome contemplation of one particular man, while sleeping off the pounding pain in her head. But first she had to get home.

The bus creaked and groaned to a stop. Tina exhaled a sigh of relief; the next stop was hers. Then again...maybe some exercise in the crisp autumn air would be as beneficial as sleep and painkillers.

"Please wait!" she called to the driver as she jumped from her seat and made a beeline for the closing door. "I want to get off here."

The driver muttered something in a tone of disgust about passengers dozing past their stops, but nevertheless reopened the exit door. Calling a sweet-voiced thank-you to the driver's reflection in the rearview mirror, Tina alighted, and not an instant too soon, for the doors swished shut again just as she took a leaping step onto the sidewalk.

Holding her breath, she waited until the exhaust fumes from the departing vehicle had dissipated, then drew in a deep breath of the fresh evening air.

Eric noticed Tina walking toward him when she got to about the middle of the block. Sitting on his bike across the street from her stop, he had been watching for her for twenty-odd minutes. After nearly an hour spent that morning on the phone with his brother, with almost half of it listening to Cameron's drawling-voiced heckling, then sitting all day fruitlessly watching the house across the street from his apartment, Tina Kranas was a delightful sight for his numbed mind and tired eyes.

Of course, with her lovely face and enticing body, the sight of Tina was also a kick to his lately reactivated libido.

Kick-starting the engine, he cruised down the street until he was opposite her, then making a U-turn, he glided up to the curb to keep pace alongside her.

"Hey, lady, want a lift?" he called over the growl of the powerful machine.

Tina tossed him a quick look, then, just as quickly, turned away to stare straight ahead. "No, thank you," she said, in a voice also raised above the bike's rumble. "I'd rather walk."

"All the way to the restaurant?" His question got its intended result—her attention.

Coming to an abrupt stop, Tina swung around to frown at him. "Restaurant?" she repeated. "What restaurant?"

Eric killed the engine before answering. "The one out on the highway with the Colonial name and atmosphere—The Continental Congress Inn."

"But why would I walk all the way out there?" she demanded, her frown deepening.

"To have dinner with me?" Eric answered, in all apparent innocence.

"Dinner?"

Eric couldn't deny the soft smile that teased his lips; she looked so darned cute in a state of bemusement. "Yeah, you know, food, drink, congenial conversation."

Tina sighed and raised a hand to massage her temple. "I have a headache."

Eric suppressed a grin. "I haven't asked you to go to bed with me," he said solemnly, "only to dinner."

She gave him a wry look and slowly shook her head from side to side. "I really don't think…"

That's as far as he let her go. "You're not hungry?"

"Well, yes, but—"

"Please come," he said in a coaxing tone, once again interrupting her. "I made reservations."

Tina stared at him for long seconds, then heaved another, defeated-sounding sigh. "Oh, all right," she said. "I skipped lunch, and I am hungry."

Despite her less-than-enthusiastic acquiescence, Eric felt a rush of elation. Before she had a chance to change her mind, he steadied the bike and leaned forward, making room for her on the saddle. "Hop on," he said, glancing at his watch. "The reservation is for seven, and it's five-to now."

* * *

Wryly reflecting that she had reservations of her own concerning the wisdom of her capitulation to his blandishments—and him—Tina shrugged, donned the helmet he handed to her and gingerly mounted the black-and-silver monster.

Surprisingly, the wild ride with the cold wind blowing into her face didn't exacerbate her headache. On the contrary. When Tina dismounted in the parking lot of the restaurant, she was amazed to discover that her mind felt clearer; the throbbing in her temples had subsided to a dull ache.

Unfortunately, though the pain had diminished, the blast of cold air had not eased the inner turmoil Tina was experiencing concerning her unusual response to Eric Wolfe. How could it, when once again her thighs tingled in reaction to being pressed to the warm strength of his body?

Of course, she had only herself to blame, Tina acknowledged, too aware of him behind her as she followed the hostess to a table placed between a window and a large stone fireplace. The crackling fire in the hearth lent both warmth and light to the ambience of the restaurant.

And the place was loaded with ambience, she silently granted, skimming an appreciative gaze around the room, which, though spacious, retained a cozy, homey appearance.

The Colonial decor did not assault the eyes or insult the senses, but rather imbued a soothing effect conducive to relaxation and low-key conversation.

Now if only she could relax and enjoy it, Tina thought, giving the hostess a smile along with her drink order—seltzer with a slice of lime. But relaxing was nearly impossible with Eric sitting so close to her, watching her every move with his striking blue eyes. Feeling his intent stare as if it were an actual touch, she could barely concentrate on the large menu the hostess had handed to her.

"You haven't been here before?" he asked the moment the hostess turned away from the table.

"No," Tina said, raising her eyes from the menu to skim another glance around the room. "Though several of my friends have recommended it to me, I just never got around to coming. It is charming."

Eric nodded his agreement. "Food's good, too." He inclined his head to indicate the menu. "The broiled seafood dinner is excellent."

Tina lowered her gaze to the menu, noting the listed items included with the dinner. "Too much food," she murmured, perusing the column for a lighter meal. "I'm afraid I overdid it with the pizza last night." She glanced up to give him a dry look. "Have to watch the calories, you know."

"Right." Eric ran an even drier look over the portion of her body visible above the table.

"But I do," Tina insisted, smiling in response to his skeptical expression. "I have to be careful, because I love food, especially fattening things—breads, pastries, pizza, stuff like that."

"So do I." Eric looked surprised. "I love Italian bread, slathered with butter. And pizza. And pastries." His lips curved into a self-deprecating smile. "My favorite is homemade lemon meringue pie."

"And mine!" Tina laughed. "And, at the risk of sounding terribly conceited, I must admit that my homemade lemon meringue is the best."

"Better than my mother's?" Eric asked in feigned disbelief and shock.

"How would I know?" Tina demanded, suppressing an urge to giggle. "I've never tasted your mother's."

"It's to die for," Eric said, his solemn tone of voice belied by a devilish grin.

"Well, in that case," Tina rejoined, "I'll take your word on it."

"You're not willing to die for pie?"

"No." Tina lost the battle against the giggle. "Not even lemon meringue."

It was silly, but it was fun.

The realization suddenly struck Tina that she was not only relaxed, but genuinely enjoying herself. Eric's whimsical sense of humor was a surprise, a very pleasant surprise, since it complemented her own.

The waitress arrived at their table with her seltzer and Eric's beer, asking if they were ready to order dinner. Tina chose the soup-and-salad combo, then studied Eric with unabashed curiosity as he struggled with the tough decision of whether to have the seafood or the charbroiled steak.

And Eric was a subject worth studying, Tina mused. With his tall, muscularly lean body, shock of sun-kissed, tawny hair, crystal blue eyes, chiseled features and downright sexy mouth, in looks alone Eric embodied the stuff of feminine fantasies. In addition to his appealing appearance, he had a great sense of humor and his fair share of charm. In total, the man possessed the power to be devastating to an unwary female. But, she concluded, as she was not one of the unwary, she was perfectly safe. She had traveled the male-charm route, she knew every one of the dangerous curves. It was all familiar territory that she had no intention of traversing again.

Eric chose the steak. Rare. A portent of some inexplicable something? Something feral, perhaps?

Dismissing the errant thought as even sillier than their banter, Tina took a sip of her seltzer and decided to indulge her curiosity about her new neighbor.

"You spoke of your mother's pie as if you regularly enjoy it," she said. "Does she live close by?"

"It depends on what you mean by close," Eric

replied, moving his shoulders in a casual-looking shrug.

Tina thought his shrug was much too casual looking, and his answer rather evasive. A warning signal flashed through her, causing a sense of unease that banished relaxation. Along with exuding charm as effortlessly as most men sweat, her ex had always been too casual, and definitely evasive. And for good reason. Glen had had a lot to hide.

Tina had admittedly been naive at the beginning of her relationship with her former husband, but she had never been stupid. She had learned her lesson fast and well. She detested lies, and any form of deceit. Now, observing Eric, she could not help but wonder what, if anything, he might be concealing behind an attitude of charm and casual evasiveness.

"I mean close," she replied, determined not to play by anyone's rules but her own—direct and to the point. "In this vicinity."

Eric narrowed his eyes slightly at the hint of sharpness that edged her tone. But he met her steady gaze straight on, and he answered at once.

"Then, no, she does not live close by. She lives in a small town north of here." This time, when he shrugged, there wasn't a casual thing about it. "Sprucewood." He raised his eyebrows. "Ever hear of it?"

"Yes." Tina nodded. "I've never been there, but I have a general idea of where it is."

Eric made a low sound of satisfaction. "Then you should understand what I meant by 'close.' I can get there in a half hour or so on my bike." He smiled. "To me that's close. It's a matter of perception."

"Hmm…" Tina murmured, taking another sip of her seltzer and asking herself if she was being too picky. Yet, while Eric now appeared quite open, she still felt he was reluctant to talk about himself. Why? It was that *why* that bothered her. In her experience, most men not only were willing to talk about themselves, they did so ad infinitum.

Unless, like Glen, they had something to hide.

Her conclusion made Tina uncomfortable, for several reasons. The most important of those reasons was the undeniable fact of the attraction she felt for Eric, an attraction, moreover, that he gave every indication of sharing.

After her crushing experience with Glen, Tina hadn't planned on feeling attracted to, or becoming involved with, any man. At least not for a good long time. Once bitten, and all that. But, most especially, she sure as sunrise had never dreamed of finding herself attracted to a man she couldn't quite trust.

Or was she being not just picky, but paranoid? she asked herself, even if she did have cause for her admittedly suspicious tendencies. Maybe Eric was reticent by nature. Yet the idea persisted that he was hiding something. But what?

"Do you get the opportunity to visit often?" Tina asked, deciding she might as well question him, since she obviously wasn't learning anything questioning herself.

"As often as I can," Eric answered, readily enough. "Which hasn't been too often lately, since the bike hasn't been running too great."

"Well, maybe you'll be able to visit soon," Tina offered in a commiserating tone. "You did say on Friday that you thought you had solved the problem, didn't you?"

"Yeah." Eric grimaced. "But now I'm not so sure." He heaved a sigh. "Looks like I'll be spending my entire vacation fiddling with the damn thing."

"Too bad. This would have been a good time for a visit," she said. "The weather's perfect."

"Oh, well." Eric shrugged. "Mom understands. I call her at least once a week since my father died and she's alone in the house." He smiled. "Even though my younger brother keeps pretty close tabs on her."

"Oh, you have a brother?" Tina said, wanting to keep him talking, now that he seemed to be opening up a bit.

"Three," Eric replied, his wry tone telling her

he was wise to her ploy. "But Jake, the youngest, is the only one living in Sprucewood."

"You're the oldest?"

Eric shook his head. "I'm third in the pecking order. What about—" he broke off, as the waitress arrived at their table with their meals. "What about you," he repeated when the waitress finished serving. "Do you have family living in the vicinity—" he grinned "—or close by?"

"No." Tina shook her head. "I have an older sister. She's married to a rancher in Montana. My parents moved to Arizona when my dad retired."

"So you're on your own?" Eric asked, heaping mounds of sour cream on his baked potato.

"Hmm…" Tina murmured, test sipping her soup for temperature. "More or less." Although the soup was good, the potato looked better. "There's got to be a zillion calories in that," she said, frowning at the vegetable.

"That's okay," Eric said, digging in to it. "I'll run it off tomorrow."

"You work out, too?" Tina asked, squashing an urge to beg for a forkful of the steaming potato.

He finished chewing and swallowed before answering. "Yeah, doesn't everyone these days?"

"Just about," Tina agreed, stifling a sigh as she unenthusiastically stabbed her fork into her salad. "From the president on down." She sighed and made a face at the sliver of carrot speared on the tines. "It seems that most folks today derive some perverse pleasure from torturing themselves with exercise and diets."

Eric grinned. "Yeah, but think of the great-looking corpses we'll all make."

Tina laughed. The laughter eased the tension inside her, and she relaxed again. There was even an added bonus from his dry wit; her headache was completely gone.

# Four

Tina hurt all over. A fine film of perspiration sheened her body. Her breath came in harsh little puffs. She was tired. She wanted nothing more at that moment than to sit down, or lie down and rest, relax…maybe die.

"Lift that leg and kick and kick and…"

The upbeat female voice blaring from the TV lashed at Tina. Gritting her teeth, she kicked and kicked, imagining the instructress as the target for her thrusting foot.

"Higher and higher. You can do it!"

Tina narrowed her eyes on the TV screen. The

physical-fitness expert was young and beautiful, with gleaming chestnut hair, sparkling hazel eyes, whiter-than-white teeth and a figure to kill for.

Tina hated her. And yet, without fail, she shoved the video into the VCR every Tuesday and Thursday evening and, like now, every Sunday morning, working off the calories accumulated on the days in between.

One oft-bemoaned bane of Tina's existence was the fact that she loved to eat...all the wrong foods.

"Now rest...and breathe...in...and out...slowly...in...and slowly...and out...slowly..."

Raising her eyes, as if seeking sympathy from the ceiling, Tina silently cursed the woman, but inhaled...slowly...and exhaled...slowly...and turned her back on the screen to gaze out the rain-spattered picture window.

Still breathing...slowly...she focused on a russet leaf the driving wind and rain had plastered to the pane. Autumn had finally decided to put in an appearance.

A blur of movement at the far side of the window caught her attention. Her gaze settled on the figure of a man, a tall man, jogging past the house.

What kind of nut jogs in the pouring rain? she wondered, moving closer to the window to get a better look.

The kind of nut who tools through traffic on a

roaring motorcycle and devours baked potatoes drowning in butter and sour cream while sipping on a light beer, she reflected, identifying the jogger as her new neighbor, Eric Wolfe.

"Rest period's over, ladies. Now let's get to work on those flabby upper arms."

"You know what you can do with your upper arms, honey," Tina muttered, feeling smug because she didn't *have* flabby upper arms. Nevertheless, since she also didn't *want* flabby upper arms, she reluctantly dragged her riveted gaze away from the elongated form of her neighbor.

He might be a nut, she mused, swinging her arms around in ever-diminishing circles, but nut or not, Eric Wolfe did possess one fantastic body.

Memory flared to vibrant life. The too-peppy sound of the instructress's voice faded into the background. A delicious chill shivered along Tina's spine. The leotard clinging to her thighs seemed to contract, confine, conjure up a response.

She could feel him pressing against her flesh, as he had on Friday morning and twice last night, zooming to and from the restaurant, the slim tightness of his tush and hips a solid presence between her parted legs.

Tina's breathing processes slowed, then raced forward. She was panting, nearly gasping. Her leaden arms fell unnoticed to her sides. Her eyes stared sightlessly at the TV screen. Her stomach muscles clenched. Perspiration trickled in rivulets down her temples and at the back of her neck. She felt drained of energy, weak all over.

"Geez!" Tina whispered, raising a limp hand to massage her nape. "Talk about chemistry!"

The video was only three-quarters over, but Tina knew that she was through for the morning. Drawing a shaky breath, she reached for the remote control and pressed the Stop button, then hit Rewind.

Nut or not, Eric Wolfe was nothing if not dynamic—at least as far as the crackling awareness the mere sight of him instilled in her was concerned, Tina acknowledged.

Eric had played the role of the perfect gentleman when he brought her home last night, even leaving the bike idling in the driveway while he escorted her to the front door, even though Tina had insisted it wasn't necessary for him to do so. He had plucked the keys from her unsteady fingers and unlocked the door for her. Then he had stepped back, not so much as touching her hand as he wished her a murmured good-night.

Tina had been rendered speechless, and she had been wide-eyed with surprise as she gazed after his retreating figure. After the sensual awareness that had simmered beneath the surface between them all evening, she had expected Eric to make a move on her when he brought her home—try to take her in his arms, kiss her, or at the very least, since it wasn't very late, suggest she invite him inside for a cup of coffee or something.

It was the contemplation of that possible something that had made Tina's hands unsteady. All the way home, she had worried the question of what she would do if Eric did attempt to kiss her...or something. Then, when he hadn't so much as brushed his fingers against hers, Tina had been hard-pressed to decide whether she felt relieved or insulted.

If truth were faced, Tina had to acknowledge that she was more than passingly curious as to how it would feel to have Eric's sexy-looking mouth pressed to her lips.

Of course, Tina had no intention whatsoever of facing that truth. She was too busy reminding herself that the absolute last thing she wanted was involvement with a man.

Now all she had to do was figure out a way to stop speculating about him, banish him from her mind.

Stealing a quick glance through the window over her shoulder, Tina admitted ruefully that ejecting Eric Wolfe from her mind would not be a simple matter. Some masculine essence of him spoke in eloquent and erotic terms to some wayward and errant feminine essence inside her.

Tina felt a hollow yearning, a blatant hunger she

had not experienced since the very early days of her marriage.

Wrong. The denial flashed through her mind, bringing with it the unwanted added baggage of self-realization. She had very recently conceded that not even with Glen, before or after they were married, had she experienced such a degree of melting arousal. Not with Glen or any man she had met since her divorce.

Ted immediately came to mind; Ted, and the drunken play he had made when she drove them home Friday night. He had pressured, cajoled, even coaxed her to allow him to deepen their friendship into a more intimate relationship.

Tina had been tactful, but she had been firm, letting him know she simply wasn't interested. And she wasn't, and never had been. Even with her husband, she had pondered her lack of burning enthusiasm for the physical act of love; hadn't Glen repeatedly accused her of being cold, devoid of sensuality? He had. And hadn't she come to accept his accusation? She had.

But that had been before she met Eric Wolfe and her hormones went bananas.

*And, except for the odd bits of information she had wrung from him last night, she didn't even know the man.*

Tina shuddered. She didn't like it. She didn't want it. She didn't need it.

Well, it had been nearly two years since…and maybe she did need *it*…but…

Both startled and shocked by her own silent admission, Tina forgot the video and took off at a trot for the shower, as if she could run away from her own thoughts.

He had to be nuts. Eric made the conclusion as he stripped the sodden sweats off his chilled body. Certifiable. No doubt about it. Grinning at his rain-slicked reflection in the medicine cabinet mirror, he stepped into the bathtub and under a stinging-hot shower spray.

*She looked sexy as hell in a leotard.*

Heat unrelated to the steaming water cascading over him streaked through Eric's body. Without appearing to look or turning his head as he jogged by her house, he had caught a glimpse of Tina standing at the wide window, her neat, curvaceous body encased in an electric blue-and-sun yellow spandex leotard. He had very nearly tripped over his own big feet.

So, she hadn't been merely making conversation over dinner when she said she worked at keeping herself in shape, too, he mused, slowly turning the tap, adjusting the water temperature from hissing hot to chilling cold.

*She'd be lithe and supple in bed.*

A shiver shot down Eric's spine. His imagination took flight. He could see Tina, feel her, her arms clinging to his shoulders, her legs clasped around his hips, her body moving sinuously beneath him.

"Damn." Cursing the near-painful response of his body, Eric twisted the tap, shutting off the gushing flow of water. A frown drew his brows together as he stepped from the tub onto the bath mat and snatched up a towel.

Last night, raw hunger for her had begun gnawing at him at the sight of her tempting mouth, so close and yet so far away across the table from him. He had fully intended to pull Tina into his arms and taste her luscious mouth when he escorted her to her front door, and he would have, if he hadn't noticed the fine tremor in her fingers when he took her keys from her. The impetus to hold her, crush her lips beneath his, had been squashed by the protective feeling that had swamped him. Suddenly certain that Tina was fearful of just such a move on her by him, Eric had backed off, leaving her untouched, unkissed—and, in the process, himself frustrated as hell.

Tossing the towel in the general direction of the hamper, Eric strode into the small bedroom. The visible physical effects of his erotic speculations had dissipated, but his mind had set on a course of action. He needed to work on calming her fear of him; that might be enjoyable. Then he would feed the beast. Sooner or later, one way or another, he was determined to make a feast of Christina Kranas. The sooner the better.

A short time later, his hair still damp from the shower, his lean cheeks close-shave shiny, his body subdued and dressed in faded jeans, a washed-out gray sweatshirt and his favorite, if scruffy, running shoes, Eric stood at the stove, whistling through his teeth as he scrambled three eggs in a shallow frying pan.

When it came to feeding, there were beasts, and then there were beasts. His empty stomach was one of them.

After finishing the meal, Eric took up his position at the window, dividing his attention between the house across the street and the one containing the beautiful object of his increasing interest and desire.

Quite like the majority of residents in the community, the couple living in the house across the street were in their middle thirties. Robert Freeman and Dawn Klinger were both well educated and career oriented. Although they had been together for seven years, they had never legally tied the relationship knot. There were no children.

Which was all rather normal by the prevailing societal standards. Bob Freeman was outgoing, easy to get along with, the type commonly referred to as a nice guy. He was a middle-management

employee with a medium-size paper products company located on the outskirts of Philadelphia.
Dawn Klinger managed the ladies'-wear department of a local discount store. She was described
as a quiet homebody type.

While still married, Tina and Glen Reber had
been close friends of Bob and Dawn. And although
Tina had withdrawn somewhat after the divorce,
her former husband had maintained the friendship,
and continued to visit the couple on a fairly regular
basis.

Again, all rather normal sounding.

But was it? Eric snorted. He was a veteran of
over ten years on the force. He had been around
the block, and not just jogging, either. If his hunch,
along with the information garnered from one of
his informants, was on target, Glen Reber and the
couple across the street had deviated from the
norm by dabbling in the dangerous business of illegal substances, initially as users, and then as
dealers.

And now the word on the street was that there
was going to be a very big deal going down soon
in the house across the way. Having met Tina, and
now wanting her, Eric hoped like hell that she
wasn't involved in the filthy business. But, either
way, he had determined to be there for the payoff.

It proved to be a long and boring morning. The

rain continued to pour from the heavy gray sky. Apart from the leafless tree branches whipping about in the gusting wind, there was absolutely nothing moving in the neighborhood.

Slumped in the one comfortable chair, which he had drawn up to the window, Eric stifled a yawn and shifted position in the padded seat to ease the numbness in his rump. He was settling in again when a black luxury car glided to a stop in front of Tina's house.

"Hel-lo," Eric murmured, sliding upright in the chair. "Look what the wind blew in." He immediately identified the man who stepped from the Lincoln and dashed to the overhang above Tina's front door. "Ah...the former husband and possible suspect, Glen Reber. Interesting."

A picture formed in Eric's mind of the investigative report Cameron had run on the possible suspect. It seemed that Glen Reber was average—height, weight, appearance, everything. Everything, that is, except for a few minor facts, such as the fact that he had a police record dating back to his late teens, and the fact that his lavish lifestyle didn't equate with his salary—not by a long shot.

Eric had a bone-deep suspicion that Reber was supplementing his legal income with rake-off funds from his association with Bob and Dawn's sideline. That suspicion didn't bother Eric to any great degree; if Reber was walking outside the law, they would nail him, along with the other two.

What did bother Eric was the question of whether or not Tina had her slender fingers in that messy pie.

The boredom of the morning banished by Reber's appearance, Eric sat forward, peering through the rain at the man repeatedly stabbing a finger into the illuminated doorbell button set in the frame of Tina's door.

"All right, all right, I'm coming," Tina called, turning away from the stove to rush to the door. "Give it a rest," she went on in a mutter, shaking her head and breaking into a trot when the bell trilled again.

"Well, it took you long enough," Glen complained when she pulled open the door. "What were you doing?" he asked irritably, walking into the house—uninvited.

"Basting a chicken." Tina gave him a wry look. "Why don't you come in, make yourself at home?"

"I am in." Glen took on what she had come to think of as his lost-puppy expression, all big eyed and sorrowful. "And I wish it still was my home."

If Tina was moved, it was to a knowing smile. "How strange," she said, in an exaggerated drawl.

"Since you spent so little time here when it was your home."

"Don't start that again," he groused.

"I'm not starting anything." Tina conveyed her unconcern with a light shrug of her shoulders. "But I do recall that you spent more time in the various houses of several different women than you ever did in this home."

"Maybe I wouldn't have if there had been a warm and willing body here," he retorted.

At one time, Tina had conceded his point. For though she had never rebuffed his sexual advances, she hadn't abandoned herself to them, either. But that time was long gone, and she was no longer buying his guilt-trip ploy.

"Yes, I think you would have," she said with gentle chiding. "You feed your ego on scoring with other women."

"It's the challenge," he admitted, with blunt and unusual honesty. "They mean nothing to me."

Tina had learned to be as blunt. "Neither did I."

"That's not true." The denial was quick. "You were the only one I ever wanted to marry."

She laughed in his face. "No, Glen, you married me because I posed the ultimate challenge. A, I was a virgin. And B, I absolutely refused to sleep with you in anything other than a bed of marriage."

"Yeah." He sneered. "You were a little prude." A smile of utter male superiority twisted his lips. "You still are. I keep tabs on you, you know." His smile went smooth with satisfaction. "I'm still the only man who ever had you."

"Big deal." Tina made a wry face. "With you I learned that sex isn't all it's cracked up to be."

"You see?" Glen pounced on her admission. "It was that attitude of yours that killed our marriage."

"Whatever." Tina was not offended; she was bored with the subject. "Was there a reason for your visit today?" she prompted, anxious to get back to basting her roasting chicken.

"I'm on my way over to see Bob and Dawn."

She turned to open the door. "Give them my best."

"I want us to get back together."

The hard demand in his voice froze Tina with her hand hanging in midair, an inch from the doorknob. Then she slowly turned to look at him, really seeing him for the first time since their divorce. Glen looked good, attractive, well dressed, properous, sure of himself.

Sure of her? Tina wondered. On the flimsy basis of the fact that she had not been intimate with any other man, did he seriously believe she would even consider a reconciliation after all this time of enjoying her freedom?

Of course, Glen didn't know how much she enjoyed her freedom; his massive ego wouldn't allow him to consider the possibility. What a jerk, Tina thought. What had she ever seen in him?

"Did you hear me?" Glen asked, testily. "I said…"

"I heard." Tina swept his five-foot-ten-inch frame with a dismissive glance. "The answer is no."

"You can't mean that," he said, closing the short amount of space between them. A suggestive smile curved his mouth, and he raised a hand to caress her cheek. "By now, even you have to be needing a little loving."

What he said was perfectly true, Tina allowed, as she had so recently discovered. But she certainly did not need Glen's version of loving, either emotionally or physically.

"My needs, or lack of them, are none of your business," she said, grasping the doorknob and swinging open the door. "Goodbye, Glen."

He looked angry for a moment, but then he flashed her a cocky smile. "Okay, baby, but you don't know what you're missing."

"That's where you're wrong," she corrected him, smiling back at him as he stepped outside. "As far as you're concerned, I know exactly what I'm not missing."

Glen looked to be on the point of exploding.

"I'm going. I'll come talk to you some other day."
He swung away and started down the flagstone
path to the sidewalk, sniping over his shoulder,
"When you're not in such a bitchy mood."

"I'll survive the wait," Tina called after him.
Slamming the door, she leaned back against it,
drawing deep, calming breaths into her constricted
chest.

The gall of the man, she railed in silent fury.
What she was missing, indeed. She didn't need
him...not for anything, and especially not for sex.
Pushing away from the door, Tina headed for the
kitchen. She was doing fine on her own. She didn't
*need* any man, she assured herself.

But she did *want* one particular man.

The unexpected thought brought Tina up short.
Standing in the center of the sparkling-clean room,
she stared into the middle distance, while gazing
inward, examining the wild idea her mental processes had come up with.

Eric Wolfe.

Tina shuddered in response to the flash of excitement the mere thought of him caused inside
her.

*What kind of lover would he be?*

That thought set the excitement to rioting
throughout her entire being. Tina could see him,
feel him, smell him, his broad shoulders, his slim

waist and hips, his long legs, his slender fingers, his masculine, sensuous mouth.

A low moan escaped the sudden tightness of her throat. A fine film of perspiration slicked her forehead. What was happening to her? Tina cried in silent wonder. She had never, ever, reacted to a man in this overheated manner.

Breathing in great gulps of steadying air, Tina raised her hand and drew the back of it across her forehead. She felt odd, strong yet weak, hot yet cold...and needful.

What to do about it? Tina pondered the question. She had options, lots of them. The safest choice being to put all speculative thoughts of Eric Wolfe from her mind.

But was that really what she wanted? Without giving a second thought to the question, Tina shook her head in denial. Her reaction to being with Eric last night, both hopeful and fearful of having him touch her, kiss her, and then the sensations she had felt on seeing him jog past her house that morning, gave ample proof that putting him from her mind was not at all what she wanted to do.

If she was brutally honest with herself, Tina had to admit that what she wanted to do was find out, once and for all, if she was the unresponsive block of ice that Glen had repeatedly accused her of being.

And Tina felt, sensed, instinctively knew, that Eric was attracted to her. If he wasn't, why pay so much attention to her at the tavern Friday night, bother to meet her at the bus stop yesterday?

But, on the other hand, if he did feel attracted to her, why hadn't he made a move on her last night? Tina frowned as she wandered back into the kitchen. Since she had never seriously participated in the male-female ritual games, she was unsure of exactly how to read the signs. For all she knew, Eric was playing it cool, biding his time, waiting for some kind of signal from her.

Okay, she decided, she'd give him that signal.

But how to proceed?

Seduce him?

Tina laughed out loud at the sheer ludicrousness of the idea. She wouldn't know where to begin.

The aroma of roasting chicken wafted to her, stirring her senses with a possible solution.

She could begin by inviting Eric to dinner.

Eric sat, still and tense, watching Tina's house through narrowed eyes.

"Ah..." His breath hissed through his teeth when he saw the door open and Glen Reber step outside. A quick glance at his functional wristwatch told Eric what he already knew; the man had been inside, alone with Tina, for less than fifteen minutes—hardly enough time for any meaningful acts of intimacy.

It was not until that instant that Eric acknowledged the emotions tying his gut into hard knots. He was feeling angry, and frustrated, and protective with regards to Tina and the man who had once shared her bed. But by far the strongest emotion gripping him was a raging possessiveness.

If he should ever learn that Reber touched Tina, in any personal way, he would blow the bastard away.

The decision so shocked and startled Eric, he bolted out of the chair.

What the hell?

Upright, Eric became painfully aware of his hard body condition, and he knew, precisely, what the hell.

All the time he had sat there on the edge of his seat, intently watching her house, Eric had envisioned scenes of Tina, pinned to her bed beneath that slimy creep.

"Only through me, you punk," he snarled at the man now crossing the street. "Tina is mine."

That statement startled Eric every bit as much as his unheard-of feeling of possessiveness. He mulled it over while monitoring Reber's progress to the house across the way.

Tina...his?

"Yes." His voice hissed through his teeth once

more. On the spot, Eric decided that if anyone was going to pin Tina to her bed, it would be *him.*

Acting on the decision, Eric pivoted away from the window. The trio across the street were closeted away from his sight. Besides, he could keep watch from any location along the quiet street. Detouring past the single kitchen cabinet, he scooped a cup from the shelf.

Eric was going to visit his neighbor.

# Five

The doorbell rang.

"Now who?" Tina muttered, pressing the fork tines into the dough edging the pie pan. "If that's Glen again, I'll..." Her voice faded on an exasperated sigh. Setting the fork aside, she turned away from the countertop.

The doorbell pealed once more. Heaving another sigh, Tina shot a helpless look at her flour-speckled hands, shrugged and, tearing off a paper towel, wiped her hands as she marched out of the kitchen, through the tiny dining room and across the living room to the door.

"Darn it, Glen, I'm—" Tina began, as she yanked open the door. Her spate of impatience dried in her throat at the sight of Eric Wolfe sheltering from the rain beneath the overhang above the front stoop.

"Hi, neighbor," he said, giving her a slow, bone-melting smile, while holding a cup aloft for her inspection. "May I borrow a cup of…coffee?"

"Grounds or brewed?" Tina returned his smile, along with an arch look.

Eric's smile evolved into a grin. "Brewed, please, with a splash of milk, no sugar."

"You want it to go or to drink here?"

"You have any cookies?"

"Yes." Laughter gave a threatening quiver at the corners of Tina's lips.

"Then I'll drink it here." He lifted one tawny eyebrow questioningly. "If you don't mind?"

"Do you mind having your snack in the kitchen?"

"No." Eric shook his head. "I come from a long line of kitchen sitters."

"Then I don't mind." Tina gave in to the laughter and swung the door wide. "Come on in."

"Thanks, neighbor."

"You're welcome," Tina replied, observing him wryly as he entered and glanced around the room.

"Nice," he said, turning to watch her shut, then lock the door. "Who's Glen?"

"My ex-husband."

Eric's eyebrow shot up again. "You were expecting him to stop by today?"

"No...yes," Tina floundered, frowning. "He was here a few minutes ago. That's his car out front, the big expensive one," she explained, even while asking herself why she should feel a need to do so.

Eric shot a glance through the large picture window. "He's not in the car," he observed, dryly stating the obvious.

"He's visiting friends across the street." Tina's smile was as dry as his tone. "When the bell rang, I thought he had come back for something."

"Something?"

There was an element contained in Eric's quiet voice that sent a chill down Tina's spine.

"He's making noises about a reconciliation." Tina shrugged, to dislodge the cold sensation as much as to dismiss the very idea of Glen's suggestion.

"You're not hearing his noises?" The chilling element in his voice was gone, replaced by what sounded to Tina like more than mere interest.

The word *interrogation* crept into her mind; Tina dismissed it at once. She had wanted some proof of Eric's attraction to her, hadn't she? she chided herself. Well, what better proof could she ask for than more than mere interest? The conclusion brought the smile back to her lips, and a lighter, careless shrug to her shoulders.

"I stopped hearing him on that topic long ago," she said, motioning him to follow as she led the way to the kitchen. "Come along if you want some coffee."

"Does this mean the subject of your ex is closed?" Eric inquired, trailing her through the dining room.

Tina felt a twinge of impatience at his persistence, but squashed it at the optimistic consideration that he just might be feeling a trifle envious of Glen.

"No, not closed," she replied, going straight to the automatic coffeemaker on entering the kitchen. "There's simply not much to say about it, that's all."

Eric watched her in silence as she went through the drill of lining the basket, measuring the coffee grounds and pouring the water into the grate. Tina could feel his steady regard. It made her nervous, in an excited way. She had to concentrate to keep from fumbling the simple routine.

"Was he abusive?"

Tina exhaled an audible sigh as she turned to face him. "If you're asking if he ever hit me, the answer is no," she said, meeting his crystal blue stare levelly.

Eric's smile told her he had heard what she hadn't said. "Verbal abuse, then," he said flatly.

Tina managed to maintain his stare, and her silence, for a few seconds. Then she turned away, moving to the fridge to get out the milk. From the fridge, she went to the food cabinet to remove a package of oatmeal cookies.

"Tina?" Eric's voice was soft on the surface, but held an inner thread steely with purpose.

"All right," she snapped, whirling to face him. "Glen was often less than pleasant."

"As in—" he arched that one tawny brow "—very recently, when he was here?"

The short hairs at Tina's nape quivered at the iciness underlying his too-soft voice. She wasn't deceived for an instant by his bland expression, either. Without knowing how she knew, Tina was certain that Eric Wolfe could prove to be very dangerous when he was riled.

"It's unimportant, really," she said, prudently deciding to do her best not to rile him. "He doesn't stop by often, only when he comes to visit his friends."

"They're not your friends, too?"

"Not really." Tina didn't try to hide the impatience she was feeling; the subject, and his persistence, was starting to get to her. "They were Glen's friends before we were married, not mine. Although we still exchange pleasantries when we see one another, I don't socialize with them." She managed a tight smile. "Any other questions?"

Eric's return smile was easy, teasing. "Yeah. Where's my coffee?"

"Coming up," she said, the tightness smoothing from her lips. She flicked a hand at the table as she walked back to the coffeemaker. "Have a seat."

"You baking a pie?" he asked, inclining his head to indicate the pan and ingredients cluttering the countertop.

"Yes." Reaching into a cabinet, Tina withdrew two gold-rimmed cups and matching saucers.

"What kind?" Eric asked in an eager, hopeful voice.

"Lemon meringue." Tina tossed a grin at him over her shoulder. "And I've got to finish putting it together," she went on, filling the cups and carrying them to the table. "So, as soon as you've had your coffee, I'm throwing you out."

"Can't I help?"

Tina laughed at the coaxing sound in his voice; it was so patently false.

"I'm serious," Eric insisted. "I'm a bachelor, and I know my way around a kitchen. Let me help."

"Doing what?" she asked skeptically.

"I can whip the egg whites while you prepare the filling," he answered immediately.

Tina gave him a considering look. "Well, maybe you do know your way around the kitchen. Okay," she agreed. "But I'm warning you right now, you mess up my meringue and you are in big trouble, mister."

"Deal." Eric grinned at her and reached for a cookie. "Am I going to get to taste this culinary delight later?" he asked, dunking the cookie in his coffee before popping it in his mouth.

"Well, of course," Tina said, sliding onto the chair opposite him. "That's what this exercise is all about."

Eric blinked and paused in the process of submerging another cookie. "What's what this exercise is all about?"

"You tasting the pie," she replied in exasperation. "How will I know if my lemon meringue is as good as your mother's unless you taste it?"

He burst out laughing. "What have you got going here, some sort of personal bake-off?"

"You might call it that."

"I already did." Eric chuckled.

"I felt challenged when you declared that your mother's was the best," she said airily, lifting her cup to take a tentative sip of the hot liquid. "Even though I suppose it won't be a true test of my skill if you help."

"Hmm…" he murmured, munching away on yet another soggy cookie. "I see your point." He washed down the sweet with the last of his coffee, then held out the cup. "Tell you what, give me a refill and then I'll get out of here, let you get on with your thing."

"Deal," Tina said, echoing his earlier remark. Taking the cup, she rose and turned to go to the counter.

"On one condition."

Tina came to an abrupt halt and spun to eye him suspiciously. "What condition?"

Eric's smile was innocent to the point of angelic. "You let me come back later to taste the finished product."

Tina offered him a heavenly smile of her own. "I'll do even better than that."

"Oh?" He raised one eyebrow.

"Hmm..." She mirrored his action. "How would you like to come for dinner?" she asked, then rushed on. "That is, if you like roasted chicken, mashed potatoes with gravy and cranberry-orange relish?"

"Oh, be still my heart," Eric groaned, dramatically clutching his flat stomach. "What time?"

Tina glanced at the wall clock. "Well, it's almost two now, and I still have to bake the pie...say, six-thirty?"

"Six-thirty's fine." He pushed his chair back and stood. "Forget the refill," he said, starting toward the archway into the dining room. "I'll get out of here now and let you get to work."

"All right." Tina laughed at his show of eagerness. "Don't forget your cup."

"I'll get it later. Don't bother to come to the door with me," he said as she moved to follow. He was midway through the dining room when he stopped to call back, "Can I bring anything to add to the meal?"

"Just an appetite."

"Count on it," Eric drawled in response. A moment later, the door shut with a gentle click.

Tina stood in the middle of the kitchen floor, staring in bemusement through the archway into the empty dining room. Nervous excitement shimmered inside her.

*Eric was coming to dinner.*

The thought jolted her from her trancelike state. She had to get moving. She had a million things to do. She had to prepare the pie and bake it. She had to tidy the house, pick up the Sunday papers, which were scattered on the sofa and the living room carpet. She had to set the dining room table. By then she'd need another shower, fresh makeup and clean clothes—something comfortable but feminine and attractive.

Tina whipped around to get to work on the pie. A sudden realization had her spinning around again and heading for the living room.

The very first thing she had to do was lock the door, because the very last thing she wanted was a repeat visit from her former pain in the neck.

The Lincoln was still there, looking half a block long next to the curb in front of Tina's house.

Eric ran an admiring glance over the gleaming black car as he loped along the walkway to the sidewalk.

The rewards of dishonesty, he thought disdainfully. Rewards not worth the high price tag they carried.

Dismissing the vehicle, he sprinted through the rain to his apartment. Both the rain and the wind driving it had turned cold. A chill shivered to the surface of Eric's body as he let himself into the flat.

A quick hot shower and a change of jeans and sweatshirt and he was back at work, ensconced in the chair at the window. Not a damn thing appeared to be happening in or around the house across the street.

The hours of the afternoon dragged by; Eric staved off boredom with thoughts of Tina, and the excruciatingly slow approach of the evening ahead.

Dinner à deux. Anticipation rippled through Eric, causing a shiver more intense than that brought on by his run through the cold rain. Unlike Friday or last night, there would be no cadre of friends, no other patrons chattering around them, no waiters or waitresses to intrude. There would only be Eric and Tina…and a roasted chicken.

And the man sitting down to dinner with Tina would be Eric the man, not Eric the cop, he decided, surrendering to a sudden, unprecedented desire for normalcy.

What the hell? Eric mused, shrugging. He was officially on vacation. On his own. He was making the rules, setting the parameters for this self-appointed assignment.

And, for the upcoming night, Eric fully intended to ignore the rules and parameters. Gut instinct told him that Tina was innocent of whatever deals were going down in that house across the way.

If, at a later date, his gut instinct proved false, deceived by his libido, and the course of events revealed Tina's involvement with illegal substances, Eric knew he would revert to form, handle the situation in a professional, intellectual manner. But for now, for tonight, he was driven by a powerful emotional fuel, and he knew it.

That knowledge made all the difference. If push came to shove in Tina's case, Eric would step around emotions and do his job. He knew himself to be incapable of anything else.

But until push came to shove, if it did, Eric was determined to follow his gut instincts…simply because that was what he wanted to do.

But Lord, he prayed his instincts were on target, because Tina was…

Eric's thoughts were interrupted by the sudden ringing of the phone. He knew who was calling; only one person had the newly allotted number. He picked up the receiver on the second ring.

"Yeah, bro?"

His brother's quiet laughter skimmed along the long distance line. "Hello to you, too," Cameron drawled. "And how are you on this fine autumn Sunday?"

"Fine, hell," Eric retorted, grinning. "It's raining and windy and cold as a witch's—"

"I get the picture," Cameron said, interrupting him. "I also have some information for you."

"On that list of names I gave you yesterday?"

"The very same," Cameron replied.

"Fast work."

"I'm nothing if not industrious." Cameron's lazy-sounding drawl appeared to belie his claim, but then, Eric knew that quite often appearances were deceiving.

"I'm impressed," he said, and in truth he was. "So, what did you come up with?"

"Zilch. *Nada.* Nothing," Cameron reported. "Every name on that list, male and female, came out squeaky-clean. There wasn't as much as one misdemeanor charge in the bunch." He gave a low chuckle. "Believe it or not, we couldn't even come up with a single instance of high school detention.''

Eric laughed. ''That is about as squeaky-clean as you can get. I'm glad to hear it, though. I liked all of them.'' Ted came to mind, and Eric quickly amended his statement. ''Well, maybe not all, but most of them, anyway.''

''You have trouble with one of them?'' Cameron rapped out, instantly alert.

''Nah,'' Eric said dismissively. ''At least not in any legal, or illegal, way.''

''Ah, I see. A woman.''

''My word, you are the perceptive one,'' Eric said in a fabricated tone of awe.

''You're too overgrown and dumb to be cute, Eric,'' Cameron rejoined in apparent amusement. ''So, you've taken a fall, have you, just like Jake?''

''Jake?'' Eric frowned. ''What about Jake?''

''You don't know?''

''Dammit, Cameron!'' Eric snapped, immediately concerned for the welfare of the youngest member of the brood. ''Would I ask if I knew? What about Jake?''

''Seems he's in love.'' Cameron's drawling voice betrayed his delight at being one up on his younger brother. ''The woman's an associate professor at Sprucewood College.''

''Well, damn,'' Eric muttered. ''So baby bro

Jake's the first of the big bad Wolfes to bite the dust, eh?''

"It would appear so," Cameron said, too wryly. "Jake says he's going to marry the woman."

Though both alerted to and puzzled by an underlying nuance in his brother's initial remark, and his tone of voice, Eric had no time to ponder it for his full attention was snagged by Cameron's follow-up statement.

"Marry her?" he repeated in stunned disbelief. "Did Jake tell you this?"

"No, Mother told me." Cameron's voice sharpened. "Haven't you talked to Mother lately?"

"No, not since I took up residence here," he said. "I was planning to call her this afternoon, but I kinda got caught up in something."

"Does the something have a name?" Cameron inquired in an amused, taunting voice.

Eric grinned at the phone. "Mind your own business, big bro," he taunted back. Then, not only to change the subject, he said anxiously, "Mother's all right, isn't she?"

"She's fine," Cameron assured him. "Practically ready to run out and buy tiny things for her first grandchild."

Eric laughed. "Have they set a date, Jake and—?" He broke off, then tossed a version of Cameron's question back at him. "Does the woman have a name?"

"Sarah Cummings," Cameron said. "Does yours?"

"Goodbye, bro," Eric retorted good-naturedly. "And thanks for the info. I appreciate it."

"Any time," Cameron drawled. "Keep your eyes open, your mouth shut and your guard up, brother," he said, concluding with his usual advice.

"Will do," Eric replied, smiling as he cradled the receiver. There were times, many in number, when Cameron's over-protective, eldest-son attitude was a large pain in the rump, but Eric couldn't deny the feelings of love and caring he always felt when talking to his brother.

Throughout the lengthy conversation, Eric had maintained his surveillance of the house across the street. As had been the scenario for a week now, not a blessed thing was going on over there.

Doubt assailed Eric. Was he on the granddaddy of all wild-goose chases here? Had he bought a pile of bilge from his informant, like some wide-eyed innocent? Was he sitting here, getting numb in the rear, wasting his vacation on erroneous or misinterpreted information?

Eric was not as a rule subject to doubts about how to proceed in any given situation. Nor was he given to questioning his decisions and subsequent actions, which were always based on intellectual consideration, spiced with a dash of instinct. The very fact that he was now indulging in those troubling doubts and questions caused a hollow sensation in his stomach. He didn't enjoy the feeling. Determined to do something about it, he reached for the phone and punched in a number.

At the other end of the connection, the phone rang once, twice, three times. Eric drummed his long fingers against the arm of his chair. The receiver at the other end was lifted on the seventh ring.

"Hello?"

Eric felt a stab of satisfaction at the sound of his informant's voice.

"Could you use a few extra this week?" Eric asked without preamble, knowing the man had a weakness for the ponies and could always use a few extra bucks.

"Yes," the man replied, then went silent, waiting for instructions.

"The intersection nearest to your office building, tomorrow morning," Eric said, then immediately hung up.

Due to the weather conditions, darkness had fallen early. Eric didn't turn on a light, but continued to sit in the darkened room, ruminating while he watched.

His informant hadn't hesitated in agreeing to a meeting, indicating to Eric that either the man was convinced of the validity of his information or his informant was playing games, entertaining himself at Eric's expense. For the informant's sake, and continued good health, Eric sincerely hoped it was the former, not the latter.

Deep in speculation, Eric took only casual note of a truck's headlights illuminating the rain-slicked macadam as the vehicle moved slowly down the street. But his attention became riveted when the medium-size truck turned into the driveway of the house he was watching.

"More company?" he muttered, leaning forward in the chair to peer through the darkness.

The decorative wall light next to the front door flicked on, but the functional trouble lights strategically placed at the four corners of the structure remained dark.

The door on the driver's side of the truck opened, and a short, burly man stepped out of the cab, just as two men came out of the house. Even in the dark, Eric could identify the men as Bob Freeman and Glen Reber.

The three men came together in the driveway, and the short man turned at once to open the back of the truck and disappear inside the dark interior.

"Hmm…" Eric murmured.

Freeman and Reber positioned themselves at the back of the vehicle. A few moments later, the other man appeared, maneuvering a wingback chair toward the opening.

Curious, Eric thought, frowning. A company that delivers furniture in the evening—Sunday evening?

While Freeman and Reber carried the chair into the house, the short man disappeared into the interior again, to reappear once more, shoving another chair into the opening. Moments later, Freeman and Reber returned to collect the second chair. The minute they had it off the truck, the driver jumped out, shut the door and hurried back to the cab of the truck. Before the other two men reached the house, the engine fired and the truck was backed out of the driveway. The truck took off down the street as the men lugged the chair through the doorway.

Altogether, from the time the truck pulled into the driveway until it backed out again, the entire process required less than fifteen minutes to complete. Of course, the rain was coming down pretty hard, so it was perfectly understandable that the men would hustle through the job.

Understandable, yet also curious, Eric mused. Curious because the job would have been made both faster and a little easier with illumination from the four trouble lights. He knew the lights would have made it possible for him to read the lettering he'd glimpsed on the side of the truck as the driver swung it around, out of the driveway.

Dark as it was, all Eric had been able to catch

was one word—Acme. Acme. Hell, he thought in disgust, was he on a stakeout or in the middle of a Roadrunner cartoon?

Oh, well, it wasn't much, but it was better than nothing, Eric thought. He reached for the phone directory to begin searching for furniture stores or companies with the name Acme. He had barely started when his stomach growled in complaint against emptiness. Glancing at his watch, he was stunned to see that it was going on seven, and Tina had told him dinner would be ready at six-thirty.

He was going to be late, Eric fumed. But if he hadn't been in a near stupor from boredom, and unconscious of the passing time, he'd have been in the shower or dressing in the bedroom, and would have missed the truck.

Tossing the directory aside, Eric sprang from the chair and dashed into the bedroom. After a record-setting shower, shave and teeth-cleaning sprint, he shrugged into a blue-on-blue striped shirt, stepped into almost-new designer jeans, and then, carrying his shoes and socks, returned to his post at the window.

Eric was watching the house, while sliding his feet into soft leather slip-ons, when the front door opened and Glen Reber emerged. Eric's eyes narrowed on the man as he hurried along the walkway, then turned in the direction of his car...and Tina's house.

Cursing aloud, Eric leapt from the chair, grabbed his jacket from the back of the only other chair in the room and tore out of the apartment and down the outside stairway. He hit the ground running, and as he whipped around the side of the garage the Lincoln's engine roared to life. Checking his headlong rush, he strolled down the macadam drive. The headlights flashed on as the car was set in motion. It cruised past Eric as he gained the sidewalk and sauntered toward Tina's place.

Dismissing Reber, the couple in the house across the street and the puzzle of a Sunday-evening delivery of furniture from his mind, Eric strode up the walk to Tina's door and gently pressed his finger to the doorbell button and held his breath. He was over half an hour late.

Eric hoped Tina didn't open the door with a heavy object in hand, prepared to bean him for ruining her dinner.

# Six

"That was great. You're really an excellent cook."

Tina felt her cheeks grow warm with a pleasurable flush at Eric's praise—not that she had needed to hear his verbal approval of her culinary efforts. The proof of his enjoyment of the meal lay in the empty dishes and decimated remains of the bird on the table before her.

No, Tina didn't need verbal confirmation, but hearing it was lovely, just the same. His vocal appreciation of her offering canceled the last lingering shred of annoyance she had felt at his being so late to arrive. Fortunately, the meal had not suffered. The chicken had been moist, the whipped potatoes had been creamy and the gravy had been smooth and unlumpy.

For herself, Tina could not have said whether the meal was good, bad or merely average. She had eaten sparingly, and had barely tasted the portion she served herself. Her meager food consumption had been due not to a lack of appetite, but to the distracting presence of the man seated opposite her at the small table.

Even casually attired, as he was this evening, and had been on the three previous occasions she was in his company, Eric presented a powerful appeal.

*Distracting?* Ha! Tina thought, trying to collect her thoughts. *Demoralizing* came closer to the mark. Demoralizing as defined by the fact that one look at him and her morals and deep-rooted beliefs were immediately ready to take a flying leap out the window in unconditional surrender.

"Thank you," she finally managed to respond. "I'm glad you enjoyed it." She lowered her eyes, unwitting provocation in the sweep of her long dark eyelashes. The unmistakable sound of his sharply indrawn breath brought her gaze back to his, a frown tugging her brows together. "Is something wrong?"

"Ah...uh, no, of course not." Eric's lips wore a suspicious twitch. "What could be wrong?"

"I don't know, but..." Tina's voice drowned in a sigh, and she shrugged her shoulders, unwilling to pursue the subject in the face of the blatantly teasing smile replacing the twitch on his lips.

"But?" Eric prompted, flashing his perfect white teeth at her.

"Nothing. Forget it." Bypassing the feeling that she had missed something, Tina flashed her own, if not perfect, at least presentable, white teeth in return. "Are you ready for coffee—and the big dessert taste test?"

Appearing to be enjoying himself immensely, for whatever inexplicable reason, Eric sat up attentively, brought his devilish smile under control and gazed at her from laughing blue eyes belying his otherwise solemn expression.

"Bring it on," he intoned in a deep and serious voice. "I vow to be impartial."

Rolling her eyes, Tina stood and began stacking the dishes. "Just let me clear this away first," she said, gathering the cutlery. "Make room on the table."

"Here, let me help." Standing, Eric scooped up the meat platter with one hand, wrapping the other hand around the gathered flatware—and her fingers.

Tina felt certain that the touch of his hand on hers was impersonal and purely accidental. At least she *reasoned* it was impersonal on his part. For her, the sensations activated, the heat generated, by the touch of his skin on hers was all way out of proportion to a simple contact of flesh.

In a word, Tina felt…branded.

"No." Tina knew at once that her denial was too strong, too emphatic. Collecting her wits or what was left of them, she carefully slid her hand from beneath his. "It'll only take a minute. I'll do it."

"But I want to help." The glitter in Eric's crystal blue eyes did not reflect his mild tone.

"But it's not necessary," Tina protested, escaping his penetrating stare by beating a hasty retreat. "You are the guest."

"So what?" he retorted, trailing her into the kitchen. "You had all the work of preparing it," he said, following her to the sink. "I can do my part by helping clear it away."

As he approached her, his eyes grazed, then fastened on the pie Tina had removed from the fridge and set on the counter before dinner. "Will you look at that?" he said in simulated awe. "That lemon meringue is picture perfect." He slid a sparkling look at her. "Lord, it's beautiful. Maybe we should have it framed instead of eating it."

Relieved by the easing of the sudden tension that had intensified in the air between them, Tina was more than willing to play along with his nonsense. She pursed her lips and made a show of giving his suggestion serious consideration. "You know, you may be right. Even though it would be a little messy to frame." She paused, as if pondering the possibilities, an impish smile teasing her lips. "I suppose I could spray it with varnish and use it for a kitchen decoration."

"Wrong." Eric laughed. "I can't wait to destroy it." He turned to head back into the dining room. "You start the coffee. I'll finish clearing the table."

The pie was an unqualified success. Eric required two good-size wedges of the sweet-tart dessert before declaring the unofficial contest between Tina and his mother a draw. He was even more lavish with his praise for Tina's dessert than he had been for the first part of the meal.

Again ridiculously pleased by his compliments, Tina fairly floated into the kitchen to rinse the dishes and load them into the dishwasher. It was after the chore was finished, the kitchen spotless once more, that her elation was tempered by a sobering realization.

Dinner was over. The night was still young. She and Eric were alone in the house.

Now what?

If that little, electrically charged moment caused by the casual touch of his hand on hers was an indication, Tina was afraid she knew precisely...what.

She still felt shaky inside from the incident, even after the brief respite that had come from distancing herself from him.

At Tina's insistence on completing the job of cleaning up by herself, Eric had made a token protest, then agreeably ambled into the living room after they finished their second cups of coffee. When she returned to the dining room to wipe the table, he had been sprawled lazily on the plush recliner set to one side of the wide front window.

Tina had experienced a sharp pang of longing at the homey, everyday, normal look of Eric ensconced in the chair. He had discarded his shoes and had his stocking feet propped up on the attached footrest, with his nose buried in the sports section of the Sunday paper.

At the time, still under the heady influence of that tense moment and his euphoria-inducing praise, but at a relatively safe distance from him, Tina had heaved a longing sigh and smiled mistily at the comfortably relaxed look of him.

But that was then, and now was now, and standing irresolute in the gleaming kitchen, Tina didn't have a clue as to what to do next. It had been so long since she was actually alone with a man, she didn't know quite how to act.

Memory stirred, rudely reminding Tina of her idea earlier that morning of seducing Eric.

Yeah. Right.

A thrill shot up her spine. Conditions certainly appeared favorable for such a plan of action. Being with Eric, talking with him, laughing with him, before and throughout dinner, had seemed so easy, effortless. Eric had conducted himself like a gentleman...if a slightly devilish gentleman. He had not stepped out of line by word or insinuation.

*Her* imagination had stepped out of line.

And yet, in all honesty, Tina exonerated herself with the fact that, from the moment she opened the door for him, there had existed a nearly tangible tension humming beneath the surface between them.

The tension was sexual in nature. Tina was absolutely certain about that. Even with her admittedly limited experience, she would have had to be utterly insensitive not to feel and understand the drawing power of the electrical currents of sensual magnetism.

In truth, Tina was not averse to the new and rather exciting sensations. She was still a bit surprised by the surge of feelings, but not nearly as startled by the onslaught as she had been that morning.

She was a female.

He was a male.

Animal attraction.

All very well in theory, Tina reasoned, acknowledging her cowardice in hesitating to join Eric in the living room. But, in light of her overreaction to that flesh-against-flesh moment, how did a relative novice go about learning the rules of the ritualistic mating game, while maintaining a modicum or, at the very least, a scrap of aplomb?

Not by cowering in the kitchen, she thought, ridiculing her timid self. Grow up, Tina. The time has come for one good woman to come to the aid of her latent sensuality. March in there and learn to be…if not bad, maybe a little naughty.

Moving before she could change her mind, Tina straightened her spine, squared her shoulders and strode from the kitchen. Midway through the dining room, she modified her stride to a graceful saunter.

Eric didn't notice. At least he didn't appear to notice. How could he, with his attention semingly riveted to the colorful comics pages? Stifling a sigh, Tina settled into the club chair placed on the other side of the window.

\* \* \*

Eric felt her the instant she swayed into the room. The short hairs at the back of his neck quivered in recognition. The fingers that had so briefly curled around hers itched to repeat the experience. His mouth went dry, as it had at the table when she lowered her eyes, innocent seductiveness in the sweep of her lashes.

Innocent?

Lord, Eric hoped so.

Keeping his eyes fastened on the page he no longer saw, he absorbed the hot shivers of awareness arrowing to every nerve, ending in his rapidly hardening body.

Tina.

Her name swirled inside his mind like the sweetest symphony, arousing a deep, never-before-felt ache of yearning in his innermost being. An image of her formed, an alluring vision exact in detail.

This evening, Tina had allowed her hair to flow free. The honey blond mane swept her shoulders when she moved, an enticement to his fingers. She had dressed casually in a cotton knit pullover and a midcalf-length skirt. But there was nothing casual about the effect on his senses of the sweater softly clinging to the enticing upward curve of her breasts and the full skirt gently swirling around her delectable hips and legs when she moved.

Her soft brown eyes beguiled him; her sweetly sensuous mouth brought a groan to his lips. His breath lodged in a tight knot in his throat and his stomach muscles clenched each and every time he glanced at her.

Eric didn't appreciate the feelings. They were too deep, too intense, way beyond a mere physical attraction. And that flat-out scared him.

Hell, when had he ever reacted with such inner disruption to the mere touch of his hand to a woman's soft flesh? Eric didn't need to struggle for an answer. It sprang into his mind full-blown, in boldface letters.

*Never.*

From experience, Eric knew he could cope with an indulgence of the senses, without losing sight of his mission at any one particular moment. But this…this stirring of the intellect and emotions along with the senses, the sensual, made him feel vulnerable, exposed, *every* moment.

By her very association with the prime suspects in this nasty business, Tina herself was suspect. And, his gut instinct and inclination aside, Eric knew that he was inviting disaster by becoming personally involved with her.

Somebody could get hurt; Eric was beginning to fear that he would be that somebody.

Therein lay his dilemma. How was he to resist

the lure of her, when every living element inside him responded to the strength of the attraction drawing him to her?

He wanted Tina with every physical, emotional and intellectual particle of his being. And, for the first time in his professional life, Eric was afraid he was about to embark on a course of action counter to every principle he believed in and stood for.

If he had any common sense, Eric reflected, he'd bolt from Tina and her house until the question of her possible guilt or innocence was resolved. At the same instant, he acknowledged that he had no intention of either listening to or following the dictates of common sense.

He was here.

Tina was here.

Whatever would happen, would happen.

Giving a mental shrug, Eric raised his eyes from the paper to find Tina staring at him, her revealing expression a study of inner confusion, conflict, and unmistakable, extremely exciting, innocent sexual interest.

Innocent?

The question again stabbed into Eric's mind.

Yes, dammit! Innocent, he stabbed back.

There was something…some quality, an aura almost virginal about her. Which, on reflection, considering the fact that she had been married, should have been laughable.

So why wasn't he laughing?

The tension simmering between then crackled, seeming so palpable, Eric felt he could reach out and coil it around his hands, examine it with his eyes.

He smiled at the idea.

Tina returned his smile with an eager hesitancy that, while endearing, held the power to activate his hormones into a frenzy.

"Hi." Eric was amazed at his ability to articulate the simple one-word greeting, considering his mental state and sudden shortness of breath.

"Hi." Tina sounded as breathless as he felt.

"Kitchen duty finished?" Eric rejoiced at his accomplishment of producing three whole words in an entire and complete sentence.

"Yes."

There was a tantalizing quality to Tina's voice that sent shards of excitement piercing through Eric's mind and to the depths of his taut body.

"Would you like to do something?" Her eyes were clear and guileless.

"What did you have in mind?" Eric's smile was slow and seductive.

"A game?"

"Like what?"

"Monopoly?" she suggested.

Eric contained the laughter that tickled the back of his throat. "Uh…no."

"Parcheesi?"

Afraid the building laughter would escape if he opened his mouth, Eric responded with a quick and decisive negative shake of his head.

Tina's eyes sparkled with a suspicion-arousing gleam of inner amusement. "Boggle?"

Eric lost it. "Boggle?" he choked out before giving way to the eruption of uninhibited laughter.

Tina managed to maintain an indignant expression for all of fifteen seconds, and then her own throaty laughter pealed forth to mingle with his.

"Okay," she said when their mutual bout of hilarity subsided to an exchange of grins. "What, then?"

Squashing the urge to voice the desire that immediately sprang to mind, Eric swept the room with a quick glance, noting with a surge of satisfaction the stereo components on a table in one corner.

"How about some music?"

"Music?" Tina revealed her incomprehension with a blank frown. "Yes, of course, but—"

"If we shove the sofa back a little," he interrupted her to explain, "we could clear enough space to dance."

"Dance?" she echoed. "Here? Now?"

"Sure. Why not?" Eric said, prudently refraining from telling her the type of horizonal dancing he'd prefer to engage in with her, while consoling himself with the hope of at least holding her in his arms if she agreed to the vertical form of erotic exercise. "I've been wanting to dance with you since Friday night at the tavern."

"But you never said a word about dancing," Tina said, frowning. "Did you?"

"No." Eric grimaced. "Hell, you could barely make your way through that mob, let alone dance." He indicated the floor with a flick of his hand. "In comparison to that floor in the tavern, this is a veritable ballroom." He gave her his most appealing smile. "What do you say?"

Tina hesitated, but only for a moment, and then she shrugged. "Well, all right. What kind of music would you like?" she asked, rising to walk to the stereo system.

The dirty-dancing kind, Eric answered to himself. "What have you got there?" he countered aloud, easing the footrest back into position against the chair, then getting up to attend to the business of moving the sofa.

"Well, I lean toward the classics," she confessed in warning, almost apologetically.

"Do you have any Rod Stewart?" he asked,

"Tonight's the Night" in particular springing to mind.

"No."

"Phil Collins?" Eric suggested, holding out hope for "One More Night"...or one night, actually.

Looking woeful, Tina shook her head.

"Well, we can hardly dance to Beethoven's *Fifth*," he said in exasperation. "What do you have to dance to?"

"I do have some Mantovani."

That stopped him in midsofa shove. Eric blinked, then stared at her in sheer disbelief.

"Mantovani?" he asked in laughter-choked amazement, after long seconds of dumbfounded silence. "My mother and grandmother have Mantovani."

"So do mine. I grew up listening to Mantovani. What's wrong with Mantovani?" Tina demanded. This time her indignation was definitely unfeigned.

"Nothing, nothing, Mantovani's fine," he said soothingly, bidding a sad farewell to dirty dancing. "It's kinda waltzy, isn't it?"

"Hmmm..." Tina murmured, nodding and giving him a droll look. "Violins, you know."

"Yeah, okay," Eric replied, returning his attention to the sofa.

A few moments later, just as he was straightening from the moving task, the strains of "Fascination" swirled in the air. Eric's pulses leapt as Tina waltzed across the cleared floor space and directly into his waiting arms.

Hey, this Mantovani guy's all right, Eric reflected, adjusting his steps to hers. Holding her in his arms was wonderful...even with the inches of space separating his body from her swaying form.

Eric wanted to pull Tina to him, to feel each movement of her body against his, but he fought the urge. Don't rush it, Wolfe, he cautioned himself. She had come into his arms willingly enough, but he could feel her uncertainty in her tense muscles. Take it slow, he warned himself. Don't blow it by coming on too strong.

Deciding his self-advice was excellent counsel, Eric raked his mind for a conversational gambit designed to relax her, ease her obvious trepidation.

"Oh, by the way," he began, struck by sudden inspiration brought on by the reminder of Friday night, "I liked your friends." Excluding Ted, he tacked on silently.

"I'm glad," Tina said, blessing him with a smile that stole his breath, and the majority of his wits. "They're a great bunch, genuinely nice." She laughed; the sound of it went straight to his senses. "Even when they're being idiotic."

"Nothing wrong with a little fun," Eric said,

laughing with her. "They're okay." And he knew, he thought wryly, thanks to his accommodating brother. He only hoped that her friends' good character was a reflection of hers.

His voiced approval of her regular companions had a loosening effect on Tina. She readily responded to Eric's expressed interest in her business, laughing with him over her descriptions of some of the more exotic, and a few outright erotic, flower arrangements she had been asked to create.

On the fourth cut of the compact disc, the tempo of the music changed from waltz time to something dreamy. Conversation ceased. Their steps slowed. Eric's arms flexed, drawing Tina's pliant form closer to his own. Surprisingly, even with the considerable difference in their respective heights, her body fit snugly, sweetly, into his.

The violins swelled...and so did Eric.

Dirty dancing—of a sort—was possible to the music of a hundred and one strings, Eric conceded, thrilling to the expectant ache.

With a murmured protest against the intimate contact, Tina took a step back.

"Sorry," he muttered, inwardly cursing the too-eager response of his flesh. Gazing down at her, he offered a rueful smile with the apology. "But I really don't have a hell of a lot of control over my body's reaction."

Tina gazed back at him, wide-eyed and solemn. "I know, but then, most men don't."

They had stopped dancing and were merely swaying to the music. The occasional brush of their bodies brought an attractive flush to Tina's cheeks. Heat flashed through Eric. The heat of desire from the tantalizing touch, and the heat of anger stirred by her remark.

"You're an expert on men and their reactions?" he asked in a deceptively cool voice, incensed by the thought of how she had gained that expertise.

"No." Tina's hair swirled with the shake of her head. "But I *was* married to one."

Eric felt slightly stunned by the power of the feeling of relief that washed over him. He was so shaken by the unique sensation he had to draw several steadying breaths before attempting a reply.

"That's right," he said, his hand gliding up her spine to her nape, as if unable to resist the magnetic pull of her shimmering hair. "For a moment, I forgot." He speared his fingers into the silky strands, gently tilting her head back.

"What are you doing?" Tina's voice was soft, a whisper on her trembling lips.

"I'm going to kiss you." Curved over her smaller body, Eric lowered his head as he answered.

"Eric."

"Hmm?" he murmured, brushing his mouth over hers.

Tina gasped, then asked in a breathless rush, "Aren't you uncomfortable?"

"A little," he admitted, once again brushing his lips back and forth against hers.

"But— Oh!"

"But?"

"You're going to strain your back."

"Who cares?" he murmured, preventing further comment by sealing her lips with his own.

# Seven

Within seconds, Tina didn't care, either, about anything, except for Eric's mouth moving on hers.

The music faded. The room faded. The world faded.

All that remained was Tina, and Eric, and the unbelievably heady sensations created by one pair of lips in contact with another.

Eric's lips were incredibly gentle in their exploration of the contour and texture of Tina's mouth.

The absence of urgency, demand, in his kiss soothed the flutter of uncertainty that had flared to life inside Tina when Eric boldly stated his intention to kiss her.

Eric held her carefully cradled in his arms. Just as his mouth did not attack, so, too, did his hands refrain from groping, probing, taking liberties Tina had not offered.

Time stood still. Time didn't matter. Time did not exist.

For Tina, existence contracted into two mouths, one instructing, one learning. After an initial hesitation, she eagerly sought the tuition, welcoming the new experience, unrestrained in her response.

Slowly, tentatively, Tina parted her trembling lips in surrender and acceptance of Eric's superior knowledge of the subject matter.

Eric's response was immediate. Unfettered desire blazed forth; sensation after delightful sensation rippled through her, stealing her breath and strength, while conversely filling her being with a newfound power.

Tina's imagination soared on the shimmering wings of sensual awareness, transporting her into a realm of glittering erotic possibilities.

With a suddenness that made her gasp, Eric's mobile mouth sparked tiny shards of pleasure throughout her body, inducing a hunger that would not be denied.

Driven by the rampant force of a sexuality set free of the bounds of self-imposed repression, Tina clung to Eric and gave unbridled expression to the voracious needs clamoring for appeasement inside her.

Tina was an apt pupil, swiftly applying the tenets of her master tutor. Her lips softened beneath the hard pressure of his, her tongue joined with his in a tantalizing duel of parry and riposte, thrust and retreat. When he tightened the fingers he had coiled in her hair, she reciprocated by spearing her fingers into the tawny gold thickness of his. And when he lowered his arm from her waist to her bottom to draw her up and into the curve of his long form, she accommodated him by arching her body into the hard evidence of his arousal.

Eric reacted with a quick sureness that set her mind and senses whirling. While maintaining his hold on her bottom, he slipped his hand from her hair to her back and, straightening, swept her off her feet, literally and figuratively.

His mouth fastened to hers, Eric unerringly strode from the living room and along the short hallway to her bedroom. No words were spoken; none were needed.

Actions spoke louder than words.

Their lips parted to explore closed eyelids, cheeks, ears and jawlines, then returned to fuse together once more, each successive joining more desperate.

Their hands fumbled with buttons, tugged at

hems, smoothed material from heated, trembling flesh.

The bed was a bower, a soft haven for their passion-weakened limbs. They fell onto it, into it, with murmured sighs of relief; at last the difference in height was nullified—they fit together perfectly.

Fit together, and yet were not joined together.

Eric did not attempt to overwhelm Tina with proof of his desire and prowess. Displaying another facet of his expertise, he proceeded to seduce her, mind, body and soul.

His hands stroked, caressed, memorized every curve and flare of her soft feminine form, while he murmured exciting sounds of encouragement for her to trace the angles and planes of his hard masculine physique.

His tongue drew a slow, moist trail from her nape to the base of her spine, then lingered to delve into the hollow he found there. In her turn, Tina delicately reciprocated the caress, her tongue dancing along his spine.

His fingers circled her eyes, her mouth, the tips of her breasts and the mound of her femininity, while enticing her to a tactile examination of the outline of his eyes, his mouth, the flatness of his nipples and the silky-smooth length of his manhood.

Inhibitions banished, Tina replied in kind to

Eric's every touch, every taste, glorying in every delirious delight derived from sensual play and erotic exploration.

The pleasure went on and on, tension curling, spiraling. Eric's kisses grew harder, hotter, more daring, on her lips, on her skin, on her breasts, on that most secret place on her body, until, writhing, mad with desire for him, Tina cried a plea to him to set her free.

Drawing back, he turned away for scant moments, reaching into the back pocket of his discarded jeans. And then, at last, Eric settled between her thighs, his hair-roughened skin sensuously abrading her satiny flesh.

Tina eagerly lifted to him, rejoicing in the fullness of him expanding to fill the emptiness inside her. With wild abandon, she embraced him with her legs, matching his unleashed passion, riding with him into the fountainhead of bliss.

"Are you all right?"

Eric's low voice intruded into the warm pool of satisfaction enveloping Tina. How long had she been floating inside that shimmering aftermath of ecstasy? she mused. Seconds? Minutes? Hours? It didn't matter, for it had been...

"Wonderful."

"Yes, you are." His hand lightly stroked her

side from breast to knee; his soft voice caressed her emotions.

She smiled and opened her eyes. "So are you," she whispered, too drained to move let alone speak in a normal tone. "I've never, ever..." Her voice drifted away on a sigh of utter repletion.

"I've never, either." Eric smiled with tender understanding. His stroking hand wandered up the inside of her thigh. "Do you think it would be possible to repeat?"

Tina blinked, gasped, then parted her legs for his seeking fingers. "So soon?"

"Crazy, isn't it?" Eric said by way of an answer, lowering his head to her breast. "But there it is." He moved his hips against her thigh to prove his claim.

An instant ago, Tina had wanted nothing more than to drift off to sleep. Now she was wide-awake, aware, aroused, shivering in response to the myriad sensations rioting inside her from the draw of his lips on the tip of her breast and the piercing play of his fingers.

This time there was no hesitancy, no slow ascent into passion. Eric *was* passion, desire incarnate.

His fingers continuing to wreak havoc upon her senses, Eric slipped between her legs, his body taut with readiness, a column of searing fire, igniting an answering flame of wanton hunger deep within her.

And this time he was not gentle; Tina refused to allow gentleness. Grasping his firm buttocks, she pulled him to her, arching her hips high in blatant demand.

"Now, at once," she commanded.

Making a growl-like sound in his throat, Eric bowed his muscle-rigid body and thrust into her, only to withdraw and thrust again, and again.

In the grip of the sudden onslaught of unbearable tension, Tina sank her nails into his flesh, urging him deeper and deeper into her, wanting more and more and yet more of him.

His teeth clenched and bared, his taut muscles quivering with strain, Eric drove himself and her relentlessly, striving for the ultimate pinnacle of simultaneous release.

The harsh sounds of their ragged breaths beat against her ears. Sweat slicked their bodies. And still they continued to hammer remorselessly at one another.

Tina was barely breathing when the gathering tightness inside her pulsed a warning of imminent release. Eric's increased efforts signaled his understanding.

A final breath, a strangled gasp, and then Tina shattered into a million thrilling pieces of cascading completion. At that exact same instant, she heard Eric's cry of triumph, and shared the throbbing attainment of his pleasure.

"Whoa," Eric murmured, levering himself away from her to flop onto the mattress beside her. "That was…" He paused, as if groping for words.

"Incredible?" Tina supplied, dragging quick breaths into her oxygen-depleted body.

"Yeah," he said on an exhaled breath.

"Tremendous?"

"Yeah." He turned his head to smile at her.

"Fantastic?" She smiled back.

"Oh, yeah, in spades." Eric would give her that much, but no more. The experience had been, still was, too new, too intense, too mind-blasting, too never-before.

He would need time, time to think about it later, to ponder the nuances of the emotional and mental effects…if he dared to think about it at all.

Time. What time was it, anyway? Eric frowned and swept the room with a searching glance. His gaze fastened on the illuminated numbers on the digital clock on the nightstand next to Tina's side of the bed.

*Tina's side of the bed.*

The thought repeated itself in ringing tones inside Eric's head. In thinking about it as Tina's side, was he therefore assuming territorial rights to the side of the bed his exhausted body now occupied?

Eric mentally backed away from that idea—it contained overtones he didn't care to contemplate.

What time was it? Although he had looked, was still looking at the clock, he had not registered the time. Focusing, he peered at the dark red digits.

It read 11:16 p.m. Four hours since dinner.

His stomach rumbled.

"I'm hungry."

Tina had drifted into a light doze. Her eyes blinked open at the abrupt and decisive sound of his voice.

"After all you ate for dinner?" she asked in tones of amazed disbelief.

Eric shrugged. "In case you haven't noticed," he drawled, "I'm a big man."

Pulling a droll expression, Tina skimmed a glance the length of his sprawled body, before coming to rest on the most masculine section of it.

"I've noticed," she replied, in a voice every bit as droll as her expression.

Laughing at the rejoinder he had left himself wide open for, Eric pushed himself upright. His laughter ceased abruptly when he saw her shiver. It wasn't until that moment that he became aware of the cool air in the room chilling the perspiration drying on his skin.

"You're cold," he said, swinging his long legs over the edge of the bed and standing to stretch luxuriously. "C'mon, a hot shower will warm you up."

The look Tina leveled at him was less than enthusiastic. "So would a blanket," she retorted.

Eric gave her his most lascivious smile. "Yeah, but it wouldn't be half the fun."

She shut her eyes and grasped the blanket with one hand to pull it around her shivering body. "I'd rather sleep— Oh! Eric, what are you doing?" she cried as, laughing, he slid his arms under her and swept her off the bed.

Not bothering to answer, Eric tightened his hold on her, to share his body warmth with her, but also because he loved the silky feel of her next to his skin.

"Eric, put me down," Tina demanded, curling her arms around his neck.

Eric caught a rough breath when her reaction caused her breasts to rub against his chest. Savoring the sensation of her nipples poking into him, he carried her into the bathroom. Kicking the door shut, he reluctantly set her on her feet, sliding her body sensuously against his.

"You are a tyrant," Tina said, but didn't protest when his encircling arms drew her closer to him.

"You feel good," he murmured into her hair.

"Smell good, too. Like a woman who has been thoroughly loved."

Tina pulled her head back to give him a look of distaste. "You mean I smell like raw sex."

"Yeah." Eric grinned. "Turns me on."

"Big deal," she retorted. "Even with my limited experience of you, I'd say it doesn't take much."

"Now that's where you're wrong," Eric said, looking offended, as he reached inside the shower to turn on the water taps. "I'm not easy, you know," he went on, in a voice raised above the sound of gushing water.

"At the moment," she drawled, blatantly staring at a point below his waist, "I'm forced to admit that you are really very hard."

"And getting harder by the second," Eric confessed, his grin turning wicked. Testing the temperature mix, he coiled an arm around her waist and, hauling her with him, stepped into the tub, beneath the spray of water.

"Eric!" Tina screeched, sputtering as the spray filled her mouth. "Do you want to drown me?"

"No." Eric chuckled and reached for the soap. "I want to lather you...all over."

Tina gave him a militant look. "Okay, but on one condition," she said adamantly.

"And that is?" Eric arched one tawny eyebrow.

Her brown eyes gleamed with inner laughter. "That I get to lather *you* all over."

"You drive a hard bargain, woman, but you leave me little choice." A contrived frown creased his brow as he held up the single bar of soap. "The only problem now is—who goes first?" he asked in a tone of consternation, marveling at the intensity of excitement the silly byplay was stirring inside him—and outside, too, come to that.

"Me." Tina made a grab for the soap.

Eric straightened his longer arms, holding the bar aloft, inches above her reach, laughing while at the same time thrilling to the feel of her wet body sliding against his.

How could this be? he asked himself, confounded by the strength of his body's response. He was thirty-three years old, for pity's sake. After the double workout he and Tina had put each other through, Eric would have thought he'd be flat on his back, physically and mentally exhausted, not stimulated, ready and eager to repeat the exercise.

Yet here he was, renewed life surging inside him with each stroke of his lathered hands on Tina's water-slicked body, quivering in response to the glide of her soapy hands on his aroused flesh.

It was unreal. But it was fun.

The baffling question was...was it the circumstances, the availability of the woman? Or was it the woman herself? Eric had a scary feeling that it was the woman herself.

But, damn, the woman herself felt wonderful, every slippery, slidy inch of her.

Despite the confining enclosure, and the awkward positioning, the pleasure mutually derived from the erotic encounter was bone deep and infinitely satisfying.

"I don't believe this," Tina said in tones of combined confusion and amazement.

Join the club, Eric thought wryly, grasping her waist to lift her from the tub.

"Does kind of blow the mind, doesn't it?" he said, ignoring his own water-slick condition in favor of vigorously applying a towel to her dripping-wet hair.

Tina's reply sounded like mumbled gibberish muffled by the folds of the towel.

"What?" Eric lifted a corner of the cloth to peer at her. "I didn't hear you."

"I said, you are smothering me," Tina groused, yanking the towel from his hands.

"Oh, sorry." Eric gave her his most contrite, ingratiating smile.

Tina was noticeably unimpressed. Tossing a wry look at him, she bent her head and wrapped the towel turban-style around her sodden hair.

Grabbing another towel from the wall-mounted

glass rod, he stepped closer to begin drying her body.

She stepped back. "I'll dry myself," she said with daunting asperity. "I'd rather you didn't touch me."

Now that really did blow Eric's mind. Unmindful of the runnels of water dropping off his body to soak the bath mat, he stared at her in sheer disbelief, not only of her statement, but also of the searing pain of rejection he felt in reaction to it.

"Are you serious?" he demanded. "How can you say that, after the last several hours we've spent together?"

"I can say that *because* of the last several hours we've spent together," Tina retorted. "Knowing what drying each other could lead to," she went on, "I'm not at all certain I could survive another *episode* with you."

"Wear you out, did I?" Eric grinned, suddenly feeling good—no, terrific—and famished.

"Well, actually, yes," Tina admitted, slanting a sparkling look at him.

"Wore myself out, too," he confessed, chuckling. "And worked up an appetite, as well."

"So did I." Tossing the towel into the wicker hamper in the corner, she walked out of the room.

"What do you have to snack on?" Eric asked,

dropping his towel on top of hers before trailing after her. "Was there any chicken left?"

"Some of the white meat," Tina answered absently, pulling on a quilted robe. "Might stretch to two sandwiches," she mused aloud, slipping her feet into fuzzy mules before walking to the vanity table to brush her hair.

"You have lettuce and tomatoes?" Eric asked, stepping into his jeans.

"I think so." Tina frowned at her reflection in the mirror. "I should blow-dry my hair," she muttered, tugging the brush through the long, wet strands.

Eric finished shrugging on his shirt, stepped sockless into his shoes, then headed for the door. "I'll make the sandwiches, you do your hair thing." Whistling softly, he started ambling toward the kitchen, only to pause to call back to her, "You want the works, Tina?"

"Sure," she called back to him. "If I'm going to stuff my face after midnight, I might as well go all the way."

All the way. The tail end of her remark replayed inside Eric's head as he gathered the ingredients and began making their sandwiches.

The words from the song of the same title came to him, and he sang them beneath his breath while he buttered four slices of bread, then slathered them with mayonnaise.

"All the way. All the way," he softly sang the song's ending, staring into space, the sandwiches half made.

Tina had gone all the way with him tonight, Eric reflected, frowning at the tomato he held in one hand and the slicing knife he was holding in the other.

She had given herself to him freely, unconditionally, in complete and sweet surrender. A memory chord of response tingled down Eric's spine.

He had set his sights on Tina, deciding he would have her, very soon after their first meeting...which he had coolly and deliberately orchestrated.

Yet he had not taken her, but had joined with her; he had not made love to her, but had made love with her. Eric understood and acknowledged the shadings of difference between the two concepts. The first represented greedy self-gratification, the second a desire to share caring, as well as pleasure.

Absently slicing the tomatoes, Eric finished making the sandwiches, then rummaged through the cabinets, hoping to find a bag of potato chips, while mulling over the possible ramifications of his deductions.

He cared for Tina. Really cared for her, Eric realized. He cared for her in a way that could, he feared, very quickly become meaningful.

A sobering thought. One that—

"Snack ready?" Tina asked, ending his reverie, as she walked into the kitchen.

"Yes," Eric answered, relieved at having his uneasy train of thought derailed.

"Good. You want seltzer water or milk?"

"Milk." Eric turned to smile at her, and felt his breath catch painfully in his throat. With her hair a shining golden halo around her freshly scrubbed face, the innocent look of her did more than rob him of breath. It had the strangest, ache-causing effect on his heart.

"What are you looking for?"

"Huh?" he asked...like a clod.

Her smile was gentle, increasing the ache in his heart. "I asked if you were looking for something in particular in the cabinets."

"Oh, yeah. You have any chips?"

"Three cabinets down," she instructed.

The chips were found, and swiftly dispatched, along with the sandwiches and several glasses of milk. Tina brought up the subject of sleeping arrangements while they worked together clearing away the debris.

"Ah...hmmm...are you, uh...thinking of staying the night?'' she asked, quickly turning away, ostensibly to stash the milk and mayo jar in the fridge.

"May I?" Eric replied, hopefully.

Tina hesitated; Eric held his breath. "You may as well," she said, unknowingly allowing him to live by allowing him to breathe again. "If you want to."

"I want to," he said. "I want to sleep with you, wake up with you." Eric caught himself just in time before adding *every night for the rest of my life*.

Tina turned to look at him, her brown eyes soft, her smile tremulous. "I want to sleep with you, too."

Eric felt like whooping. He didn't. Instead, he forced himself to be practical. "What time do you have to get up in the morning?"

"Around seven-thirty."

"That's a good time for me, too," Eric said, recalling his appointment with his informant. "I have to go into town early, so I can drop you off at the shop."

Tina shook her head. "The shop's closed on Mondays, but I still want to get up early. I can get my car from the garage anytime after they open at eight."

"Okay." Eric shrugged. "I'll drop you at the garage before I go into town."

His stomach was full. The kitchen was clean. The hour was late. He held out his hand to her.

The temperature in the bedroom felt to be somewhere around forty degrees or so. Goose bumps prickled Eric's skin as he shucked out of his clothes. Tina, on the other hand, appeared unconcerned with the cold. A wry smile tickled his lips when she removed the quilted robe. She had not only dried her hair while he made their snack; she had also slipped into a long-sleeved, high-necked, voluminous flannel nightgown—the kind his grandmother favored.

"I was chilly," Tina said defensively.

"Uh-huh," he murmured. "Are you actually going to sleep in that tent?"

"Yes." She said, lifting her chin defiantly. "Do you have any objections?"

"No." Eric grinned. "It is your bed."

"And I intend to *sleep* in it."

"I hear you," he said, his grin dissolving into soft laughter. "I'm not...er, up to anything else, anyway. That is, anything more than a good-night kiss." He arched a quizzing eyebrow. "Okay?"

"Okay." Tina's lips twitched.

In a concession to her sudden modesty, Eric crawled into bed beside her wearing his briefs. The good-night kiss they shared was short in duration, but oddly tender and comforting. The instant their lips parted, Tina whispered good-night and turned onto her side, her back to him.

Eric lay on his back, contemplating their kiss, his shoulders and chest exposed to the chill air. A shiver had him reaching for the blankets, tugging them up to his collarbone.

*He was sleeping with a suspect.*

The thought jarred him from his reverie. Some undercover cop you are, Eric chided himself. Turning to her, he curled his arm around Tina's waist and curved his body into the warmth of hers, spoon-fashion.

Well, hell, he definitely was a cop, he mused around a wide yawn, snuggling closer to her pliant body. And he certainly was undercover...or covers, as it were.

# Eight

"**D**inner?"

"Fine," Tina answered calmly, repressing an impulse to leap into the air and shout, *Yes, yes.*

"Are you in the mood for anything in particular?" Eric's voice again sounded disembodied coming from behind the black helmet. "Italian, Chinese, Greek?"

Tina removed her own helmet and ruffled her flattened hair. "No. Are you?" she asked, handing the helmet to him, then smoothing her palms down her wool slacks.

"Seafood," he said, balancing the bike between

his thighs as he turned to fasten the helmet to the saddle. "Lobster tail, and maybe a dozen or so steamed clams to start." He turned in time to catch her smile. "Let's not go through that routine again about my appetite," he warned, amusement evident on his voice. "Does a seafood restaurant meet with your approval?"

"Yes." Tina gave her smile free rein, just out of sheer good spirits. "What time?"

"Six too early?"

"No, six is fine," she said, reluctantly raising her admiring gaze from his muscular legs to his tight butt to his slim waist to his broad chest and shoulders and up to the dark mask concealing his expression from her.

"Knock it off." Eric's voice was low, rough edged, revealing his response to her visual evaluation of his physical attributes. "I've got to get moving, and you've got to get your car." He indicated the repair shop behind her with a movement of his head. "I'm going to let you chauffeur for me this evening."

"How kind of you," she drawled, surrendering to the laughter bubbling inside her.

"Yeah, ain't it?" Eric's muffled laughter mingled with hers. "I'm a real sweet guy."

"Your modesty underwhelms me," she gibed, swinging around and heading for the repair shop.

"See you at six," she called over her shoulder. *"And drive carefully."*

"I always do," he called back to her on a note of inner laughter.

Oh, sure, Tina thought, wincing as he roared away from the curb and down the road. She suffered a few moments of anxiety for his safety as she recalled the harrowing ride he had given her on Friday morning, weaving in and out of the rush-hour traffic. Then, on deeper reflection, she also recalled his expertise in handling the monster machine and she relaxed.

The car was repaired and ready for her. Tina was feeling so good, so lighthearted, she didn't even balk at the sizable bill the mechanic presented to her. Smiling serenely, she wrote a check, handed it to him, claimed her car and, humming softly, drove away.

Not at any time did the tires leave the road. And yet, riding the winds of euphoria, Tina felt as if she were soaring, the car's tires cushioned by fluffy pink clouds.

It was a lovely sensation, heady and warm. Tina didn't even feel the bite of approaching winter in the stiff autumn breeze that had pushed yesterday's storm clouds away.

The sunlight was weak but glaring, sparkling on the rain-washed air. Tina was sparkling, too. A casual observer might have concluded that she was in love.

Tina herself had not as yet arrived at that earth-shattering conclusion. She felt good. She felt happy. She felt deliciously satisfied, emotionally and physically.

Eric sat on the rumbling but motionless bike, one foot propped on the curb, his watchful expression hidden behind the dark visor. The center-city morning traffic inched past him on the street, while the pedestrian horde surged by him on the sidewalk.

From his position a quarter of a block away from the intersection, he searched the crowd for the familiar figure of his informant. When he spotted the man, Eric lifted his foot and moved the bike forward along the curb, timing his movement to coincide with the man's arrival at the corner.

The contact had the innocent appearance of a driver requesting directions.

"What's the word?" Eric muttered, glancing around, as if thoroughly confused.

"There's been one small shipment," the informant said, raising an arm and pointing, as if indicating his verbal directions. "I hear the demand for more is high, and that there'll likely be one or two more small shipments before the big one's delivered.''

"Thanks." Eric extended his right hand, slipping several bills into the informant's palm.

"I'm sure you'll have no trouble now, sir," the man said in a louder voice.

The traffic light flicked to green; Eric waved his hand in a quick salute, then gripped the handlebar and shot through the intersection.

Ten minutes later, Eric drove the bike down the ramp to the underground parking garage beneath a large apartment complex, and brought it to a stop in the two feet of space between the wall and the front bumper of his midsize car. Venting his frustration by kicking the stand into place, he strode to the elevator and rode it to the fourteenth floor.

All the while, his informant's words replayed in his mind: *Before the big one's delivered.*

Delivered.

Delivery.

Damn, Eric fumed, letting himself into his one-bedroom apartment. He'd known there was something fishy about that furniture delivery on a Sunday night.

Too bad he hadn't been able to get the license number on that truck, Eric railed in disgust. Because he'd be willing to bet a ten-spot against a

plugged nickel there'd be no listing of an Acme
Furniture Co. in the directory.

It didn't take long to confirm his suspicion.
There were listings for Acme Dry Cleaners, an
Acme Siding Company, Acme Markets, but no
Acme Furniture.

Big surprise, Eric thought wryly. Setting the directory aside, he sat staring out the wide window,
not seeing the panoramic view of the art museum
and the distinctive buildings on boathouse row
along the river.

The informant had guessed that there would be
at least one, maybe two, small deliveries before the
big one.

How big? Eric wondered, adrenaline surging
through his system. He had been right to take a
flier on this tip, and he'd be there to intercept the
big one. All he had to do was wait them out, extend
his vacation if necessary, but wait them out. The
haul would be worth the wait.

Deciding that after the next delivery he would
call his superior and invite him in for the kill, Eric
grunted with satisfaction and pushed the button on
his answering machine to replay the tape.

There were a couple of messages from friends,
demanding to know what hole he had disappeared
into, then one from his mother. Unlike the commonly held stereotype of the complaining parent,

Maddy Wolfe never whined about being ignored. A smile erased the grim set of his lips as he listened to his mother's brief, directly-to-the-point message.

"Eric, assuming you are still alive, since I haven't heard anything to the contrary, will you give me a call within the foreseeable future? I have some good news."

Laughing softly, and deciding it was in all probability now the foreseeable future, Eric reset the machine then picked up the receiver and dialed his mother's number. Maddy answered on the fourth ring.

"Hello?"

"Hi, beautiful," Eric drawled. "It's me, Eric, your still-alive offspring."

"Gosh, I'm so glad you told me," Maddy said, matching him drawl for drawl. "I'd have never guessed."

Eric absolutely adored his mother. In his admittedly biased opinion, Maddy was the most with-it woman he knew. And he loved the rare occasions when he already knew a juicy piece of information before she could tell him herself.

"Does the good news you mentioned have anything to do with Jake's love life?" he asked, too casually.

"Oh..." Maddy said on an exhalation of consternation. "You too? When did you talk to Cameron?"

"Yesterday," he answered, frowning. "And what do you mean, me too?"

"I had a call from Royce not a half hour ago," she said, which explained everything.

Eric laughed. "Big bro stole your thunder, did he?"

"Doesn't he usually?" she asked rhetorically. "I swear, that brother of yours is more a mother hen than I am."

"Yeah," he agreed, grinning. "The Lone Wolfe does keep pretty close tabs on all of us." His grin gave way to a chuckle. "Makes you feel all warm, and cared for, and protected, and even...henpecked at times."

"Now, Eric," Maddy said reprovingly. "Cameron's only looking out for our best interests."

"I know, I know. And I appreciate it...even if it does get a bit wearing now and again." Deciding it was time to change the subject, he referred to the intent of her message. "So, little Jakey's in love, is he?"

"Well, if he isn't, Jake is certainly giving a good impression of a man in love," Maddy replied, amusement evident in her voice. "And Sarah is a lovely woman."

"Like her, do you?" Eric asked purposely,

knowing his mother's knack for reading a person's character.

"Very much," she answered at once, saying much more than she had actually said. "And I believe that you, Royce and even Cameron will like her, too."

"Whoa, lady, are you speaking about the same female-hating Cameron I know and tolerate?"

"Oh, Eric, really!" Maddy exclaimed with a hint of maternal exasperation. "Must you be so cynical? Cameron does not hate females, and you know it."

"No? Could've fooled me," Eric said dryly. "And if I'm cynical...well, I've earned the right."

"Maybe it's time for you to transfer to another department on the force," she suggested gently.

"Not just yet, Mom," he said, thinking about the delivery truck that had visited his neighbors on a Sunday night. "But maybe in the foreseeable future," he went on, thinking about the loving warmth of another, blond and beautiful neighbor.

"I hope so, son." Maddy's sigh was soft, but Eric heard it. "Any police work is dangerous, I know, but undercover narcotics is especially—"

"I gotta go, Mom," Eric interjected, gently but firmly cutting her off.

"I'm sorry," Maddy murmured. "I do so dislike a nagging female. But I am still a mother."

"The best," Eric assured her. "I really have to go now, Mother. But I'll be up to see you soon."

"All right," she said. "Let me know in advance, and I'll bake a lemon meringue pie."

"It's a deal," Eric said, thinking that if he wasn't careful he'd have lemon meringue oozing out of his ears. "Take care, Mom. I love you."

*I love you.*

The phrase came back to haunt Eric off and on throughout the morning, but not in a familial way. Oh, without doubt, he loved his mother and his three brothers, but the phrase playing hide-and-seek with his mind had, chameleonlike, metaphorically changed into a different shade of love.

Tina. Her name whispered through his mind.

Tina of the honey blond hair and soft brown eyes and enticing sweet lips. Tina of the quick humor and throaty laughter and old-fashioned but nice musical preferences. Tina of the warm body and hot kisses.

Damn, Eric mused, just thinking about her made him feel all hot and bothered, weak and strong, possessive and protective, tender and fierce.

Was that love?

Eric honestly didn't know, because he had never been in love. He had been in deep like, but he had never before believed himself in love...except with the blue-eyed, raven-haired minx who'd sat at the desk next to his in the fourth grade, and that didn't count.

So then, Eric quizzed himself while riding the elevator to the apartment lobby to collect his mail, did the warm and wonderful feelings he experienced merely thinking about Tina denote the presence of that elusive, indefinable emotion called love?

Eric reflected on the question on the return trip to his apartment, and came to the conclusion that, in all truth, he simply didn't know the answer.

Putting speculation aside, he riffled through his mail, which mainly comprised bills and junk. And he kept further introspection at bay while writing out the necessary checks to cover the bills.

But even as he affixed the required postage to the last envelope the question returned to haunt him.

Was he, could he possibly be, in love with Tina?

Probing his emotional feelings was not one of Eric's usual practices. But unless he did a little psyche-digging, examining the available evidence, as he would have in relation to his police work, how else could he form an intelligent opinion?

Eric shot a glance at his watch; it read 10:28. Okay, he thought, he'd allow himself one hour of contemplation, but then he'd have to get moving, because, since Tina was not working today, he had promised himself the treat of having lunch with her.

Hell, if truth be faced, he had kind of promised himself the treat of *having* her for lunch, Eric recalled, growing warm all over at the possibility.

There was a clue there, he mused. A bit of evidence for him to examine. Despite the rigorous workout he and Tina had engaged in last night, Eric acknowledged, his passion still ran hot and wild, and his desire for her was unsated.

A frown of concentration creasing his brow, Eric got up and went into his bedroom to collect the suit, dress shirt, tie and shoes he wanted to wear for dinner. While he was arranging the clothes in a garment bag, another clue swam to the surface of his consciousness.

In addition to his strong physical reaction, Eric had to admit that he genuinely liked Tina as a person, despite the unpalatable fact that he still had no definite proof either way concerning her involvement in this drug business.

All of which left him where?

Looping his index finger through the hook and slinging the garment bag over his shoulder, Eric left the bedroom, and then the apartment. Striding along the hallway to the garage elevator, he concluded that, all things considered, if his feelings were a true reflection of his emotional status, he could be in very deep trouble.

Eric felt a sinking sensation unrelated to the swift descent of the elevator. The sensation warred with the anticipatory feelings simmering inside him.

After all these years of unencumbered, uncomplicated, uninvolved bliss, why had he gone and fallen for a suspect, of all females?

The question popped into Tina's mind later that morning. She was stripping the sheets from her bed, dreamily reliving the delightful education in erotic play she had experienced there, when the idea struck.

Was she in love?

Giving a sharp shake of her head, as if to dislodge the ludicrous thought, she gathered the bedding and carried the bundle into the laundry room.

But the seemingly simple question was not so easily banished. Throughout the day, at odd, unexpected moments, it wormed its insidious way to the forefront of her consciousness, insisting she recognize its presence.

In love?

It was suddenly there while Tina was vacuuming the bedroom carpet.

In love?

It whispered through her mind while she was cleaning the bathroom.

In love?

It danced into her thoughts while she shoved the sofa back into place in the living room.

Love!

It finally ambushed her when she paused in her flurry of housework, clanging like a bell inside her mind as she stood irresolute in the kitchen, trying to decide whether she wanted soup or a sandwich for lunch.

Tina knew when she was beaten. Surrendering to the nagging persistence of her consciousness, she considered the euphoria-dousing question of love.

How could she be in love? Tina demanded of herself, dropping like a stone onto a chair. She hardly knew him.

Tina squirmed in the chair, suddenly uncomfortable with the fact that she had willingly made love with, slept with, a man she knew almost nothing about.

She didn't even know what Eric did for a living, Tina reminded herself. All he had said was that he was on vacation leave; Eric had never specified from what type of employment he was on vacation. For all she knew, he could be anything from a corporate CEO to a cat burglar. Tina frowned, made even more uncomfortable by her last thought.

Did cat burglars take vacation leave? Tina wondered vaguely, the distracted thought indicative of her growing sense of unease with the subject matter.

Recognizing the mental ploy for what it was—an attempt to dodge the issue at hand—Tina determined that at the first opportunity she would question Eric directly about his employment. Then she sternly told herself to get it together and get to the point.

The point, of course, being: Was she in love?

Tina sighed, but forged ahead with the self-examination. She had been in love once, and what she was feeling now in no way resembled the feelings she had had for Glen Reber...at least not the feelings she had experienced after the intimacies of their wedding night.

Tina shuddered in remembrance.

Although it was true that there were similarities between the only two men she had ever been intimate with, Tina felt positive that those similarities were few and strictly superficial. Both men were physically attractive, even though, to her eyes, Eric was definitely the handsomer of the two. And they both possessed a certain charm and style.

But that was where the similarities ended. Tina

knew from experience that Glen was shallow, unfaithful and often, deliberately cruel. Instinct, intuition, something, made her certain that Eric possessed the opposite qualities, that he was deep, abiding and gentle.

And Eric was one magnificent lover, the inner voice of satisfaction whispered.

Of course, again, Tina acknowledged the irrefutable fact that her only basis of comparison was her former husband. But, she thought, it sure didn't take the intellect of a rocket scientist to arrive at a judgment concerning the differences between the two men in that regard.

While engaged in the intimacy of lovemaking, Glen Reber had proved to be selfish, demanding, ungiving and, when thwarted in any of his desires, sadistically inclined.

In sharp contrast, while making love, Eric had displayed a fiery passion, generating intense erotic excitement, while at the same time conveying a gentle caring, a tender concern and a genuine desire to give pleasure, as well as to receive it.

On reflection, Tina reversed her original assessment; in actual fact, there were no comparisons between the two men. To her regret, she knew that Glen's charming persona was a sham, a mask he donned and discarded at will, to suit his purposes at any given moment.

On the other hand, Tina felt positive, to the very depths of her soul, that Eric's charm, humor and caring style were not in the least surface facades, but were instead integral facets of his true personality.

And she trusted him implicitly.

Tina's sudden realization of the extent of the trust she felt for Eric gave her the answer to her own question.

She *was* in love with Eric Wolfe.

But having the answer did not automatically ease the weight on Tina's mind. She didn't want to be in love—with Eric or any other man. She had allowed herself to be swept away once before by that emotional whirlwind. The aftereffects of disillusionment and pain were devastating, and not worth the transitory thrill of the brief, giddy ride.

So...what to do? Tina asked herself, frowning at the package of luncheon meat she held in her hand, and wondering when she had left her chair to walk to the fridge.

Heaving a despairing sigh, Tina shoved the package back into the fridge; she wasn't hungry for a sandwich. Come to that, she mused, returning to the chair, after gnawing on her unpalatable emotional state, she wasn't hungry, period.

What to do? The new question replaced the old

in Tina's mind, goading her into contemplation of her situation, and the options available to her.

She could stop seeing Eric, nip their tenuous relationship in the bud before it had sufficient time to blossom into something infinitely more serious, thus avoiding the possibility of being hurt again, more deeply than before.

Tina pondered the consideration for a moment, then shook her head. What would distancing herself from Eric prove? She would still love him, and the separation would very likely hurt as much as it eventually would if Eric turned out to be as false and insincere as Glen had been.

Getting restless, Tina deserted the chair to pace in a circle around the table. Another, less wrenching alternative would be to continue seeing Eric, but only contingent upon the understanding that their relationship reverted to one of platonic friendship.

*Fat chance!*

Tina grimaced at the immediate and derisive inner response, but was forced to accept the validity of it. All Eric had to do was look at her and she became all warm and squishy inside. All he had to do was smile at her and her resistance dissolved.

Well, so much for options, Tina thought, figuratively throwing up her hands in surrender. Besides, she didn't want to stop seeing him, being with him, sleeping with him. Simply because she not only loved Eric, she *liked* him.

Even though Eric had not mentioned one word about either loving or liking her.

Tina soothed the sting of that painful truth with the rationale that men in general were always hesitant about revealing the depths of their emotions. It appeared to be a built-in species thing.

Feeling exhausted by her spate of introspection, Tina decided a shot of caffeine was in order. She had scooped the grounds into the basket and was in the process of running cold water into the glass pot when the doorbell rang.

Tina glanced at the dining room archway, then back at the pot, determining to ignore the summons. The bell rang again. Thinking it might be the mailman with something she had to sign for, she turned off the water, set the pot aside and took off at a trot for the door.

It wasn't the mailman.

"Hungry?" Eric asked, brandishing a brightly patterned red-and-white cardboard bucket with one hand and a matching paper bag with the other.

"Yes," Tina answered, her appetite restored by the sight of him. She raised her eyebrows as she stepped back to let him enter. "What have you brought?"

"Chicken wings, hot and spicy," he said, giving

her a lascivious grin, along with the bucket. "And mashed potatoes, gravy and biscuits." He held the bag aloft.

Tina's mouth watered and she groaned. "All low-cal, low-fat stuff," she observed wryly.

"Aw, c'mon, live it up," Eric said, handing the bag to her and shucking off his jacket.

"That's easy for you to say," she muttered, sweeping a glance over his lean body. "You don't have to worry about every morsel you put in your mouth."

"Maybe not, but I've got the solution to your problem." He grinned again, more suggestively than before. "We can work it off with vigorous exercise this afternoon." His expression left no doubt about the type of exercise he had in mind. "And if that doesn't ease your cal and fat worries, you can have broiled fish and a salad for dinner."

"I planned to, anyway," Tina retorted, excitement flaring inside her as she led the way into the kitchen. "And it's a good thing, too," she said, prying the lid from the bucket and sniffing appreciatively at the spicy aroma wafting from inside. "This smells wonderful, like an automatic ten pounds to the hips."

As it turned out, the food was tasty.

The afternoon exercise was delicious.

Although Tina still didn't know what Eric did

for a living, she did know he was well versed in the art of lovemaking.

She soothed her conscience and excused her lapse by assuring herself that a good opportunity really hadn't presented itself; Eric had kept her rather distracted.

# Nine

The opportunity was at hand.

Eric was replete, from the afternoon's endeavors and from the enormous seafood dinner he had consumed. Relaxed, he lounged back in his chair and smiled at her over his coffee cup.

Tina seized the moment. "How much longer will you be on vacation?" she asked, casually lifting her own cup to her lips to blow on the steaming liquid.

"This week...officially," Eric replied, readily enough. "But I could extend it another two weeks—" he smiled with obvious sensuality "—if I wanted to."

"You have four weeks' vacation a year!" Tina exclaimed, grateful for the opening he had given her. "What are you, the president of a bank or something?"

"Not hardly," Eric drawled. "I work for the city."

"Philadelphia?"

"Uh-huh." He nodded.

"You must have some position." Tina couldn't imagine him in the role of a clerk, pushing papers behind some license-applications counter. "Appointed?"

"Naw, nothing so exalted." Eric laughed. "I'm just a city employee, with the option of using my accrued vacation time all at once."

Very likely because of his lean, muscular physique, Tina immediately thought of the waste management department, the hauling and lifting required in trash disposal.

No wonder he could eat like a racehorse and show not an inch of excess flesh, she mused. If, indeed, he was employed in the area of waste management.

Tina opened her mouth to ask point-blank, but Eric beat her into speech.

"More coffee?"

"Er...no, thank you." Tina shifted mental gears. "I'm stuffed to the gills."

"You ate the flounder's gills?" Eric opened his eyes wide in feigned horror.

"No, you idiot," Tina said, laughing. "The broiled flounder I ordered came sans gills."

"I didn't notice." He grinned at her. "But I am relieved to hear it."

"Of course you didn't notice," she gibed. "You were too busy inhaling two dozen steamed clams, a one-pound lobster tail, a baked potato, literally swimming in butter and sour cream, and a Caesar salad that looked large enough to feed a family of four."

"Only if they were on a strict diet," Eric protested in an injured tone.

Tina was helpless against the offended expression he pulled, and the laughter teasing her quivering lips. The question of his work went right out of her head. She didn't notice its departure, because she was too caught up in the sheer joy she experienced just being with him.

When Eric flashed his wicked grin, Tina's amusement escaped. They exited the restaurant laughing together, her cares forgotten, for tonight, at least.

That week alternately sped up or crawled by for Tina. When she was with Eric in the evening, the hours flew, seemingly contracting into mere moments. The opposite applied when she was away from him, minutes expanding into long hours.

Like greedy Midas, Tina and Eric hoarded their gold of hours; their favorite hiding place was Tina's bed.

And there, with all the verve and enthusiasm of intrepid adventurers, they eagerly explored the alluring terrain of each other's bodies, while probing the depths of their individual sensuality.

Tina had never before known such happiness, had never before basked in the unadulterated joy of just being alive.

Questions and doubts no longer picked with nervous little fingers at the fabric of her mind. Tina unhesitatingly admitted that she loved Eric with every particle of her being.

That is, she admitted it to *herself;* she had not murmured one word of love to him. Not because she was afraid to broach the subject; she wasn't. She firmly believed that he was as much in love with her as she was with him. His actions, his attitude, the glow in his crystal blue eyes when he looked at her, all spoke in silent eloquence of his love for her. No, she was not in the least afraid to speak the words.

Tina was simply waiting for Eric to speak them first.

* * *

The jury was no longer out; the verdict was in and emblazoned on his mind like the legendary words carved inside crudely rendered hearts on countless tree trunks.

*Eric Wolfe loved Christina Kranas.*

While he sat perched on the edge of the chair at the window, watching the house across the street, Eric came to the acceptance of his love for Tina. It was Friday afternoon, one week to the day after his initial approach of her.

Was it really possible to fall in love in a week? Eric mused, stifling a yawn triggered by utter boredom. Must be, he reasoned, shifting to ease the numbness in his posterior. He was living proof of the possibility.

You ain't quite right, Wolfe, Eric chided himself, stretching his long legs out in front of him. Only a slightly bent cop would be dumb enough to fall for a suspect.

But was Tina still a suspect? Did he believe…

*No.* The denial leapt into Eric's head before the question of her association with the drug dealers was fully formed. Eric wasn't sure exactly when he had reached the conclusion that Tina was innocent of any involvement in the illegal operation, but the precise date and time didn't matter.

He'd had a gut feeling about the veracity of the

tip from his informant, and he now had the same gut feeling about Tina's innocence.

Bottom line was, Eric trusted Tina, as well as loved her. He knew, unequivocally, that should the necessity arise he could trust her with his life.

Eric did not expect such a necessity to ever arise. He was capable of taking care of himself. And yet the rock-solid belief he now held that Tina would be there if he should need her assistance, regardless of the possible danger, was both comforting and exciting, for one thrilling reason.

*Tina loved him.*

Though she had not once mentioned the word *love* to him, Eric was as certain that Tina loved him as he was that the sun would continue to rise in the east.

He knew. How could he not know? Eric mused, sketching an image of Tina inside his mind, while keeping a sharp-eyed watch on the quiet street outside.

Tina had betrayed herself, her love, to him in a hundred ways, some barely noticeable, others so obvious they were soul-shattering...shattering *his* soul.

Tina had given the gift of herself, all of herself, to him in sweet and hot surrender. Eric treasured her gift, and her, and had offered the gift of himself in return.

Tina was his; he was hers. Her softness buffered his hardness. Her gentleness tempered his cynicism. The radiance in her lightened the darkness in him.

And the hardness, cynicism and darkness had been there, a living part of him, for a long time.

Eric shuddered, recalling the bitter hatred that had seared his mind, coloring his perception, on the day the minister intoned the service of burial over his father's casket.

He had lived for years with the bitterness and hatred eating away at him like an acid toxin.

Tina's very softness, her loving and laughter were Eric's antidote, the remedy that made him feel whole again. And, from his new perspective, he saw himself as the protector of her softness, the rock-solid strength between Tina and the harmful, seamy side of the world.

They were made for each other.

Someday soon, hopefully very soon, Eric would feel free to speak the four words he would not allow himself to say aloud until this surveillance was over, and she knew exactly who he was, what he was. Until then, he held them close, in his mind, in his heart, keeping them pure, for her alone.

*I love you, Tina.*

Some cop he was. The derisive thought brought a whimsical smile to Eric's compressed lips. He had spent more time loving Tina this week than watching the neighbors for continuing illegal developments.

Oh, well, it was his own time that he was squandering, he reminded himself.

Thing was, Eric didn't consider the time squandered. He regarded it as time well spent on every hope and dream he had once held for the future.

There would undoubtedly be many more undercover stakeouts down the road for him, Eric knew. But there was only one Tina.

She came first. As Maddy had always been to Eric's father, Tina was his top priority.

Love sure did strange things to folks.

The thought amused Eric, and he was still grinning some time later when the phone rang.

Since Eric had only given the number to two other people besides Cameron, the caller had to be either his boss or his love. Anticipation caused a tingle in the fingers that reached for the receiver.

"Eric?" The upbeat sound of Tina's voice did a tap dance on his nervous system.

"You were expecting Kevin Costner?" Eric asked in a teasing drawl.

"What would I want with him, when I can have you?" Tina asked in a solemn, serious tone that stole his breath, liquefied his insides and made mush of his brain.

"Eric?" she prodded uncertainly when he didn't respond for a couple of long seconds. "Did I say the wrong thing?"

"No, love," he assured her, pulling his wits together. "You said exactly the right thing."

"I meant it."

"I know." Eric grabbed for a steadying breath. "The knowing's driving me nuts."

"What do you mean?" Tina sounded confused, and a little worried. "I mean, why is it driving you nuts?"

"Because you're there, and I'm here," Eric said. "I'm missing you like hell."

"I'm missing you, too." Tina's voice was throaty, soft, and misty sounding.

It went to Eric's head, and his heart, and other vulnerable parts of his anatomy. Telling himself to lighten up before he started babbling his feelings to her like a love-struck teenager, he cleared his throat and said the first crazy thing that jumped into his head.

"You wanna have phone sex?"

Tina's laughter sang along the wire to him, tickling his ear, and his fancy. "Heavens, no!" she exclaimed. "Maybe I'm just old-fashioned, but I prefer the genuine article."

"Yeah, so do I," he purred. "When?"

"You're insatiable," she accused, still laughing.

"Yeah," he growled. "When?"

"Later tonight," she promised, in a thrill-inducing whisper. "But first…" She hesitated; he jumped in.

"First?"

"I was wondering if you felt like going out for a while this evening."

Things clicked in Eric's mind, bits of information came together. It was Friday, the night Tina usually spent in the company of her friends.

"The tavern?" he asked, knowing the answer.

"Yes," Tina answered, as expected. "Ted called me a little while ago to ask if I needed a lift tonight." She gave a half laugh. "To tell the truth, until he called, I'd completely forgotten about meeting the gang tonight."

Her admission pleased Eric very much. Enough to make him feel willing to share a portion of their time together with her friends.

"Okay. What time?"

There was a brief but telling silence. Eric smiled with tender understanding. Tina had expected him to balk at her suggestion of an outing.

"You want to go?" Tina's voice conveyed her surprise.

Eric smiled. "Sure. Why not?"

"Well, I thought that—" Tina paused, as if

gathering her thoughts "—I thought you might prefer to stay in."

"A change of scenery couldn't hurt," Eric said in a slow drawl. "We haven't been out of the house together since Monday evening." He chuckled softly. "Hell, we've hardly been out of the bedroom since Monday evening."

"I wasn't bored." Tina's voice was so low he could barely hear it, and yet the message came through loud and clear. "Were you?"

"You know better than that." Eric's voice was also low, velvety with intimacy. "I loved every minute of it." Then he turned the tables on her. "Didn't you?"

"Yes," Tina whispered. "That's why I thought..." Her voice faded away.

"You thought correctly," Eric said, filling in the void. "But we must eat, too, keep up our strength." He paused for a reaction from her. When there was none, he continued. "I was assuming we were going to have dinner at the tavern."

"We were."

"Okay, then, we'll go," he said. "We can always come home early, you know."

"Yes, I do know," she agreed, in a purring tone that set his imagination on fire. "Suppose I swing

by and pick you up after work? Say about six-
thirty?''

"Or I could take the bike and meet you there,"
he suggested, to save her the run out of her way.

"But then we couldn't go home together," she
pointed out in a senses-stirring purr.

"True," Eric said, not only taking her point, but
running with it. "I'll be ready and waiting."

Agreeing to Tina's suggestion was the easy part
for Eric. Getting through the rest of the afternoon
was the hard part. Not a damn thing was happening
in or around the house across the street. But that
no longer bothered or surprised him.

Eric's familiar and trusted gut feeling had come
back into play, and he had arrived at the conclusion
that nothing was going to happen—not before the
weekend. Instinct, or intuition, or something, had
convinced him that whatever was going down over
there was going down on Sundays.

Still, Eric watched, bored but diligent, until it
was time to get himself ready for Tina.

All in all, the evening turned out to be rather
enjoyable for Eric. Disarmed, so to speak, by the
information his brother had provided about the
members of the group, Eric felt more relaxed in
their company, less constrained in joining in with
the banter and harmless fun.

And he did have fun, more than he had allowed himself to indulge in for some length of time. He laughed at their jokes, even the lame ones, and even loosened up enough to offer a few dry witticisms of his own.

Yet, true to form, even as he relaxed and enjoyed, Eric dissected the reasons he had lowered his guard. First and foremost of these, of course, was the very fact of Cameron's verbal report that from all he could gather, every member of the group was clean, in the legal sense.

The second reason was the confirmation of Eric's initial perception of the members of the bunch being average, normal, genuinely nice people.

The third reason, and by far the most important to Eric, was the reflection on Tina's character by her very association with them. A reflection of character that coincided with his own independently drawn conclusions.

Birds of a feather, and all that.

So the evening proved a double success. Eric enjoyed himself, and Tina was happy. He was content to bask in the overflow of her happiness. She displayed it in the most exciting ways—after they had returned to her house, and to her bedroom.

It began snowing in fits and starts of flurries early Sunday morning. By midday the fitful snowfall was dusting lawns, shrubs and tree branches, but was still melting on the sidewalks and streets.

"Isn't it pretty?" Tina said in delight. "I have always loved the first snowfall of the season."

"It won't last," Eric predicted, softening his observation with a smile. "Too early."

"I suppose," she murmured. "Thanksgiving is still over a week and a half away."

"Yeah," he murmured, turning his gaze from the window to the paper he held in his hand. "Besides, the bad-driving weather will come soon."

Tina shuddered. "That's the minus side of snow, driving in it. I get nervous just— Oh, hell!" she muttered.

Eric raised his glance from the sports page to frown at her. "What's the matter?"

"It's my ex-husband." She grimaced and indicated the street with a sharp movement of her head. "I hope he's not thinking of stopping in here—" Tina broke off on a groan, then said in disgust, "Oh, nuts, here he comes."

"So I see." Eric was already on his feet, the paper still clutched in one hand. His brain shifted into high gear as his eyes narrowed on the confident-looking man just then stepping onto the front stoop, beneath the protective overhang.

Well, surprise, surprise, Eric thought wryly. It must be Sunday…day of deliverance.

The doorbell rang.

Tina groaned again.

"Are you afraid of him?" Eric sliced a hard look at her. "Because if you are, there's no reason for you to be, not as long as I'm here."

"I'm not." Tina shook her head and stood up as the bell rang once more. "I'm tired of telling him I'm not interested—not in him, or his friends." She jerked her head, indicating the house across the street. "I want him to leave me alone."

"Would you like me to convey that message to him from you?" Eric asked in a soft, deadly-sounding voice.

Tina looked startled for an instant. Then she laughed, a little shakily. "Good heavens, Eric, lighten up. You look positively lethal." She started for the door, tossing over her shoulder, "You don't want me to be afraid of you, do you?" she said teasingly, turning away to open the door.

Good advice, that, so back off, Wolfe, Eric told himself. It was going to be hard enough telling her about himself when the time came. He certainly didn't want her afraid of him, not now, not ever.

Taut but controlled, Eric listened to the exchange between Tina and Glen Reber filtering to him from the doorway.

"No, Glen," she was saying adamantly. "I am not going to invite you in."

"But why not?" he persisted angrily. "It's snowing and it's cold out here."

"Go visit your friends across the street," she said with obvious impatience. "Their house is as warm as mine."

"This used to be my house, too."

"Used to be is as dead as the bad relationship we once shared," Tina retorted. "I told you before that I don't want you coming around anymore, Glen. I meant it. If you do, I won't answer the door."

"You always were a cold bitch," he snarled.

*He'd deck the bastard.*

Fury impelled Eric into motion. He was halfway to the door when Tina shut it in Glen's face. Fortunately for Eric, she stood staring at the solid panels for a few moments, long enough for him to return to his position near the window and conceal his dangerous intent behind an expressionless mask of calm.

*You'll get yours, creep. Someday. Soon. And the pleasure will be all mine.*

Through eyes glittering with the promise of retribution, Eric watched Glen storm away from the door, down the glistening walk, and then to the house across the street.

"He's gone."

"I know." Consciously relaxing his battle-tightened muscles, Eric consigned Glen Reber to a day of reckoning and turned from the window to smile at her. "If he bothers you again, let me know," he said, careful to keep his voice cool and steady, his smile easy.

"I don't think he will." She sighed tiredly. "At least I hope this time I got through to him."

"And if you didn't, I'll take care of it," he assured her, feeling the weight of her sigh.

"No!" Tina said sharply, her face paling. "I don't want you involved with him."

Eric frowned, feeling an instant's doubt about her own involvement with Reber. Then he immediately dismissed it. He wasn't wrong, but something was.

"Why?" he demanded.

"Because I don't want you hurt!" Tina exclaimed.

Eric smiled.

"Oh, men and their damn macho image!" Tina glared at him. "Eric, you don't understand."

"So enlighten me."

"Glen is dangerous." Her eyes lost their sparkle, growing dark and bleak. "I...I learned after the divorce that Glen had been arrested, several times. Once for nearly killing a man with a knife."

Beginning to tremble, she sank onto the edge of the sofa. "I couldn't bear it if you—" Her voice broke, and she stared at him in abject fear.

Eric crossed to her in three long strides. Grasping her shoulders, he drew her up and into his arms. "Tina, don't look like that," he murmured, soothing her with a gentle stroke of his hand down her back. "Honey...honey, nothing's going to happen to me." He grinned. "I'm tough."

"But, Glen's—" She broke off once more, shuddering.

"A two-bit hood," Eric said with casual unconcern. Then he frowned. "And I'm damned if I can figure out how a woman like you ever got tangled up with a lowlife like him."

"I was a fool." Tina's pale cheeks flared pink. "A young, naive fool." She lowered her eyes in embarrassment. "And Glen can put on quite a performance. He can turn on the charm until it practically oozes out of his pores. He set a romantic scene, and cast himself as Prince Charming. I bought the play from opening night. He swept me off my feet, and kept my head spinning right up to the altar." She expelled a short, harsh laugh. "I learned the meaning of duplicity on my wedding night."

"Dare I ask how?"

"No." Tina shook her head. "I don't want to

think about it, let alone talk about it. It's over. Done. And I'm no longer a naive young fool.''

"No, you aren't," Eric murmured, slowing lowering his head. "You are a beautiful, exciting temptress.''

She started to laugh at his description of her, but her laughter got lost inside his mouth.

It wasn't far from the kiss to the floor.

Holding her as if she were made of the most delicate china, Eric gently drew her down with him to the carpet; it made a viable subsitute bed.

Following the lead of an emotional need he had never before experienced, Eric did not so much make love to Tina as give physical expression to how much he cherished her.

Nevertheless, the results were the same.

Murmuring to her, caressing her, stroking her silky skin with feather-light brushes of his hands and lips and tongue, he kindled a spark that quickly burst into flames that swiftly went racing out of control.

"Eric."

His name on her lips, softly pleading, enticing, set Eric's pulses beating against his eardrums. The glide of her fingertips down the length of his spine drew a shuddering breath from his constricted chest.

Eric fought against the tide of desire threatening to overtake them both. It was a losing battle.

Passion escalated. Hands skimmed. Mouths fused. Tongues dueled. Bodies joined.

*Hold on. Hold on.*

Eric repeated the words to him himself in a desperate bid to draw every drop of sweetness from the moment. Loving Tina, giving of himself, as he had never loved or given to any other woman, he expanded the moment to the outer limits of endurance.

Then the moment exploded.

Eric felt shattered. Undone. Wonderful.

The descent from the heights was slow. When his breathing leveled and his heart felt as if it would stay inside his chest, instead of hammering its way out, Eric stretched out on the floor beside Tina, drew her close to his quivering body and was asleep within seconds.

The chill in the air woke Eric. He felt stiff, and cramped, but most of all he felt cold. The room was dark except for the pale glow from the picture window. Beyond the pane, he could see large, lacy snowflakes swirling in the wind.

Shivering, Eric swept his hand along the carpet until he found his shirt. Sitting up, he spread the shirt over Tina. Then, groaning silently at the stiff-

ness of his muscles, he rolled away from her and
stumbled to his feet.

Standing stark naked in the middle of the room,
stretching and flexing to work the kinks from his
body, Eric stared through the window at the snow.
He was about to turn away, intending to scoop up
Tina and carry her into the shower, when the flare
of headlights, reflecting brightly off the snow,
snagged his attention and kept him still. Behind the
snow-sparkled pool of light crept a full-size, closed
van.

Suddenly alert and taut with expectancy, Eric
watched the van come to a halt, then slowly turn
into the driveway of the house down the street.

*"Damned fool."*

Cursing himself aloud for surrendering to his
clamoring senses on this night of all nights, Eric
turned this way, then that way, searching the darkened floor for his pants, unaware that he was firing
off a string of colorful curses of self-condemnation.

"Eric, what's wrong?" Tina's voice was blurry
with sleep and confusion.

"I've got to hurry," he muttered, zipping his
pants as he shoved a bare foot into a shoe.

"But...why?"

"Because I want to get closer to watch," he
answered distractedly, searching out his other shoe.

"Closer?" Hugging the shirt to her, Tina scrambled up off the floor. "Watch for what?"

"The delivery of drugs," Eric said without thinking. "In that house of your ex's friends, across the street."

"Drug delivery?" Tina cried. "You can't be serious!"

"I'm dead serious." Eric was nearly growling now, furious at himself and the elusive shoe. And he didn't think to guard his tongue. "I witnessed a delivery there last week."

"I can't believe it." Tina shivered, and pulled the shirt tightly, protectively around her shaking body.

"Ah..." Eric purred, spying the shoe. He pushed his foot into it, then headed for the dining room and the small closet where Tina had hung his coat earlier.

"Where are you going?"

Eric wasn't startled by her sudden appearance; quiet as she had been, he'd heard every move she made. He shrugged into his jacket as he turned to her.

"I told you. I want a closer look." Stepping around her, he started for the kitchen, which was dimly lit by the night-light on the stove. "I'll go out the back."

"Eric!" Tina called, running after him and

clutching at his arm. "If there is some sort of drug dealing going on over there, you could be in terrible danger."

"I must go, Tina," he said impatiently, pulling his arm back to loosen her grasp; she hung on tight.

"Why?" she shouted, giving a yank on his arm hard enough to turn him halfway around. "Why you?"

"Who, then?" Eric snapped, out of patience.

"The police!" she shouted, wincing as he jerked his arm free of her clutching fingers.

"I *am* the police."

# Ten

*I am the police.*

Eric's flatly voiced statement echoing in her head, Tina stood, still as a post, staring at the back door in wide-eyed disbelief.

"A cop," she murmured dully. "Eric's a cop."

Questions tumbled into her mind.

How had Eric known there would be a delivery of drugs tonight to the house across the street? How long had he known? Had he moved into the neighborhood to keep that house under surveillance? Why hadn't he told her? Had he had her under surveillance, real close surveillance, as well?

*Could Eric possibly have believed that she was involved with whatever was going on over there?*

Tina could handle the barrage of questions; what she couldn't deal with were the obvious answers.

A queasy sensation invaded her stomach. A chill ran the length of her small form, a chill unrelated to the scant protection of the cotton shirt draping her otherwise nude body from shoulders to mid-thigh.

Eric's shirt. And Eric was a cop.

So, what did that make her?

A dupe…again.

"Oh, God." Tina's stomach lurched, and, flinging a hand up to clap it over her mouth, she whirled and made a headlong dash for the bathroom.

Eric watched the red taillights blink, and then the van turned right at the end of the street. He pushed up his jacket sleeve and glanced at his watch. The hands stood at 8:16. His lips twisted into a wry smile.

Later than last week…but still in the ballpark, he mused, recalling the previous Sunday's delivery. But then it had been furniture. Tonight it had been small white cartons marked Fine Crystal in large black letters.

Crystal. Right.

Eric snorted. And then he sneezed.

Hell, he was freezing. And no wonder, he thought, sliding his hands into the jacket's slash side pockets. He'd run out of Tina's little more than half-dressed.

Tina!

"Oh, sh—" Eric's voice was carried off by the wind as he turned away from his position at a corner of the house directly across the street from the one under surveillance.

Retracing his tracks along the unpaved alley behind the homes lining the street, Eric approached Tina's back door with a mounting sense of apprehension. His unease owed everything to his sudden recollection of having blurted out not only his suspicions about the drug dealing, but also his true occupation.

"Damn," Eric cursed, grasping the doorknob. He had one whole hell of a lot of explaining to do. He only hoped Tina would be willing to listen.

No, his first hope was that she had not thought to relock the door. Holding his breath, he twisted the knob and gave a gentle push. The door swung open.

"Thank you, Jesus," Eric whispered fervently. "Now, I may not deserve it, but if you'll only hang in there with me a mite longer, I'd surely appreciate it, Sir."

Moving as silently as smoke, Eric stepped into the kitchen and quietly shut the door. He saw her even before he reached the archway into the dining room. Apparently she had showered, for her hair was a dark and damp mass of loose waves cascading around her shoulders. She was dressed in faded jeans and an oversize green-and-white Eagles sweatshirt.

Eric sighed; she had looked so damn sexy in nothing but his shirt. He stared at her longingly a moment, then strode through the dining room.

"Tina."

Tina started at the sudden, unexpected sound of her name, but caught back the scream that filled her throat.

*Eric!*

She had deliberately curled up on the chair by the window so that she couldn't possibly miss his approach to the front door—if he had the gall to return. And here he was, standing bold as sin in her living room!

Scrambling out of the chair, Tina drew herself up to her full five-foot-two-and-three-quarter-inch height, planted her hands on her hips and glared him straight in the eyes.

"How did you get in here?" she demanded. "Do you have a damned master key or something?"

"Of course not." Eric took a step closer. She narrowed her eyes. He stepped back. "You forgot to relock the door after I went out."

"Well, you can just go right back out again," she said in an emotionally strained voice. "And believe me, I won't forget to lock the door after you."

"Tina, listen..." he began in a soothing tone.

"I don't want to listen to anything you have to say," Tina cut him off. "I just want you to go." A curl of disdain lifted the corner of her lip. "Officer Wolfe."

"I couldn't tell you." Eric raked a hand through his snow-dampened tawny hair. "You have to understand—"

Tina again ruthlessly interrupted him. "Oh, I understand. Boy, do I understand. I worked it all out while I was waiting for you to show your face again...if you had the nerve."

"Nerve has nothing to do with it," Eric said, trying another tentative step.

"Stay right where you are!" Tina's barely controlled voice cracked like a whip.

Eric came to a halt...two steps closer to her.

It was much too close for Tina's peace of mind. She wanted to punch him out, tear into him with her fingernails, do severe bodily damage to him.

She wanted to score his skin, make him hurt on the surface as much as she was hurting inside.

"Tina, please," he said with edgy patience. "If you'd just let me explain, talk to you."

"Now he wants to talk to me, explain," she said to the air around her. "He thinks I'm stupid.... Ha! What am I saying? I *am* stupid!"

"Tina!"

"You lied to me!"

"I didn't."

"Oh, right." She laughed derisively. "You just conveniently omitted telling me what department you worked in for the city. Lord only knows what else you omitted telling me. Things like suspecting me of being involved with drug dealing...or whatever is going on across the street...simply because I was once married to Glen."

"But only at first," he said defensively.

"Only at first," she repeated, feeling sicker with each passing second.

Eric was beginning to look harried, and tired. "Can't we sit down and talk this out?"

"No." Tina shook her head, and swallowed the acrid taste of loss. "No, Eric. I don't want to talk to you. I can't bear the thought of talking with a man who will go to any lengths, even to making love to me, to use me."

"I did not." Eric's voice was hard; his eyes

were harder, glittering like frozen chunks of morning sky.

Tina knew she had to end this, get him out of her house. Because she was weakening, beginning to long to believe him, she was vulnerable.

"Get out of here, Eric," she said, in a voice made cold by the fear of her love for him.

"All right." He sighed, and it was then that she noticed he was shivering. "I'll go."

"Don't forget your shirt." Tina moved her hand to indicate the garment draped over an arm of the sofa.

Eric grabbed his shirt and strode to the door. Then he turned to look at her. "But I'll be back, Tina, after you've had a chance to cool down."

"That'll be never," Tina said, wishing he would just go, before the tears stinging her eyes betrayed her by spilling over onto her cheeks. "Twice burned, and all that."

He just stood there, staring at her, staring, as if imprinting every one of her features on his mind. Then, finally, he turned, pulled open the door and left.

And not an instant too soon. Tina collapsed onto the carpet, wrenching sobs racking her trembling body before the door clicked shut.

Eric sneezed. Then he coughed. Then he swore. He had developed a head cold. Happens when a man stands in the snow only partially dressed, he thought, sneezing again.

Some two inches of snow had accumulated on the ground by late Sunday night. It had turned to mush, then melted entirely by sundown Monday...along about the time Eric began sneezing in earnest.

By Tuesday night, he felt lousy...but not only from the effects of the viral infection. Tina had adamantly refused to talk to him...twice.

Eric had called her early Monday morning... between sneezes. In a tone of voice at least twenty degrees colder than the outside temperature, Tina had told him, in a scathing tone, to drop dead.

By the next morning, Eric had felt that he just might comply, but, undaunted, he'd dialed her number again.

She'd hung up on him.

Deciding that perhaps Tina needed a little more cooling-off time, Eric resisted the gnawing desire to call her on Wednesday. He called his boss instead.

His trusted gut feeling had joined forces with his standby hunch, and both were telling him the big shipment was due...probably this coming Sunday. Eric figured it was time to apprise his superior of the situation.

"I had a sneaky suspicion you were up to something," Lieutenant Dan Phillips drawled after Eric finished telling his story. "You, on vacation. Ha."

"You wound me." Eric grinned, then sneezed.

"Yeah, well, get yourself and your wound downtown," Dan retorted. "We've got an operation to set up."

By Friday, everything was in place. Eric was feeling slightly better...at least as far as his head cold was concerned. But he was missing Tina more than he would have believed himself capable of ever missing any one individual.

Wanting Tina, wanting just to be with her, was driving him crazy. Eric consoled himself with a promise to confront her as soon as this drug business was over, and convince her of his love for her, on his knees, if necessary.

He fervently hoped that wouldn't be necessary.

Tina had a miserable week.

Business at the shop was brisk. She was making money. But she couldn't work up any enthusiasm about either the business or the profits.

She missed Eric so badly she felt like screaming...primarily at him for not being the man he had led her to believe he was...damn his lying soul.

By closing time on Friday, Tina was exhausted.

It was hard work acting as if she didn't have a care in the world, to stave off speculation and questions from her assistant, and being pleasant and helpful to her customers.

Using the old-standby excuse of a headache, Tina did not join her friends at the tavern on Friday evening. By Saturday evening, the excuse had become a reality.

Tina swallowed two aspirins and crawled into bed as soon as she got home from work.

She didn't sleep; she cried.

By morning the headache and the tears were gone. Tina had found something more important to replace them. It was Sunday. She knew from what Eric had let slip that he suspected the drug deliveries were made on Sundays.

Tina didn't have time for a headache or tears; she was too busy worrying herself frantic about Eric.

By sundown, Tina was pacing the house like a crazed lioness forcibly separated from her cubs.

It was after six-thirty when she saw Glen's distinctive Lincoln moving slowly down the street. She held her breath, then let it out on a relieved sigh when, instead of heading straight for her door after parking his car in front of her place, as he had the two previous Sundays, he crossed the street and went directly to his friends' house.

Afraid to move away from the window, and too keyed up to sit, Tina stood back a ways from the glass pane, waiting, and watching, and wondering if Eric was watching, too.

It was nearing nine-thirty when Tina saw the vehicle lumbering down the street. Without pausing to consider or even think, she flew to the phone and dialed Eric's number. The minute she heard his voice, she blurted out the information.

"Eric, there's a motor home coming down the street!"

"I see it." He voice was terse, clipped. "Stay inside, Tina. And that's an official order."

"Be careful, Eric. I—" Tina broke off; Eric had disconnected. "I love you," she whispered too low for him to hear. Then, replacing the receiver, she ran back to the window.

Eric was tense with anticipation, poised for the coming action. Yet inside, a glimmer of hope sent tendrils of warmth curling around his heart.

Tina had cared enough to warn him.

It wasn't as good as a declaration of love, but it was something to hang on to.

His full attention now on the business at hand, Eric watched, a satisfied smile quirking his lips, as Glen Reber and Bob Freeman exited the house and strode to the RV. As the two men drew close to the vehicle, the door opened and another man handed out two large suitcases.

Eric activated his two-way radio.

"Company's here." he said tersely. "I'm going to a party. Wanna come?"

Turning from the window, Eric made his way unerringly through the dark room to the door.

An RV, of all things, he thought, shaking his head as he descended the outside stairs three at a time. Before he had traversed the short distance from the stairs to the end of the driveway, the street was swarming with cops, every one of them converging on the RV and the men lugging the cases toward the house.

How Glen Reber managed to slip through the human strands of that closing net, Eric would never figure out, but slip through it he did.

Eric had crossed the sidewalk, blending into the darkness next to a curbside tree, when he spotted Reber, hugging the inky darkness around the home next to the target house, inching his way down the street to his car.

Leaping into the road, Eric took off at a run after the retreating man. By the time he arrived in the general area where he knew his quarry should be, Reber had vanished.

Taking slow, quiet, measured breaths, Eric began a game of hide-and-seek.

Eric lost. His quarry found him first. He was four houses down from the action, across the street from Reber's car, and Tina's house, when he felt the unmistakable feeling of a knife point pressed against the side of his neck, directly above his jugular vein.

"No heroics, tall man," Reber warned in a grating whisper close to Eric's ear. "If you want to keep the blood flowing inside that vein, you'll move slow and careful toward that car over there." He backed up the threat with an added bit of pressure from the knife.

Eric's parents had not raised any fools. Biding his time, watching and waiting for the right moment, he began moving, slowly, carefully, toward the big Lincoln.

With his attention divided between his captive and his car, Reber never gave so much as a glance to his ex-wife's house. He should have. He didn't see her.

But Eric did. And his blood ran ice-cold.

*Jesus, Tina, stop!*

The cry rang inside Eric's head as he watched her emerge from the shadows beneath the overhang. Her hands gripping the handle of the large black iron frying pan she was holding high over her head, Tina came running down the walkway toward them.

Right or wrong, his moment was upon him. Eric seized it. He moved with blurring swiftness. Ignoring the pinprick of the knife point puncturing his skin, he raised his arm and his knee as he turned.

Three things happened simultaneously.

The hard outer edge of his hand slashed down into the curve of Reber's neck.

His knee smashed into the man's groin.

And the frying pan landed with a thunk on Glen's head.

Reber grunted, then dropped to the street like a stone.

"Oh my god!" Tina cried. "Is he dead?"

Hunching down, Eric pressed his fingers to the side of Reber's throat. "Nah," he said, springing upright. "But he'll hurt like hell when he comes to."

"Eric...I..." She broke off, staring at him through eyes widened from reaction. "You're bleeding!"

Raising his hand, Eric touched his fingers to the wet trickle seeping from the wound. "It's nothing."

"It—it's over?" Her voice quavered, her body shook, the pan hanging at her side from her limp hand swayed.

"It's over." Eric was fully aware of the commotion around the house up the street, the raised voices calling back and forth, the red-and-blue lights flashing atop the police cars filling the roadway. And yet he saw only Tina, and he saw red, a surge of anger born of fear.

He opened his mouth to give her a blistering lecture, dress her down one side and up the other for endangering herself by disobeying his orders to remain inside.

The words caught in his throat, as through his mind flashed the memory of his thoughts the previous week, his belief that he could trust Tina with his life if necessary.

She had run to his defense.

But she had put herself in jeopardy, Eric reminded himself. She could have been seriously injured...or worse. The feeling inside him swirled again, now more fear than anger. He had to make her understand the magnitude of the risk she'd taken. His lips parted once more.

"I love you, Tina."

She gasped and stared at him, dumbfounded, and then the pan hit the sidewalk with a clang and she turned and ran back into the house.

It was late when Eric was at last free to leave the police station. A co-worker dropped him off at his center-city apartment.

Forty minutes later, showered, shaved and dressed in brown slacks, a white turtleneck and a tweed jacket, Eric emerged from the underground parking garage driving his late-model midsize car.

Now that the drug-shipment business was over, he had a real job of work to do...that of convincing a certain small, beautiful, risk-taking, breathtaking blonde that they were made for each other.

Eric prayed she would listen.

Tina sat curled up in the chair by the window. Hers was the only house on the block with lights spilling into the one o'clock a.m. darkness.

Her features were composed. Her hands lay at rest in the velvet softness of the green ankle-length robe covering her lap. Her eyes stared into the night. Watching. Waiting. Listening for the low roar of the monster machine.

A tiny frown line appeared between her pale eyebrows when, instead of the bike, a silver-gray car came down the street and made the turn into her driveway.

Tina's pulse leapt with combined anticipation and panic on sight of the tall form that stepped from the car and moved with purposeful strides to her front door. She sprang from the chair, the full skirt of the robe swirling around her legs as she took off at a run. She was at the door before the sound of the first ring of the bell faded on the air.

"May I come in?" Eric's voice was tense, strained; his sharply defined features were drawn to a fine edge.

Tina couldn't speak, for the emotion clogging her throat. Nodding in answer, she slowly backed away, all the way into the middle of the living room. Mute, she stared at him, absently noting how very handsome he looked.

His eyes, clear as a crisp, blue autumn sky, boring into hers, Eric stalked her to a standstill at the arm of the sofa.

"Are you ready to listen now?" His voice, low and taut with urgency, tingled from her nape to the base of her spine.

"Is that your car?" Tina moved her head a fraction, indicating the driveway.

"Yes." Eric frowned. "What does that have to do with anything? I asked if you were willing, now, to listen to my explanation?"

"No."

He went absolutely still. His face paled. A fine tremor shook his strong fingers. "No?"

Still unable to form words, Tina slowly moved her head back and forth in denial.

"Tina." Eric's voice was a whispered cry of agony torn from his throat.

Tina couldn't bear the sound of it. She took a hesitant step toward him.

He extended a hand, as if in supplication.

"I love you, Eric."

He froze. Then, a light bursting like blue fireworks in his eyes, he strode to her and pulled her into his arms.

"Tina...Tina, you had me so damned scared," he groaned, kissing her hair, her temple, her eyes, her cheeks. "If you ever endanger yourself like that again..."

"I'm sorry," Tina murmured, smoothing her hands over his hair, the high bones of his cheeks, his hard jaw. "But I was afraid, terrified Glen would hurt you."

"God, I love you." His mouth brushed hers. "Can you forgive me for not telling you who and what I am?"

"I have," she whispered, raising her mouth to his.

"Love me." It was not a question, but a plea.

"I do." Tina brushed his lips with her own. "Oh, Eric, I love you more than my own life."

"Then show me." Sweeping her up, close to the revealing thump of his heart in his chest, Eric strode for her bedroom.

She did.

*  *  *  *  *

**SILHOUETTE®**

*Desire®*

Do you want...

**D**angerously handsome heroes

**E**vocative, everlasting love stories

**S**izzling and tantalizing sensuality

**I**ncredibly sexy miniseries like **MAN OF THE MONTH**

**R**ed-hot romance

**E**nticing entertainment that can't be beat!

You'll find all of this, and much *more* each and every month in **SILHOUETTE DESIRE**. Don't miss these unforgettable love stories by some of romance's hottest authors. Silhouette Desire—where your fantasies will always come true....

DES-GEN

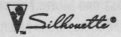

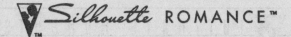
# Silhouette ROMANCE™

**What's a single dad to do when he needs a wife by next Thursday?**

**Who's a confirmed bachelor to call when he finds a baby on his doorstep?**

**How does a plain Jane in love with her gorgeous boss get him to notice her?**

From classic love stories to romantic comedies to emotional heart tuggers, **Silhouette Romance** offers six irresistible novels every month by some of your favorite authors! Such as...beloved bestsellers **Diana Palmer, Annette Broadrick, Suzanne Carey, Elizabeth August** and **Marie Ferrarella,** to name just a few—and some sure to become favorites!

Fabulous Fathers...Bundles of Joy...Miniseries... Months of blushing brides and convenient weddings... Holiday celebrations... You'll find all this and much more in **Silhouette Romance**—always emotional, always enjoyable, always about love!